KEY RIDGE

ALLISON SPEKA

Chapter One

"Seriously, Garrett, wake up! You're going to be late." I threw a pillow at my boyfriend's head and tried to coax him out of our bed for the third time that morning.

"What time is it?" he groaned.

"Seven fifty-five."

Even though we had been together for eight years and lived together for two, his inability to get moving in the morning still irritated me. He always slept through his alarm, so it was up to me to ensure he got up in time for work every day.

I was a morning person through and through and couldn't relate to his zombie-like demeanor. Waking up early to work out, read, or go for a walk was the highlight of my day.

Garrett finally spilled out of bed and went straight for the tiny bathroom the two of us shared. Once I heard the shower start, I breathed a sigh of relief and returned to the living room to savor one more cup of coffee. Settling into our sectional couch, I resumed working on my crossword puzzle.

A warm breeze hit me square in the face through the window I had left open. Now that it was almost October, the intense and humid heat had at last settled down in Florida. It was a luxury to go outside again and *enjoy* the weather without sweating through whatever shirt I was wearing.

"Hey, Mattie." A damp and shirtless Garrett poked his head out of our bedroom doorframe. "We've got dinner with the crew tonight. You'll probably have to head there straight from work."

My mind quickly scanned through all my upcoming social commitments.

"Tonight? I don't remember you telling me that."

"It's kind of last minute. We're celebrating." Garrett looked at his feet sheepishly and rubbed his short brown hair with a towel. "Will and Lauren got engaged last night."

"What?" I exclaimed, springing up from the couch. Will was Garrett's best friend from the college we had both attended. "But-but they've been together for like five minutes."

"It's been a year, babe. Lauren was really riding on him to propose."

"I didn't know riding someone to propose was an effective strategy." I crossed my arms and glared at him.

"Don't even go there. You know how swamped I am with work. Once I make partner, I'll be able to think about marriage."

My chest tightened in that familiar way it always did whenever marriage came up. The subject of our relationship status was an ever-looming issue between the two of us.

I could recite Garrett's excuses by heart at this point. First, it was "But we're too young." Next, it was "We don't have enough money for a wedding." Now, he had moved on to the "Once I make partner" narrative.

"It's getting old watching friends who've been together a fraction of the time we have beat us down the aisle," I muttered.

He walked over to me and cupped my chin in his hand, attempting to get me to look at him. I relented and stared back into his blue eyes.

"I love you," he said and planted a kiss on my forehead. "I promise when I do propose, it will be the grandest gesture you ever saw. It will put everyone else's to shame."

"It's not just about the proposal. I want to get married to *you*. I want to start our life together."

"We already have a life together," he responded, turning away from me, and heading back to the bedroom to change.

It was pointless to argue with him anymore about this. I knew I was fighting a losing battle. I should have been more insistent earlier on in our relationship. Once a guy knew he could get away with not asking you after four years, or six years, he certainly wasn't going to suddenly have a change of heart after eight.

I walked into our bedroom and shoved past Garrett to get into our cramped bathroom and closed the door. Gripping the side of the countertop, I took a deep breath and scrutinized myself in the mirror.

My long, wavy hair was thick and constantly trying to double in size with the Florida humidity. I fingered a blonde highlight that I had recently added to my light brown hair. I thought it popped against my tan skin, but Garrett had said it made me look high maintenance. My blue eyes were almost as light as Garrett's. When we met in college, I remembered thinking that our future children would look adorable with the blue eyes they were sure to inherit from us. Somehow the thought of children felt further away now at twenty-nine than it did back then at twenty-one.

A soft knock echoed through the tiled room. Sighing, I opened the door to face my boyfriend, or some would say, roommate. He met my gaze with pleading eyes.

"Please, let's not fight, okay." He grabbed my hand and pulled me into his chest. "I love you."

"Who's fighting? Not me." I gave him a weak smile, knowing the argument wasn't worth it. It never was.

"You're the best." He gestured for me to exit the room first and smacked my ass when I passed him. "We need to get going. How many times do I have to tell you we're going to be late?"

Chapter Two

"I COULD USE SOME HELP WITH THE HOUSEKEEPING TEAM. They don't respect me and it's causing issues. I have to double-check every room they turn over to make sure they've done a good enough job."

I nodded sympathetically at a property manager I had worked with for years as she rattled on about the latest issues she was facing at one of our resort properties.

"Have you tried setting up a meeting with the owner of the company?" I asked her.

"He keeps giving me the run-around. It's useless. Our old company was so much better."

"Well, we have a contract in place with these new cleaners, so we need to make it work. Their rates were much better, and we're going to close out the year with huge savings. It looks great for our department."

She bit her lip and looked unsure.

"Trust me. It just takes time to build these relationships. You're doing a great job. Keep up the amazing work."

I gave her my brightest smile and continued to reassure

her. By the time our meeting was over, I hoped some of my optimism had rubbed off on her. I was known for my sunny disposition and positive attitude at Brook's Boutique Property Management Firm.

I swiveled around in my plush chair and surveyed the view outside my window. Our firm occupied the twenty-fifth floor of a high-rise. When I got my own office last year, I thought I would never get used to the fantastic view. Sometimes I had to pinch myself to make sure I wasn't dreaming. I had gotten a job here right out of college in operations and had risen through the ranks to Director of Property Management.

Despite my best efforts, my mind wandered back to my conversation with Garrett this morning. If only my personal life was on the same trajectory my professional life was on.

There was a knock at my door before it cracked open, revealing a tall redheaded woman looking disheveled.

"Hey girl, how was your weekend?" she asked, sitting opposite my pearly white desk. Sharon from the finance department was the only person I might consider a friend instead of just a coworker.

"Just the usual. Garrett and I went out to dinner, and I hit up the farmer's market on Sunday. What about you?"

"I went to this cute little pop-up bar on Friday and met the coolest guy. Very starving-artist vibes, but he was so hot. Anyway, we ended up going out on Saturday, and you won't believe where he took me." Sharon rambled on about her adventurous weekend.

I felt a pang of jealousy. She was constantly trying new things and meeting new people. It made me feel like such a dull square. I had lived in Florida my entire life, and the only people I hung out with were my friends from college. I thrived on routine, and my idea of an adventure was trying the new sushi place that had just opened up on our block. I was twenty-nine going on fifty.

Actually, my parents were in their fifties and were more adventurous than I was. They had just gone on a two-week Alaskan cruise and snowshoed on a glacier. I hadn't even *seen* snow in real life before.

"Do you want to grab drinks after work?"

Sharon's question ripped me from my thoughts.

"Can't. Garrett and I have dinner plans." I chewed my lip before continuing. "His friend Will and his girlfriend Lauren just got engaged."

Sharon sat up straight at the news. "Excuse me. They met, like, fifteen seconds ago."

"I know."

"And didn't you tell me Will was a bit of a player?"

"Yep."

"What the hell."

"Trust me. I feel the same way."

"What did Garrett say about it."

"He said Lauren really wanted to get engaged." I wrinkled my nose as if there was a putrid stench in the air.

She scoffed. "And what about his devoted girlfriend of almost a decade? What she wants doesn't matter?"

"It's fine, really. We're just waiting until we're at a more secure point in our lives." My closed-lip smile felt tight.

Sharon rolled her eyes but didn't press the subject further. I knew that she knew what I was saying was bullshit, but she was kind enough not to point it out. I had cried one too many times over a bottle of wine with Sharon for her to fall for the same excuses I rattled off to everyone else.

"Are you ready for the new client pitch this afternoon?" she asked, graciously changing the subject.

"I was just about to go through the deck again. Did you see pictures of this property? It's gorgeous. It looks straight out of a movie. Almost makes me want to move out to the mountains."

She snorted. "Right, and give up your beach days? Not likely."

"Snow just seems so romantic, though."

I sighed and stared at the pictures of the property I had pulled up. It was located next to a ski resort in Colorado. The Key Ridge Ski Lodge. We managed resorts across the state of Florida and had recently opened our portfolio to other states. The prospective client's town was growing in popularity, but they were having trouble scaling. The property was large, and a huge potential money grab for the winter months. I had to nail this pitch.

"I can picture Mike in a Speedo better than I can picture you in snow."

"You're only saying that because he *did* wear a speedo at last year's holiday party."

We both doubled over, cackling, until a knock at the door interrupted our outburst.

"Mattie." My boss, Mike, stepped into my office. "Are you ready for the Colorado pitch? The clients just arrived from the airport. I know we scheduled the meeting for this afternoon, but they're earlier than expected, and I don't want to keep them waiting."

Just then, a gray-haired woman, maybe in her early sixties, and a thirty-something guy walked past my office. The guy was lean and muscular with dirty blond scraggly hair and stubble. He looked rugged and athletic. Although attractive, the scowl he was wearing and the hard set of his jaw were a turnoff for me. Mysteriously moody was not my type, but he was undeniably good-looking, none-theless.

Sharon gasped. "Was that Giles Stone?"

"Who?" I asked at the same time Mike nodded.

"His family owns the property. He came with his aunt to hear the pitch." Mike made a move to follow them before turning back to me. "I'm going to go with them to the conference room. Meet us there in five."

With that, he rushed out of the room before I could object.

"Who is Giles Stone?" I asked again.

"He's a professional snowboarder," Sharon whispered despite the subject of our conversation being nowhere within hearing range. "Or he was. I think he retired, but he was in the last two Winter Olympics. How have you never heard of him?"

"Oh right, *that* Giles Stone. I'm such a huge fan of snowboarding. I *totally* forgot I have his poster hanging in my room."

Sharon rolled her eyes at my sarcasm. "I'm not a winter sports fan either, but he's gorgeous. There's something extra attractive about a guy that does winter sports."

She came around to my side of the desk and pulled my keyboard toward her. She opened a search engine and typed his name in. Pictures of him filled my screen. They mainly consisted of him in winter clothes contorting his body into crazy positions high up in the air.

I stared at her. "Um, what's attractive about winter sports? You can't even see him underneath all those layers. I can't believe you even recognized him."

She clicked on a picture of him shirtless on the cover of a sports magazine to enlarge it.

"You were saying?" she asked.

"He's okay there, I guess."

"You should read up on him so you're prepared."

"By 'read up' do you mean stare at half-naked pictures? I only have five minutes." I closed the window she had opened. "I need to review this deck one more time. I'm sure snowboarding, or his career, is not going to come up in our presentation."

"If you say so." She walked back around toward my office door. "Hey, if it comes up organically, mind slipping him my number in case he's looking for something to do while he's in town?"

I laughed and tossed a balled-up piece of notebook paper at her.

"Out."

SITTING ACROSS FROM GILES STONE WAS DIFFERENT THAN looking at his pictures online. Sharon was right. He *was* gorgeous. And intense. From the moment I entered the room, his deep brown eyes hadn't stopped searing a hole right into me.

His aunt, Bev, seemed nice enough, but she had a slight edge to her. My hand was still throbbing from her firm handshake. All I could do to hide my nerves was plant a massive grin on my face and pretend I was completely at ease.

"Hello, I'm Mattie," I greeted them cheerily. "How was your flight."

"It was fine. We appreciate you flying us out for this," Bev said.

Giles just grunted in response.

I extended my hand to Giles, and he eyed it like I had an infectious disease. After a few heartbeats, he engulfed my hand in his and gave it a quick shake before dropping it. I noticed him flexing the hand that had touched me.

"So, Colorado, huh? I've always wanted to visit. Must be a beautiful place to live."

"It is," he replied flatly.

His short remark and hard stare had me on edge. This was not the typical demeanor of potential clients.

"What do you think of Florida? It must be pretty different, huh?" I cleared my throat nervously.

He narrowed his eyes. "Obviously."

Bev nudged his arm before turning back to me with a smile. "It's lovely here. Always nice to be in a tropical climate, even if it is just for a quick trip."

"Well, Mattie is our director of Property Management. She's put together a great presentation for you. I think you'll find it all very informative," Mike said.

"Thanks, Mike. I'll just get us started, then." I plugged in my computer and my slide deck appeared on the screen in front of us. "Feel free to stop me at any time with questions, but for now, let's just dive right in."

The first few slides outlined our basic structure. We would place a property manager on-site at their lodge to handle all the daily operations. They would manage the housekeepers, order supplies, and go above and beyond to keep guests happy.

"And because your property hasn't been updated in a while, our team will make improvements as we see fit to make the space appealing to guests and ensure we capture as many new customers as possible."

Giles mumbled something under his breath. His presence made me uneasy.

"I'm sorry, what was that?" I asked, my voice dripping with politeness.

"I don't think you, or your team, has the first idea what would make us appealing to our customers," he spat. "Our customers *like* our vintage charm. None of them want to stay in a place with the same aesthetic as a sterile doctor's office." He gestured to the conference room we were sitting in.

My lip twitched as I tried to maintain my smile.

"Of course, sir. I didn't mean that the lodge didn't already possess a certain charm. And we would certainly work to create a feel that would appeal to your customer-"

"Please, spare me." He waved his hand as if to dismiss me. "You're so full of shit."

"Excuse me?" I choked out.

"What would a couple of suits that live in Florida know about running a ski lodge? Do you even ski?" He crossed his arms.

"Well, no," I sputtered. "But I know a lot about hotels and prop-"

"That's what I thought. I've heard enough."

He stood from his chair and circled around the table toward the exit.

"Giles, please sit down. You're being rude." Bev shot me an apologetic glance as she tried to talk down her nephew.

"No, I'm done here. I'll be outside."

With that, he stormed out, leaving me flabbergasted. While I didn't always nail every presentation, this was undoubtedly the first time I had lost someone's interest within the first five minutes.

At least Mike looked just as shocked as I felt. A sure sign that it wasn't my pitch that was the problem. Just that the person I was pitching to was an asshole.

"I'm sorry about him," Bev said, rising from her chair. "It's not you. He's got other things going on."

"It's not a problem," I said through gritted teeth. It most certainly was a problem. I had spent days on this pitch, and he never intended to listen to it—the nerve of that jerk to waste my time.

"Look, despite that scene he just caused, I'm the decision-maker, and I'm drowning."

My ears perked up at her desperate tone. Was there still a shot of landing this?

"We would be happy to take some of that burden off you," I said. "Trust me. This is exactly the type of work our firm was made for. We'll organize all your processes. When we're done, I promise we'll have your lodge running like a well-oiled machine."

I slid a packet of papers toward her.

"Maybe you and your nephew would like to review our numbers and mission privately to see if we'd be a good fit. I've outlined the details here."

"I appreciate a prepared woman." She winked at me.

Mike was sitting so far forward in his seat that I thought he might fall out of it. I could tell he was eager to intervene, but he knew I had a way of reading people. Bev seemed like the type of person that valued her privacy and didn't like to make a production of things. The raw numbers and no bullshit information were precisely what she needed to make a decision.

She took my packet and paused in the doorframe. "I'll review this on our flight home and get back to you. Again, I'm sorry for the outburst. I hope we can move past this if we do decide to go forward."

"Of course," Mike and I said in unison. I'm not sure which of our smiles was bigger.

As soon as Bev was out of earshot, Mike raised his hand, and I gleefully high-fived it.

"What a save. I thought we were screwed when he walked out of here like that. Good job having that write-up prepared."

"We're not in the clear yet," I reminded him. While I was an eternal optimist, I did try to keep a realistic perspective on things.

"When she sees those estimated returns and reduced working hours, it'll be a no-brainer."

"Fingers crossed," I replied. "Let's just hope if we do land this account, there will be minimal interaction with that pro snowboarder asshat."

Chapter Three

I TAPPED MY FINGERS IMPATIENTLY ON THE STEERING WHEEL as I stared out into the endless sea of tail lights. I planned to leave work early and change before meeting Garrett and our friends at dinner, but unfortunately, an issue at one of our properties forced me to stay late. Now I was stuck in traffic trying to get to the restaurant.

"Shoot," I muttered.

There was no way I'd be there on time. I loathed being late, even if I *was* barely given any notice.

It occurred to me at some point during the day that Garrett must have known Will was going to propose long before it happened. Maybe it shouldn't have bothered me that he didn't mention it, but part of me knew his exclusion of information was tied directly to how he knew this would make me feel.

I desperately wanted to be happy for them, but I couldn't wrap my head around it. Will, his perpetual bachelor friend—the one who didn't know what a top sheet was and still ate bologna sandwiches—was getting married before us.

Garrett probably figured I would obsess about it and read too much into it.

Well, he was wrong.

I'm fine. I told myself as my knuckles turned white from gripping the wheel.

Fifteen minutes later, I arrived at the Italian bistro where Garrett had texted me to meet them. I was already a few minutes late, but I sat in the car for a few moments attempting to collect myself.

I pulled down my visor mirror and practiced smiling.

"I'm so happy for you," I whispered.

Fake, you look fake.

I closed my eyes and took a deep breath before plastering on a smile again.

"Congrats," I hissed.

It was pointless. Hopefully, at this point, everyone was halfway into a celebratory glass of wine and wouldn't notice my half-hearted congratulations.

I walked briskly through the double doors, and the host directed me to a large table in the back. The restaurant was bustling with life. Before I even approached, I knew that most of the noise was coming from my friends.

"Mattie." Garrett stood and greeted me with a kiss on the cheek.

"Hey." I made the rounds, giving quick hugs to everyone seated.

Will and Lauren were at the head of the table. Across from them was Ben, Garrett's other best friend from college, and his wife, Jennifer. Jennifer and Ben had also been together since college, so I was close with them. Jenifer was one of my best girlfriends.

To Jennifer's left was Nadine. Nadine was Jennifer's childhood best friend and also went to school with us. She had broken up with her longtime boyfriend last year, which made me feel a little bit of relief at not being the only unengaged, or unmarried, one in the group.

I settled into my seat, and Garrett handed me a glass of wine before raising his own drink.

"Now that we're all here, I want to congratulate Will and Lauren. I think I speak for everyone when I say we all thought this day would never come. Cheers, buddy."

We all shouted cheers and clinked our glasses. I detected the tiniest bit of irritation when I caught Lauren's eye. Even though they had been dating for a year, I hardly knew her. Whenever we hung out as a group, she always seemed to have an excuse not to come. I sensed she didn't like us all that much, especially Garrett. Honestly, I couldn't blame her. Garrett loved to bring up Will's crazy single days any chance he got. I'd be annoyed with him too.

"How's work going?" Jennifer asked me, handing over a basket of bread.

"Just the typical grind." I grabbed a roll. "Oh, but maybe you'll think this is exciting. Today I got to pitch to a professional athlete. Apparently, he's a former Olympic snowboarder."

"No way." Now Nadine was also leaning in, listening to my story. "Who was it?"

"Giles Stone."

Jennifer squealed. "Oh my god, I know exactly who that is. He's so hot."

Nadine nodded her agreement.

"Who are we talking about?" Garrett asked, slinking a hand behind my chair, and leaning in. "Me, I hope."

I rolled my eyes. "Giles Stone. He's a professional snowboarder and apparently a professional asshole. I had to pitch to him today about that Colorado property I was telling you about. He stormed out after a few minutes and couldn't have been ruder."

"Bummer," Nadine said.

"Why are the hot ones always shitty people?" asked Jennifer.

"Except for us, right?" Garrett gestured to himself, Will, and Ben.

"No, you guys were pretty shitty." Jennifer laughed. "It just took our hard work to turn you into upstanding life partners, right girls?"

"Cheers to that," I said, grinning.

We both clinked our glasses and offered them to Lauren who looked uncomfortable. After an awkward few seconds, she tapped her glass on ours and returned to staring at the menu, not saying a word.

I caught Jennifer's eye, and we shared a knowing glance. It was always like this with Lauren.

"Oh my god. Look at the picture Steven just posted." Nadine shoved her phone into Jennifer's eyesight, and they both peered over it.

"Stop. That cannot be his new girlfriend."

They started to gossip about an old acquaintance. I smiled politely and waited until they were ready to discuss something different. One of the cons of having two best friends that had grown up together was that I would never be caught up on their inside jokes or know all the same people they knew. They almost reminded me of sisters, which made me feel a pang of sadness.

I was close with my sister, Frankie, who was a few years younger than me. She moved to Atlanta after college, and now we only saw each other a few times a year. Thank god for texting, or I'd be distraught about it.

"Lauren looks pretty miserable for having finally got what she wanted," Garrett whispered into my ear.

I snuck a glance in her direction.

"I think her misery is because we're here, not because of that gorgeous ring on her finger."

He chuckled. "If a sparkly piece of jewelry is why you care about being engaged, I'd be happy to shell out money on some nice earrings."

My spine stiffened in disbelief that he would bring that up now. We were out with friends.

"You know that's not it," I hissed and gave him a death glare, letting him know he'd gone too far.

He ruffled my hair, oblivious to my irritation, and turned his attention back to Will and Lauren.

"Hey, Will. Remember that time you slept with a cocktail waitress and ended up getting locked inside the bar until the next morning?"

Ben roared with laughter. "That was hilarious. Lauren, have you heard this story?"

Lauren looked like she wished she could disappear as Ben and Garrett rambled on about Will's drunken escapades.

I tried to shoot her a sympathetic glance, but she wouldn't make eye contact with me. I sighed and turned back to Jennifer and Nadine, who were still obsessing about people I didn't know. Taking a big sip of my wine, I waited patiently to be included.

"Bye, drive safe, okay? This was so much fun." Jennifer and Ben hugged each of us before piling into their car.

"Thanks for setting this up. We really appreciate it," Will said as he also hugged us each goodbye.

Lauren looked in pain, but to her credit, she tried to disguise her discomfort and gave us each a hug too.

"Shoot, I think I forgot something inside," Nadine said, heading back to the entrance. "I'll see you all later."

"I'm going to run to the bathroom," Garrett announced. "See you at home, babe?"

We had driven separately, so I nodded as Garrett also disappeared into the restaurant again.

When I turned back to Lauren and Will, she was eyeing me as if trying to decide something.

"Everything okay?" I asked her, getting a little annoyed with her attitude.

"You don't sense anything off?" she asked.

"What are you talking about?"

"We've got to go." Will laughed nervously and tugged Lauren away from me. "We'll see you around, Mattie."

I gave a small wave and walked over to my car. What had Lauren been talking about? What had seemed off? She must have meant the vibe of our friend group in general.

"Whatever," I muttered, starting the car. Between her and the Giles mess earlier today, I was pretty fed up with shitty attitudes.

I pulled out of the restaurant and headed home, the day playing on repeat in my mind. Nothing terrible had happened, but it was still so mediocre. A pit formed in my stomach.

Ever since I was a little kid, my parents always fussed over my upbeat personality. Anytime something bad happened to anyone in my family, I would always try to be right there with a smile and a solution.

Lately, though, I worried my bright demeanor might be fading. I had been pretending that everything was great for so long that when I finally took a step back and looked at my life, I realized I might not be as happy as I thought.

Yes, I was great at my job, but it was the only real one I had ever known.

Yes, I loved Garrett, but did we even want the same things out of life? I would never admit this to anyone, but deep down, I was worried he would never ask me to marry him.

When I pulled up at a stoplight, I took a deep breath and closed my eyes, willing this strange feeling to leave me.

I was fine.

Everything was great.

Chapter Four

SHIT, I WAS RUNNING LATE AGAIN. THERE WAS SOMETHING about the fall season that made it so hard for me to stay in a good routine. It could be the shorter days. Or maybe it was the weather finally becoming desirable again. Whatever it was, I found myself constantly rushing out the door lately.

"Babe, don't forget we've got dinner tonight," Garrett reminded me. "We've got to celebrate my promotion."

I had forgotten. Why was I so scatterbrained this week?

"Of course. Where are we going again?"

"I didn't tell you."

I glanced back at him from the mirror in the doorway. He looked especially smug.

"Um, I'm not a mind reader."

"I got reservations at Vino."

Vino was a new restaurant in town that I had been dying to try. It was crazy expensive and ridiculously tough to get a reservation. My lips tugged into a smile at the news.

"That's amazing, Garrett."

He waved off my praise. "Just make sure you're there at

seven-thirty exactly. They'll give up our table if we don't make it there on time."

"Shoot, I have to go to one of our properties at six today." I chewed my lip, thinking. "Let me just grab a change of clothes in case I need to head straight there."

I raced to our walk-in closet and ran my fingers along my dresses, trying to decide which one to wear tonight. I held up a red one and examined it as my eyes shifted to my freshly manicured nails.

I gasped and dropped the dress.

My nails were freshly manicured because I went to get them done with Jennifer and Nadine a few days ago. While this wasn't abnormal for the three of us, I had tried to bail, and they insisted I join them.

Garrett had been promoted.

Reservations at a fancy restaurant.

My friends had demanded I get my nails done.

Did all this mean what I thought it meant?

I jumped up and down and let out a silent squeal of delight. It was finally happening.

But what should I wear to get engaged?

Now I scrutinized my closet much more closely. My eyes danced past a white chiffon option, too obvious, and stopped at a flouncy silver number. I selected it and smiled. This was the one. I hadn't had a chance to wear this yet, and I knew it made my body look insane.

Shit, my garment bag was still at work from when I picked up dry cleaning last week.

I remembered I had a steamer in my office and placed the dress carefully inside my almost empty leather tote bag. Not the most glamorous carrying case, but it would have to do.

I raced for the door and stopped to plant a big kiss on Garrett's lips on the way out.

"What was that for?" he asked, grinning.

"Just excited for tonight," I said, wiggling my fingers at him. "I'll see you later."

"ARE YOU SURE?" SHARON DEMANDED.

"Pretty sure. Why else would Jennifer have practically forced me to go to the nail salon when I was swamped that night?"

"That *is* compelling."

"I'm telling you, I have a feeling it's coming." The smile hadn't left my face all morning.

"Well, I'm happy for you. It's about time he manned up."

"Agreed," I said. "Maybe it took Will taking the plunge for him to finally wake up and realize it's time."

Sharon looked unimpressed.

"Knock, knock." Mike stepped through my open doorway.

"Morning," I greeted him.

"I'll talk to you later, Mattie." Sharon waved before slipping past Mike.

"So." Mike sat in the now unoccupied chair. "Do you remember that pitch we made for the Colorado property last week?"

"How could I forget?" I was still irritated we never heard back from them. It's one thing not to hire us but to ghost us completely? Rude. Especially after the way Giles Stone acted in our meeting.

"Well, I decided to follow up with Bev one last time, and low and behold, she answered. She was drowning in work when I called and was completely overwhelmed. She apologized for not getting back to us earlier—the time just got away from her or something like that. Anyway, she agreed to a trial period."

I sat up straighter. Sometimes we allowed clients to use our services for a few months to ensure they were pleased before signing a contract.

"A trial period. For how long?"

"Just thirty days. They want us there before ski season is in full swing, so I said we'd have someone in place by November first. It's a short one, but given how stressed she sounded over there, I'm guessing any help will be a godsend."

"That's amazing. Do we already have a property manager contact in Colorado?"

Mike shook his head. "That's the thing, our closest property right now is in Utah. The company we use out there doesn't have anyone in Colorado. We will need to hold a round of interviews remotely for the position and hire someone in-house."

"That's going to be tough on such short notice." I bit my lip. "Wait, what if we hire someone and we don't get the contract after the temp position?"

Mike shrugged. "We'll just have to be upfront about that. It will be a contract position with the opportunity to go full-time."

I nodded, although I wasn't sure we would get many qualified candidates in this market without the promise of full-time benefits. "I'll contact HR today to get a job posting online."

⸺

"Lunch?" I looked up to see Sharon at my door.

"Is it already noon?"

"It's one."

"Shit, sorry. I've been back and forth on this job posting with HR all morning." I got up from my chair and grabbed my bag.

"I heard we got the ski lodge. Nice work."

We walked toward the elevator.

"Assuming we can find someone who will take the PM job on insanely short notice and be okay with no full-time perks."

Sharon snorted. "Sounds easy enough."

The elevator pinged as we arrived in the lobby. I stepped forward and was immediately met with a barrier and a squeal.

An intern holding a coffee cup carrier had rushed onto the elevator and collided with me. Everything seemed to happen in slow motion as the lava hot liquid soared in my direction. I threw my bag out in front of me for protection right before the coffee made contact with me.

"Oh my god. Oh my god. Oh my god. I'm so sorry." The intern was frantically picking up the now almost empty cups.

"You should wait to see if people are coming off the elevator before you burst into it," Sharon told her, irritated.

"I know, I'm such an idiot. I was running late. I'm so sorry."

I looked down to see that I was basically unscathed, except my bag was soaked with coffee.

"It's alright. Just be more careful next time." I smiled at

her, still remembering what it felt like to be young, ambitious, and nervous as hell to mess anything up.

She apologized several times before rushing out the door to get replacement beverages.

"Let's hop in the bathroom before lunch. I need to clean off my bag."

Sharon and I steered ourselves down the hallway and into the luxurious marble bathroom located in the lobby.

I grabbed some paper towels and set my bag on the counter to inspect it. It was a nice bag, but I bought it years ago. It already had a decent amount of wear and tear. I started to dab at it and then peeked inside to see if any damage was done there. As soon as I saw it, the blood drained from my face.

"*Shit*," I said.

"What?" Sharon stopped primping her hair in the mirror and gave me her full attention as I held out my gorgeous silver dress, now covered in coffee stains.

She gasped. "Was that what you were going to wear tonight?"

I nodded, trying not to panic. "I meant to hang it up in my office, but I got so sidetracked when Mike told me about the Colorado Property I completely forgot."

"What are you going to do? You can't get engaged in that."

I groaned. "Maybe this is a sign. Garrett was never going to propose to me tonight. This is the universe punishing me for my optimism."

"Um, first off, even if there is only a one percent chance of you getting engaged tonight, you absolutely cannot wear a stained dress. Second, it's not optimistic to think that your boyfriend of *almost a decade* is going to propose."

I chewed my lip, weighing my options.

"I'm sorry, but I can't do lunch. I've got to run home and get a new dress before my next meeting," I said, already rushing out of the bathroom.

"Run like the wind," she called.

Chapter Five

RACING HOME, I KEPT GLANCING AT THE TIME. I KNEW I was cutting it close to my next meeting, but I'd be damned if I was going to get engaged in a coffee-soaked dress.

Suddenly it hit me, and warmth flooded into my stomach.

I was going to get engaged to the man I'd been with since college. I was going to have the beach wedding of my dreams. I was going to get to call someone my fiancé. Then, soon, my husband.

Since I was a little girl, I had dreamed of my wedding, and I had been planning it ever since. Despite it being normal now for my generation to not marry, or wait until they're older, I had always wanted to get married young. So, it surprised everyone when I fell in love with someone who had no timer on such things.

But now the moment I had been waiting for was here. The moment that would send my life spiraling in the direction I had been dying to go ever since I met Garrett.

I bit back my grin as I pulled into a street parking spot

in front of our apartment. I rushed up the one flight of stairs and opened the door, ready to be in and out of there as quickly as possible.

As soon as I set my keys down, a soft thump came from our bedroom. I froze, my eyes glued to the bedroom door. After another minute passed, I heard footsteps. I panicked and fished my pepper spray out of my purse. Just as I was about to aim it in the intruder's direction, Garrett slipped out of our bedroom, wearing nothing but sweatpants.

I breathed a sigh of relief and brought my hand to my heart, lowering the pepper spray.

"Garrett, what the hell are you doing here? You almost gave me a heart attack."

He looked flushed. He ran his hand through his hair, and didn't move from his spot in front of the bedroom door.

"I, uh, I wasn't feeling well, so I came home early."

I looked at him, puzzled.

"Are you sick? Why didn't you text me?"

The few times a year when Garrett did get sick, he was a complete baby about it. Last year he begged me to drive home from work just to bring him soup.

"I was going to. I just got home." He leaned his back against the door. "What are *you* doing here in the middle of the day?"

His whole demeanor felt off to me.

"Someone spilled coffee all over my bag, and the dress I was planning to wear tonight got ruined. I came home to grab something else, but maybe I don't need to anymore."

"Why's that?"

"Um, if you're sick, I'm assuming dinner is off," I replied, disappointed.

"I think it's just something I ate not sitting right. We should still do dinner later."

He wasn't meeting my eyes. What was going on with him?

Then I realized. What if he had the ring in there? Maybe he came home to get it and didn't want me to see it.

I bit the inside of my cheek to keep from smiling.

"Okay, well, if dinner is still on, I need to get another dress. I'll grab it from the closet and be in and out so fast."

"No," he cried and gripped the doorknob behind him.

"C'mon, Garrett. I *really* need a different dress." I stepped toward him and gave him my best puppy dog eyes. I didn't want to spoil my surprise, but I needed to look my best tonight.

Before he could answer, I heard another thump coming from inside the bedroom. I froze.

"Is someone else in there?"

Garrett looked down at his feet.

I felt panicky now. "Garrett, what's going on?"

I tried to shove past him and get to the door. He didn't budge.

"Mattie, please just go. Let's talk later."

There was a thud now, and I was sure someone else was in there.

"Why the hell is someone else in our bedroom, Garrett? What's going on?" I demanded, shoving his bare chest.

"Mattie—"

"Move," I said, giving him a death glare.

"Please—"

"Move," I shouted, shoving him harder this time.

Finally, he relented and let me get past him. I swung open the door and gasped.

Nadine was there, wearing only a skirt and a bra. She appeared to be looking frantically for a top.

"What the hell is going on?" I yelled, my voice shaking with horror at what I had just walked into.

Nadine covered her mouth, and tears sprung into her eyes.

"Mattie, I'm so so sorry. Oh my god. I'm so sorry." She started to sob.

I whipped my head around to find Garrett just standing there, arms across his chest, still not looking at me.

"Will someone please start talking?" My voice cracked as I continued to yell at them.

"We never meant for this to happen," Nadine responded through tears. Thankfully she had located her top and was now fully dressed.

"Meant for what to happen?"

Nadine glanced at Garrett for help, but he remained mute.

"We're together, Mattie," she cried. "I'm so so sorry. God, I'm sorry."

My jaw went slack.

"No, *we're* together." I gestured frantically between Garrett and myself. "We've been together for *eight years*. And you're supposed to be my friend."

She started choking on her sobs and didn't say anything in response.

"How long has this been going on?" I demanded to know.

"Since the Cabo trip." Garrett finally broke his silence.

My mouth hung open in shock.

"The Cabo trip was six months ago," I whispered.

Back in April, our whole friend group decided to take a

long weekend trip to Mexico together. I had to stay back at the last minute because of a work emergency.

Black dots flooded my vision. I raised my hand to my forehead and slowly lowered myself onto the floor.

"We never meant to hurt you." Nadine was hovering over me now, grabbing my shoulders.

I wanted to tell her not to touch me. I wanted to tell them both to go to hell. But I felt like I was going to pass out, and the only thing keeping me conscious were deep breaths.

Through spotted vision, I saw Garrett exit the room, not even saying one word in his defense. Not begging for forgiveness like I would've expected.

I wanted to cry as all my dreams came crashing down at once—as my heart shattered. But I couldn't feel any of that. I couldn't even feel Nadine's touch on my arm. All I felt was numbness wash over me.

Chapter Six

STUFFING THE LAST OF MY CLOTHES INTO AN OVERSIZED suitcase, I glanced around the room to ensure I hadn't missed anything. I spotted an old sweatshirt of mine in Garrett's laundry pile and snatched it.

"Do you have everything?" Garrett asked from the doorframe.

I zipped up my suitcase without looking at him, not bothering to respond.

"Mattie, please at least look at me. It doesn't have to be this way."

I inhaled sharply. "Actually, Garrett, this is exactly the way this has to be. You decided that as soon you started fucking one of my best friends behind my back."

He hung his head and held his hands up as if surrendering before retreating back to our—his—living room.

Being cheated on was never something I fantasized about. However, if I *had,* the fantasy would have certainly included Garrett crying and begging for my forgiveness. He would have professed that he couldn't live without me and that he would die if I ever left him.

It definitely would not include him ignoring me and giving me no explanation. It also wouldn't include me moving out the day after finding out about his affair only to have his mistress, *my friend*, move in.

"It just makes sense this way," Garrett had said when I started to pack. "This way, you won't lose any money from the lease."

So generous of him to get me out of my lease payments. Really, what a stand-up guy.

I rolled my last suitcase out to the living room and took my key off my key ring.

Garrett got off the couch and walked over to me. "All done?"

"That's the understatement of the century."

He hesitated, glancing at my eyes and then back to his feet. "Where are you going to stay?"

"Don't pretend like you care."

"I do care, Mattie."

I glared at him. "I can't believe I wasted eight years on you."

With that, I slammed the front door in his face. If I never saw him again, it would be too soon.

"You've arrived at your destination," the automated voice on my phone announced.

A tan stucco home with dark brown shutters and a palm tree out front loomed in front of me. It looked like every other house on the block, except they all had slightly different features. Golf carts, every color of the rainbow, sat in each driveway. They were the preferred method of transportation for the residents here.

"You made it." An older woman with bleached blonde hair and a permanent tan rushed toward me and scooped me into a hug. "I'm so happy you're here. Ron, come outside and help with your daughter's bags."

Yes, this is what my life had come to—almost thirty and moving back in with my parents, who now resided in a retirement community.

Everything was fine.

I returned my mother's hug, grateful to be comforted. When I called and shared the news of my happiness's demise with them, they were surprisingly not as shocked as I had expected them to be.

"We never trusted that boy," my dad had said.

"Any man that can't commit to you after that long is a dud," my mom so helpfully chimed in.

So glad I was getting all these opinions now after wasting years with him.

My dad, Ron, rushed out wearing one of his signature Hawaiian shirts and golf shorts.

"Stop yelling, Mary. You'll disturb the neighbors."

"Oh, pish."

My mom led me inside the front door while my dad was left to deal with my car full of luggage.

Their house was open, bright, and airy. Exactly what you would expect to find in Florida. There were pictures of sea turtles on the walls, and the kitchen had been painted a blue that resembled the sea.

"Sit, sit, honey." She pulled out a bar stool that lined the kitchen's peninsula.

A plate of freshly baked cookies appeared in front of me, and I snatched one.

"So work is okay with you taking some time off, then?"

I nodded. "Mike was pretty understanding. I'll go back on Monday, though."

"You sure you don't want to take some more time off?"

I shook my head. "I broke up with my boyfriend. No one died or anything."

"Honey, it's a bigger deal than that. You two were practically married."

"Except we weren't," I said flatly.

"Well, you lived together. You had to move out. That's a huge life change. I'm sure they would understand if you needed to take a few extra personal day—"

"Mom, stop. I'm fine. Yes, I have to find a new place to live, but I'll manage. Did I expect to be planning a wedding this holiday season instead of signing up for dating apps? Maybe. But there's nothing I can do about my situation except move on. Going back to work and keeping busy is exactly what I need. The last thing I need to do is fester and be sad over this while Garrett and Nadine play house in my old apartment."

Just thinking the last thought made me fume. I took a few deep breaths to calm down. The fact that as I was moving into my parent's guest bedroom, they were probably popping a bottle of champagne to celebrate their new chapter together made my blood boil.

"Well, I don't want you to bottle anything up. It's okay to be upset about this." She came around the peninsula and kissed the top of my head. "I would say for your situation, at least a week of wallowing in self-pity would be appropriate."

I rolled my eyes. "I promise I'm fine. That's hardly necessary."

A few hours later, I was unpacking the contents of my suitcases into a tiny dresser only intended for overnight guests. My jeans were overflowing out of the bottom drawer as I struggled to jam it closed. I would have to find some more storage if I was going to make this work for any extended amount of time.

The vibration coming from my phone was a welcome interruption. I picked it up to see Jennifer's name flashing across the screen. I was dreading this conversation but figured it would be better to get it over with. Since she and Nadine were so close, I wondered if she had already been informed.

"Hey, Jen," I said.

"Hey, girl. How are you holding up? I called as soon as I heard what happened." The sympathy oozing from her voice made me cringe. The last thing I wanted was everyone in my friend group to pity me.

"I'm as good as can be expected. Better now than yesterday." I fell back onto the plush bed. "I guess I'm still in shock a little bit. I can't believe Garrett isn't in my life anymore. And then the fact that he and Nadine were sneaking around all this time? It makes me sick to think about it. I feel like an idiot."

"Ugh, I can't even imagine what you're going through."

I paused before responding. "I thought he was going to propose to me yesterday. Instead, I found him half-naked with someone I thought was my friend."

"She *is* your friend," Jennifer insisted.

I snorted. "Not anymore."

"Oh no, you can't let this break up a friendship. You just need some time to adjust."

Her relaxed tone made me shoot up in bed. "Um, excuse me? I don't just need *time to adjust*. They had been having an affair behind my back for months. They're dead to me."

"That's so dramatic," Jennifer whined.

"How are you being so casual about this? They were lying to all of us. I know you've known Nadine longer, but you should be on my side."

The call went silent. I checked my phone to make sure we hadn't gotten disconnected.

"Jen?"

"Mattie…"

There was another long pause. I held my breath, anticipating what I feared she would say next.

"I knew about them. I'm so sorry I didn't tell you, but it wasn't my place."

"You knew?"

"Yes," she sniffled. "I feel terrible. I know this isn't fair to you. I've always begged them to tell you, even right after Cabo. I even threatened to tell you myself once."

The blood drained from my face.

"You've known since Cabo?"

"Yes, and I'm so sor—"

"Screw you," I snapped before pounding the red 'end' button.

I got up and paced the small room. Was I the biggest idiot on the planet? All my friends were in on this huge secret that affected my entire life, and no one even bothered to give me a hint.

Lauren and Will's engagement dinner flashed through my mind.

What had Lauren said? 'You don't sense anything off' or something like that. I hadn't known what she was referring to at the time, but looking back, it must have been regarding Garrett and Nadine.

"Shit. Shit. Shit." I groaned. Literally, everyone knew.

Now I didn't just have a relationship to mourn. All of my friendships had also gone up in flames.

Chapter Seven

THE SUN PEAKED OVER THE HORIZON AS I DUMPED MY WORK bag onto my desk. My eyes were puffy, and my head felt groggy. I hadn't been sleeping well since the incident, and I figured what better way to spend my morning than getting to work before everyone else. Today when I arrived, the front door was still locked. The maintenance staff had to let me in.

I had spent the weekend buying every organizational tool I could think of and transformed the guest bedroom into a color-coded compulsive dreamland. After that, I found some new recipes online and meal prepped for the week ahead. When I finished cooking, I realized my parent's back patio could use a freshening, so I spent hours deep cleaning it.

My mom had begged me to sit on the couch, watch a sad movie, and relax. But ceasing to be productive sounded like defeat to me. Garrett and Nadine had already taken so much from me. I would be damned if I let them take my positive attitude too.

I stared out the window at the view I had always adored. Something about it felt off now. I looked around my office. All of this felt off.

Shaking my head, I tried to rid my brain of the intrusive thoughts. I opened my laptop and got to work screening resumes for the new PM hire we desperately needed in Key Ridge, Colorado.

"Morning, sunshine. What are you doing here so early." Sharon poked her head into my office with a bright smile.

"Just trying to catch up on some work."

"Oh, right. Mike said you were sick on Friday." She plopped down in the seat across from my desk. "I thought it was weird when you never came back to work after you went home to get a new dress. I just figured you might be playing hooky to celebrate an engagement. I can't believe you never texted me to tell me what happened. So, spill. Did Garrett finally grow a pair and propose?"

"Not exactly." Shit. I should have texted her a brief summary to avoid the awkwardness of telling her the news in person.

"Not exactly? What's that supposed to mean?"

"I caught him cheating on me, and we broke up," I said.

She choked on the sip of coffee she had just taken. "What?" she exclaimed.

I nodded and recounted the tale in as little detail as I could manage.

"Now I'm staying at my parent's house while the new lovebirds enjoy their honeymoon phase."

"That's insane, Mattie. How are you at work right now? How are you even *functioning* right now?"

I shrugged. "What am I supposed to do? If I just lie around and cry about it, then they've won."

"This is hardly about winning and losing. You've just had your heart broken, and your life upended. It's okay not to be okay right now."

"Obviously, I've been better, but I promise you I'm fine." I faked a smile for good measure. "Besides, I'll probably be able to meet someone online, date them for a while, and still get proposed to faster than if I had stayed with Garrett. Let Nadine deal with that commitment-phobic man-child now. He is so not my problem anymore."

Sharon still looked unconvinced. "Well, can we at least get wine drunk one day this week? That's a non-negotiable after a breakup."

"Obviously."

"I SEE ON YOUR RESUME THAT YOU WORKED AT THE DAILY Inn. Can you describe your experience there?" Mike asked.

We were in a conference room interviewing the tenth candidate for the position at The Key Ridge Ski Lodge.

"Totally." The candidate had long unkempt hair. I could only see the top half of his body over video chat, but I was willing to bet he was wearing a pair of ratty flannel pajama bottoms. Honestly, his top half wasn't much better. "I worked in their kitchen for a couple of months. Didn't work out, though. The hours were kind of long."

I snuck a glance at Mike.

"Well, these hours would probably be long too. You'd also have to live on-site," I replied, trying my best to keep the perkiness in my voice.

"Oh, I don't want to move."

"Then why did you apply? It was clearly noted in the job description."

"It was? Huh. I must have missed it."

After a few more grueling minutes, we ended the call.

"Christ, how bad can these candidates get? That was the least professional one yet." Mike took off his glasses and rubbed the bridge of his nose.

"He wasn't so bad."

"What are you talking about? He was abysmal."

"At least he showed up for the interview." Aside from the ten people we had interviewed, an additional five hadn't even shown up for the call.

"That's where the bar is set? We're screwed."

I wanted to chime in with words of encouragement, but I was concerned he was right. It had been two weeks of searching nonstop for candidates, and we weren't any closer to finding someone than when we started. And we were *not* being picky.

"It's a tough job market right now." I gave him what I hoped was an uplifting smile. "We'll find the right person."

"We're running out of time."

"We've still got a week. I'll figure something out," I insisted. "You know me, and you know that I refuse to lose this property."

"You're the best we've got, but I'm not sure that even you can pull this off."

"Just trust me."

We left the room and parted ways. As soon as I was on my own, I felt the panic settle in. I had my game face on when Mike was present, but I wasn't sure how I would find someone to start in a week.

***

"Get off your phone and watch this movie with us, Mattie." My mom and dad were cuddled up on the couch, and I was sitting in the chair, scrolling through pictures on social media.

I had been living with them for a couple of weeks now, and while it wasn't terrible, it was a tad suffocating.

Every morning I was met with an ambush of questions.

"What are you up to today?"

"Did you empty the dryer?"

"Do you want to go to a yoga class later?"

"What are you thinking for dinner?"

It was sweet, and I loved them, but it was exhausting.

"I am watching," I said while still not looking up from my phone.

"You kids and your technology," my dad huffed.

I rolled my eyes. "Dad, I'm hardly a kid."

"You're still a kid to us."

Before I could reply, there was a commotion at the front door. I jerked my head around to see a mess of long blonde curls tangled in the straps of a duffel bag.

"What in the world—" My dad stood up.

"Frances," my mom exclaimed and raced to the door.

My sister, Frankie, threw her arms around our mother. They embraced as if it had been years since they'd seen each other instead of months.

I got off the chair to hug my sister. "What are you doing here? Why aren't you in Atlanta?"

She hugged me hard before replying. "With everything going on, I just wanted to be with family for a few days."

I crossed my arms over my chest. "You mean you felt bad for me when mom told you what happened, so you decided to drive down to take pity on me."

She shoved my shoulder. "Excuse me for wanting to be there for my only sister."

In truth, I was happy to see Frankie. It had been too long, regardless, and a friendly face amidst the mess that was my life was much appreciated. However, anytime I did see my sister, I was always reminded of how put together her life was. Sometimes it made me feel inadequate.

Yes, I was successful in my career, but Frankie was the youngest marketing VP in her company's history. Yes, until recently, I had my own place, but I rented and lived only miles from where we grew up, while Frankie moved to Atlanta and owned her own condo. The only thing we had in common was that we were both single. But even then, she one-upped me because her relationship status had always been her choice. She liked her independence and couldn't be bothered with the idea of marriage.

"You two okay with bunking together?"

I grinned. "Of course, let's get you settled."

Grabbing her duffel bag, I led the way into the room we'd now be sharing.

As soon as we walked in, Frankie shut the door behind her and perched on the bed.

"Alright, spill. I need all the details. I know you've been evading my texts."

I sighed. She didn't waste any time. "I told you it was over with Garrett. I'm not trying to hide anything."

"According to Mom, there's *a lot* more to the story. I can't believe it took me driving all the way down here to get you to talk."

I groaned, joining her on the bed. "What did she tell you?" I asked.

"Just that your asswipe, shit for brains, boyfriend cheated on you, and you moved out."

"Mom didn't tell you who with?"

Her eyebrows shot up. "No. Was it someone you knew?"

"It was *Nadine*."

"Shut the fuck up."

"I walked in on them."

"Stop. Tell me everything."

I rattled off all the details, even down to the fact that Nadine wasn't even fully dressed when I entered the room and caught them.

"What a bitch."

"I know."

"I never liked her. She totally gave off mean girl energy."

I shrugged. Had she? I always thought of her as nothing but a good friend until all this happened.

"Want to know the worst part?"

She nodded, her eyes wide.

"They had been sleeping together behind my back for *months*."

"No."

"Since Cabo."

"This is too much." Frankie was shaking her head in

disbelief now. "What did your other friends say when they found out?"

I felt tears pricking at the corners of my eyes.

"They knew," I said.

"Oh, Mattie." Frankie threw her arms around me and embraced me tightly. "You're better off without all of those assholes."

I held up my phone that I had been scrolling on earlier.

"Look," I said pathetically. "They were all at a house-warming party for Nadine and Garrett last night. That was *my* house."

She snatched the phone out of my hand.

"You cannot look at this. It's unhealthy." She tapped the screen a few times. "There, I deleted the app. No more cyberstalking for you."

I nodded solemnly.

"Now, come on. Let's go break into the good stuff Dad keeps at the top of the liquor cabinet."

Chapter Eight

I stared at a blank screen as Mike furiously checked his watch for the hundredth time.

"What is with the lack of respect these candidates have? I can't believe we have another no-show."

I closed my laptop and gave him a defeated shrug.

He sighed. "I think we have to call it."

"We can't," I said, panicked.

"Mattie, what other choice do we have? It's Friday, and we promised we'd have someone there late next week to start the trial. We have no options other than to let Bev know that we can't fulfill our commitment to her. I'm sure that nasty nephew of hers will be pleased."

I bristled at the memory of Giles. Letting him feel like he won made this all feel like even more of a failure.

"We've never had to back out like this before," I whispered.

Mike's face softened. "I hope you know that none of this is your fault. It's hard to branch out into new markets."

"Of course," I replied as he got up to leave the room.

He gave me an encouraging thumbs up. I nodded and tried to smile, but it didn't reach my eyes. Despite Mike telling me this wasn't on me, I couldn't help but feel like a complete failure. Why was nothing in my life working out for me right now?

I thought I had it all together. Clearly, I was falling apart.

<hr>

"MAKE SURE YOU GIRLS TIDY UP THE ROOM BEFORE everyone gets here," my mom called through a crack in the sliding glass door.

Frankie and I looked at each other and rolled our eyes before returning to sipping our wine. We had been sitting around the fire table on the patio catching up while our parents scampered around in the kitchen, getting things ready for a neighborhood party they were hosting.

"I swear she still thinks we're teenagers." Frankie lifted her legs and held them against her torso.

I snorted. "I can't believe she's still making me clean my room."

"At least you're getting free rent."

"Amen to that."

We clinked our glasses and laughed.

"I'm going to go the bathroom and get more wine," she said, getting up. "Don't worry. I'll throw our clothes under the bed while I'm in there."

"Bless you."

Once she was gone, I stared at the flickering fire, trying not to let any negative thoughts break down my mental barrier. This week at work had been a tough one. It was hard not to feel like a loser lately.

I glanced at the door to make sure Frankie wasn't close to returning. Quickly, I pulled out my phone and redownloaded the social media app she had deleted. I knew it was unhealthy to want to see what Garrett and my ex-friends were up to, but I couldn't help it. I was a masochist. Pictures filled my screen, and I started scrolling, desperate for updates.

My heart stopped, and my finger froze as I came across Nadine's latest post. My wine glass almost slipped from my other hand as I sat there in shock.

Filling up my screen was an image of Nadine's left hand. Her ring finger was adorned with a beautiful oval-shaped solitaire diamond set in a thin gold band. The kind of ring I had always dreamed of having. Panicking, I scrolled to her caption. This could not be real.

This may come as a shock to many that I'm not close to, but I'm engaged! We've been keeping our relationship private, but now I'm ready to scream it from the rooftops. I love this man, and I'm so excited to spend our lives together.

I flipped to the next picture she had posted. It was one of her and Garrett dressed in cocktail attire, posing with her hand outstretched to show off the ring.

My mouth hung open in shock. How could this be happening? We broke up *three weeks ago*.

The slider door opened, and I scrambled to turn off my phone before Frankie caught me.

My haphazard mannerisms warranted a strange look from her. "You good, Mattie?"

I grinned like a murderer who had just stashed the body underneath a blanket. "Of course." My voice was unusually high-pitched. I cleared my throat to try to cover it up.

"You're acting a little squirrelly."

"I just almost dropped my phone, is all."

She eyed me. "You better not be texting anyone you're not supposed to or be looking at any pictures you're not supposed to."

"Of course not." My smile was frozen on my face. I made a conscious effort to blink so I wouldn't look so psychotic.

"Do you have something in your eye?"

I stopped blinking.

"Let's see if Mom and Dad need help with anything." I sprang up out of my chair, desperate to move my body. If I sat under my sister's stare for a second longer, I knew she'd see right through my weak facade.

***

"So you're the one visiting from Atlanta? How exciting. I love it there. Isn't it just such a fun city?" Kathy, one of my parent's neighbors, had cornered me while I was making a fresh drink.

People had shown up an hour ago, and their house had turned into the fifty-five-plus version of a college frat party.

"That's my sister, Frankie. I'm Mattie. I live—well lived—just a few towns over."

Kathy's face immediately fell, and I knew my mother must have given her the scoop on my pathetic life.

"Oh, Mattie, sweetie. Your mom said you were staying with them. I'm so sorry about what happened. Men are scum, after all. I'm on husband number three, and let me tell you, it doesn't get any better."

"Great." My lips hurt from keeping them upturned as I dumped a shot of whiskey into the plastic tumbler my dad had given me. I normally didn't mix liquors, but tonight it felt like a great idea to sample everything.

"Darlene, come over here and meet Mattie."

A woman with fire engine red hair wearing a bejeweled sweatshirt joined Kathy's barricade.

"Oh now, aren't you just stunning? I already met your sister. I can't believe how gorgeous you two are."

"Thanks." I laughed out of discomfort.

"Darlene, Mattie is the one Mary told us about. The one that's staying with them for a while."

"Oh my god, of course. Terrible what happened to you. And with your best friend too. You know I got cheated on before I met my Stuart."

Kathy nodded sympathetically. "The world of dating is just horrendous. I've heard it's gotten even worse now with online dating. You can't pay most men to commit."

They continued to carry on about the horrors of modern-day dating while I sloshed my drink back and chugged almost all of it in one giant gulp. Tonight was not the night to watch my intake.

"AND NOW THEY'RE LIVING TOGETHER IN THE apartment *we* lived in together. Can you believe that?" Kathy, Darlene, and I were sitting on folding chairs in the driveway. I had lost count of what cocktail we were on hours ago.

"Unbelievable," Kathy replied.

"They're going straight to hell," Darlene slurred.

Kathy and I cackled.

"C'mere." I leaned into my newly captivated audience. "You want to know the worst part?"

Their eyes got wide as they waited for me to continue.

"They're"—I paused to hiccup—"*engaged*."

They gasped in unison.

"What a little punk." Kathy spilled a little of her drink while attempting to take another sip. "Oopsie."

"He can't do that after making you wait around all those years," exclaimed Darlene.

"I know." I nodded aggressively. The sudden movement of my head made me slightly nauseous.

"You know what you should do?" Kathy grabbed my arm, and I looked at her, eagerly anticipating her advice.

"What?"

"Call him. You need to tell him off."

"You know what, you're right." I burst out of my chair and immediately clutched the back of it for support as my vision doubled.

"You okay?" Frankie was at my side then, looking concerned.

"I'm fine," I slurred.

She raised her eyebrows and crossed her arms. "You're drunk."

"So?"

"So, we're at a party at our parents' house with a bunch of retirees, and you're wasted. What are you doing?"

"Is'not my fault." I pointed to Kathy and Darlene, who were suddenly—and conveniently—deep in conversation. "They were feeding me drinks."

Frankie rolled her eyes. "Don't blame Mom's friends."

"Well, whatever. The damage s'done. I'm going to pee."

"When you're done, just go drink some water and lie down."

I saluted her and pushed past the rest of the party attendees to get inside. A few people were in the kitchen, but they paid me no mind as I slipped into the guest bedroom.

With my inhibitions thoroughly shattered, I pulled out my phone and dialed Garrett's number. He picked up almost immediately.

"Mattie?"

My breath caught at the sound of his voice.

"Mattie, are you there?"

The rage I was feeling minutes ago dissolved into a puddle.

"How could you do this to me?" I whimpered.

"I'm sorry." He let out a slow breath. "I should have been honest with you a lot sooner. But we had been together for so long and I just didn't want to hurt you."

"Great job with that. Just s'ya know I was always suspicious," I lied.

"Are you drunk?" he asked.

"Does it matter?"

"I'd rather speak when you're sober."

"I'd rather not learn about your engagement through social media, but here we are."

There was a long pause on the other end of the line, and tears welled up in my eyes.

"Mattie—"

"How could you? That should have been us." The tears were now freely falling down my cheeks.

"All I can say is I'm sorry."

"Please, Garrett. Just tell me why. You owe me that much."

There was a moment of silence before I heard him sigh on the other end.

"She's pregnant," he whispered.

A sob escaped my lips before I clasped my hand over my mouth.

"It's early. We haven't told anyone yet. I didn't want you to find out this way."

I didn't even bother responding as I let the phone fall to the bed.

Pregnant?

My mind went completely blank.

Through my tears, I tripped out of the bedroom and back into the living room. I was about to be hysterical. I couldn't be here around all these people. Throwing open the front door, I walked to the end of the driveway, ignoring the glances of everyone around me.

"Mattie? What's wrong?"

I ignored my mother and continued to walk until I was on the street.

Golf carts were lined up in a neat row. I stumbled into the first one. My mother once told me that everyone left their keys in the ignition. There was no crime to worry about here. Sure enough, a keychain with fuzzy dice was dangling by the wheel, tempting me. I turned the keys without a second thought.

Frankie and my mother were running down the street waving their arms.

"Mattie, what are you doing?" one of them shouted as I

pulled the cart away from the curb and slammed on the gas.

Pregnant?

The word kept running through my mind. I started gasping for breath as my sobs became more and more frenzied. The tears blurred my vision as I whipped the cart onto the first turn out of the neighborhood. I needed to get out of here.

I threw the cart around the next blind turn, only to be met with another driver looking shocked to find me in their lane. I screamed and whipped the wheel in the other direction.

With the speed at which I was going and the force at which I turned, the cart started to tilt toward the passenger side. I tried to correct the wheel back but failed. The cart tipped sideways as if in slow motion before I felt myself flying out of it and crashing to the asphalt below.

"WHAT THE HELL WERE YOU THINKING?" MY DAD ROARED.

I was sitting on the medical exam table, waiting for the doctor to come back to stitch the large gash in my forehead.

"Stuart's cart is completely wrecked. Do you know how much money it's going to cost to fix that? Do you know how *embarrassed* we are?"

"Ron, don't yell. Everyone will hear you."

"I don't care," he barked. "Our daughter drunk drove our friend's golf cart and crashed it. I'll yell if I want to. You're lucky no one called the cops, and they aren't pressing charges."

My head was pounding from both the alcohol and the injury. I closed my eyes and willed my parents to disappear.

My mom got up and put a hand on my dad's arm. "Why don't you wait outside until you can calm down? Yelling isn't helping anything. I'll talk to Mattie."

He threw his hands up in exasperation and stormed out of the examination room.

A hand squeezed my knee, and I looked up to see my mother's concerned eyes.

"What happened?" she said in a comforting tone that I didn't deserve.

Her soft words caused me to break down all over again.

"Mommy," I sobbed through tears.

She pulled me to her and hugged me tightly.

"They're engaged," I choked out, unable to admit the rest of it.

She held on tighter, not needing more clarification than those two words.

"It's going to be okay, sweetie. You're stronger than this."

She held me while I cried until the doctor finally came in to stitch me up.

Wincing, I dabbed my forehead with a washcloth. I had to get five stitches last night, and the doctor instructed me to keep the area clean and dry.

I hardly recognized the reflection that stared back at me in the bathroom mirror. Aside from my scarred forehead, I had an angry patch on my chin where the skin had met the ground. My eyes were also swollen and puffy due to the hours upon hours of relentless crying.

It was almost noon when I emerged into the kitchen, desperate for caffeine to wake me from my coma-like trance.

"Nice of you to join us," my father grumbled as soon as I stepped into the main room.

My entire family was sitting at the dining table looking rather sullen.

"Is this an intervention?" I asked jokingly before sitting down to join them.

My mother reached across the table and grabbed my hand.

Oh boy. I was in for it.

"Matilda, sweetheart." This wasn't good. She hardly ever called me by my full name. "You know we love you. And we want nothing but the best for you…"

She trailed off and looked to my sister for support.

Frankie sighed and looked at me. "It's time to move out. You need to get back on your feet."

I groaned. "Is this about the crash? I know I fucked up, but I'll pay for it. In case you all don't remember, I had to deal with some very difficult news yesterday." Of course, they didn't know about the *most* difficult news I heard last night.

My father's face was red, but he continued to sit there, stewing, while my mother and Frankie handled the conversation.

"I know it was a tough pill to swallow, sweetie. Trust me. I would love nothing more than to wring his neck for you. But the reality is, they've moved on. And us babying you, letting you stay here? It isn't helping you anymore. It's been almost a month. It's time for you to start figuring out what's next. I haven't seen you so much as look at an apartment ad since you've been here."

"I've had a lot on my mind," I mumbled.

"Mattie, you need to do this," Frankie continued. "How would you feel if Nadine and Garrett could see how you reacted last night? Moving on is the best revenge, trust me."

I glared at Frankie, irritated she wasn't on my side.

"Excuse me for having a few issues right now. My life was completely upended just *weeks* ago." I turned my attention back to my mother. "You were the one encouraging me to wallow, remember?"

"But you haven't been wallowing. You've been pretending everything is fine until you finally blew up yesterday." She shook her head. "Look, Mattie. We're not saying you need to be okay just like that. We're just saying that you need to start making an effort."

"It wouldn't kill you to try something new," my dad finally spoke. "You've lived within the same twenty-mile radius your entire life. You've had the same boyfriend and friends for nearly a decade. Maybe it's good that you're being forced into a bit of change."

My mouth hung open. "Are you implying it was good that my boyfriend cheated on me with my best friend?"

He shrugged. "If it gets you to expand your horizons a little—"

"Dad!" I exclaimed.

He held up his hands, and my mom quickly stepped in.

"No one is saying that. We're just saying that maybe you, Ms. Optimistic, can turn this awful situation into an opportunity."

They all eagerly nodded in agreement at my mom's words.

I crossed my arms. Opportunity? What opportunity could I possibly make of this?

My whole life sucked. Even work was going terribly right now. I'd have to call Bev on Monday to tell her that we failed to find a property manager. How humiliating.

All of my buzzing thoughts started to settle as an idea began to form. Maybe I could solve my work problems *and* find some new opportunities all at the same time.

Chapter Nine

"THIS IS YOUR CAPTAIN SPEAKING. WE'RE GOING TO BE experiencing quite a bit of turbulence as we approach the mountains. Please stay seated and keep your seat belt fastened."

Leather might be permanently embedded underneath my fingernails from how hard my grip on the armrest was.

"You alright, young lady." The elderly man seated next to me looked genuinely concerned for my well-being.

I nodded but didn't even attempt to open my mouth for fear of vomiting all over him.

This was only the fourth flight I had ever taken in my entire life. The third one being the flight from Orlando to Denver. And this was *definitely* the smallest plane I had ever been on. I had no idea they even made airplanes with only fifteen rows and no middle seats.

The plane was enroute to Key Ridge, Colorado. My new home base. At least for now, that is. When I told Mike I wanted to take the PM position out here, his initial reaction was to say no.

"But it's a demotion," he had said while trying to talk me out of it.

I told him it didn't matter. I needed a change of scenery, and I needed it now. Besides, what could be more of an adventure than moving to a small mountain town with only a few days' notice?

My family wanted me to find an opportunity, and I sure as hell found one. Despite the terrifying plane ride, I could feel my positivity returning as if someone had plugged an IV full of sunshine directly into my veins.

I was excited to try something new, to meet someone new, to *live* somewhere new. I was most excited to see the mountains and *snow*. I had never seen snow before, but from what I had seen in Christmas movies, it looked magical.

I clutched my windbreaker tightly around me. Underneath it, I had layered two sweatshirts. Hopefully, I wasn't too cold upon arrival. I had no heavy coat, and Florida wasn't exactly the best place to buy one at the last minute. Acquiring weather-appropriate clothing would be high on my to-do list upon arrival.

"Alright, folks, please take one last look at those seat belts and make sure they're fastened nice and tight. It's going to be a bumpy landing."

The man sitting next to me leaned as far away from me as our seats would allow as I started my intentional breathing. So what if I sounded like a pregnant lady in a Lamaze class? It was worth it if it got me through this flight without being ill or passing out.

The plane jerked to the right, and I screamed involuntarily. The last minute of the ride felt like ages, but when we finally hit the tarmac, I sank back into my seat in a puddle of relief.

"Relaxing flight, eh?" the old jokester sitting next to me asked.

"Very." I tried to smile at him, but I still felt a little queasy.

When we arrived at the gate, I realized I hadn't once leaned over to look out the window. I cursed my fear of flying. Now I had missed out on the view of a lifetime.

After a few minutes, we deplaned, and I entered the tiniest airport I had ever seen. Sure, I hadn't had much experience, but this building was only one room. I could see the singular security line, the exit, and the world outside as soon as I stepped through the gate's threshold.

It should be easy enough to find baggage claim.

"I'M SORRY, BUT I CAN'T LET YOU RENT THIS CAR." The woman at the rental car agency looked between me and my Florida driver's ID and shook her head.

"What do you mean?" I asked, my friendly smile waning.

"Have you ever driven in the snow before?"

I shook my head. "No, but I promise I'm an excellent driver."

She didn't look convinced. "All of you warm weather folks flock to our small towns for vacation, and you get into accidents on our icy roads. Causes problems for everyone."

I guess I had to add winning over less-than-friendly locals to my list of things to accomplish.

"I'm actually moving here for a while," I informed her.

She gave me a bored look before typing something into her computer. "In that case, you better take one of our SUVs. They have four-wheel drive and snow tires." She eyed me one more time. "You'll need both."

"Great," I said with more cheerfulness than I felt.

After another fifteen minutes, I managed to talk the reluctant woman into handing over the keys to the car that I had paid for and made my way to the lot. As soon as I exited the building, I was pelted with the coldest air I had ever felt.

I wrapped my arms around my body. The windbreaker wasn't doing anything against these frigid temperatures. Maybe I hadn't known what I was getting myself into. They never looked cold when they walked through snow-covered, candlelit streets in the movies.

Before I could think of another negative thought, I looked up and witnessed the most stunning views I had ever seen. I was surrounded on all sides by jagged white-capped mountains. They towered over the airport and everything surrounding it.

"Wow," I breathed.

I forgot for a second how cold I was as I stepped in a small circle, taking in all three-hundred-sixty degrees of gorgeous views.

This was the right decision.

A short uneventful drive led me to The Key Ridge Ski Lodge, where I had told Bev I would meet her. For all the fuss the car rental lady made about driving, I expected a lot worse. The roads were clear, and I felt no less comfortable driving here than I did in Florida.

I parked the car in the front lot and took in my new surroundings. The lodge was a Bavarian building that looked like it was plucked straight out of the Swiss Alps. It was a shade of cream that stood out against the white snow and it had dark brown trim everywhere with a brown pointed roof to match. It was even better than the pictures.

"Mattie."

I looked up to see a tall woman in a green parka, Bev, waving at me from the lodge's entrance. To my dismay, an annoyingly attractive man with a permanent scowl etched on his face was next to her. Giles.

Waving, I approached them. "Bev, hi. It's so good to see you again."

"Glad you made it okay." She shook my hand.

I then extended my hand to Giles, who eyed it with distaste. Great, guess his attitude hadn't changed.

"What are you wearing?" he asked.

"A windbreaker. But don't worry. I plan to buy some warmer things now that I'm here. Florida didn't exactly have a lot of options."

"Clearly," he replied, looking at my forehead instead of my eyes.

I touched my stitches self-consciously.

"What did you do to your head?" he asked, leaning in closer to inspect. He had his hand up as if he was about to move my fingers out of the way but then recoiled when he realized how close he was to me.

"Oh, you know. Just the standard golf cart accident."

His eyebrows shot up into his messy dark blonde hair. "I definitely do not know."

He waited for me to elaborate, but I just snickered awkwardly and cleared my throat, shifting from side to side.

"Okay, then," he finally said when he realized I wasn't going to say more.

Bev shot a glance between the two of us and smirked before pinching my thin windbreaker. "You really don't have anything warm? Not even something you might have bought for a trip?" Concern crept into her voice.

"This is my first time visiting somewhere with a colder climate," I exclaimed, grateful for the change in subject. "It's so exciting to see snow up close and personal like this."

Giles scoffed. "You're telling me this is your first time seeing snow and we've entrusted our ski lodge to you?"

"Oh, don't worry about that." My cheeks hurt from either the cold or the fake smile. "I promise I'm very good at what I do. I'm confident this place will be sold out well into the spring months. I also did a ton of research on ski lodges while working on the pitch for this place."

"Whatever you say, Florida." He shrugged and turned back toward the entrance.

Bev grabbed my arm and led me in the same direction. "Let's get you inside before you freeze to death."

Crossing the threshold led us into the lodge's main lobby. The brown woodwork continued into this room and up to the beams on the high ceiling. The space was open, with a giant fireplace at its center. There were comfy armchairs surrounding the fire. To the right was a large reception desk.

Beyond the fireplace was another expansive room with a few folding tables and chairs. That area was nowhere near as grand as the rest of the room. I made a mental note to add that to the list of possible improvements.

"This is beautiful. It's the perfect cozy atmosphere." I noticed Giles rolling his eyes at my delight and tried not to let it affect me.

Bev sighed. "It is, isn't it? This place has been in the family for decades. I remember being a little girl, wandering these halls while my parents ran the place."

"What a wonderful place to grow up."

She nodded. I could see the memories flashing across her eyes as she probably tried to take in the room from a newcomer's perspective.

"Well, this is the heart and soul of the place, but there's a lot more to see. I know you had an overnight layover and must be exhausted, so I don't want to overwhelm you. Why don't you get some rest today and get settled? I can give you the official tour tomorrow."

"That sounds great," I said.

"Giles, let's take Mattie over to her apartment."

I winced and glanced in his direction.

"Sorry, no can do," he replied in a decidedly unapologetic tone. "Need to head to the office."

"Office?" I asked before I could stop myself.

He made eye contact as he was walking past me. "The office at the ski resort. I have some work to do."

"I thought your family only owned the lodge."

He crossed his arms impatiently. As if my genuine interest in his life and town offended him. "The resort used to be owned by a different family in Key Ridge. It got bought out by a big ski company a few years ago. I've been working there ever since I got back."

"Right, you just retired—"

"I really have to go," he said before nodding at his aunt and spinning on his heel.

"Okay, then. Great," I muttered under my breath.

"Don't worry about Giles." Bev waved her hand at his departing back. "He's got a lot going on, and he's handling it like an ass. He'll warm up eventually."

My throat itched to ask her more, but I held back, not wanting to seem too interested in her mysterious nephew.

"Um, so we were talking about my apartment."

"Right, yes. Looks like I'll just take you there by myself."

I followed her out of the main entrance and back to the front parking lot.

"This you?" Bev asked, pointing to the insanely large SUV the rental agency had given me.

"Yep." I unlocked the doors, and we stepped inside the oversized vehicle.

"They must have taken one look at your Florida license and insisted you take this."

"That's pretty much what happened."

I started the car, and Bev directed me out of the lot, past the building, and down a block. I could see the main street of town in the distance.

"Oh, is that the town? It's adorable. I can't wait to explore."

"I'll have Giles show you around."

"Great." I smiled back at her.

Just what I wanted. To spend time with the town jerk that already hated me. Maybe I could still win him over despite his bitterness at my company being here.

"Pull in here." Bev pointed to a modest tan house, and I drove up the driveway.

"Just keep the car on the left side of the driveway so I can get in and out of the garage."

"This is your house?" I looked at her, puzzled. I knew my accommodations were prearranged, but I assumed I would stay either at the lodge or an apartment in town.

"I've got a rental above my garage. It's a small space, but I think you'll find it—what's that word you love? *Cozy.*"

I laughed nervously. "Sorry, I tend to romanticize everything."

"Don't apologize. That kind of attitude is exactly what we need around here."

We walked up the driveway. To the left of the garage was a staircase that led to a small landing with a door. She handed me a key.

"I have a spare, but I promise I won't be barging in on you. Try not to lose this, alright?"

"Of course." I took the key from her and jiggled it in the old lock until there was a click.

The door opened up into a small entryway with slate tile. There was a bench and coat hooks on the wall and a rack for my boots—as soon as I bought some. The slate continued into the kitchen, which took up the entire left side of the apartment. The wood cabinets matched the wood floors in the living room and bedroom area. The space had no walls, but that added to its charm. A plush bed was situated in the far right corner of the room, and in front of that was a comfy-looking loveseat that faced a tv.

"You're right. This place is the definition of cozy." I took a few steps into the kitchen and looked out the window above the sink.

"I can see the mountains from here!" I exclaimed.

Bev chuckled. "You can see the mountains from almost every angle in this town."

"Well, this is amazing. I can't believe I get to stay here."

"It's all yours. I've left you some clean towels in the bathroom, and there's also a small washer/dryer combo in there. There are a few snacks in the fridge to tide you over, but you'll need to hit up a grocery store soon. Anyway, you've got my number, and you know where I live. Let me know if you need anything."

"I will. Thanks again, Bev. I'm so excited to be here."

I squealed as soon as she left me alone. This place was everything I had dreamed of and more.

Getting over my old life was going to be easier than I could have ever imagined.

Chapter Ten

BEEP BEEP BEEP

My phone continued to go off. I groaned in protest. My eyelids were heavy, and it was difficult to pry them open. When I finally did, I almost forgot that I was in a new room. The bed was heavenly. I had passed out almost as soon as my head hit the pillow.

BEEP BEEP BEEP

I reached for my phone to shut off the pushy alarm. Stretching my arms over my head, I rolled out of bed. As soon as my feet hit the floor, I recalled just how chilly my new surroundings were. Grabbing the blanket off the bed and wrapping it around myself, I went in search of a thermostat.

The white device was tucked away on the tiny sliver of wall between the kitchen and bathroom door. I cranked it up to seventy-two in the hopes that it would remove the inner chill that had grabbed onto my bones.

The moody blue sky shone through the window in the living room. It all looked so magical with the sun having just slipped behind the mountain tops. I glanced at the clock on the wall. It was only four pm. Apparently, it got dark here early. A glimmer caught my eye, and I gasped, rushing to the windowsill to get a closer look.

It was *actually* snowing.

I gleefully jumped up and down as I took in the white flakes falling softly from the sky. I needed to get out there and experience this firsthand.

I pulled on a long sleeve t-shirt and layered a green hoodie on top of it. I grabbed my windbreaker and keys. Checking the map on my phone revealed there was a super-store just fifteen minutes away. I could head there now to pick up some food and, hopefully, some warmer clothes.

I slipped into my ankle-length furry sheepskin boots—which, according to Frankie, were not actually a practical footwear choice for the snow—and headed out the door.

As soon as my boot connected with the ground outside, it shot out from beneath me. I shrieked. The thin layer of snow must have iced over while I was napping. My boots, while cute, didn't provide any traction on the slippery stairs.

This is what Frankie had meant by impractical.

I gripped the railing and took the steps slowly, one at a time. When I reached the bottom, I felt momentarily proud of myself for not slipping before realizing it was freezing outside. I waddled as quickly as I could manage to my new monster SUV and hopped in.

The leather seats were shockingly cold, and I let out another yelp. Thank god Bev wasn't around to witness this or she would be even less confident in my ability to run her ski lodge effectively.

The keys stuck when I put them in the ignition but the engine eventually started, and I blasted the heat. It wasn't until I was about to put the car in drive that I realized I couldn't see out the front window.

"What the—"

Upon closer examination, the window appeared covered in a layer of snow and ice. I turned on the windshield wipers only to be met with an angry scraping sound and a still-obstructed view.

Huh. I wondered what people did about this. Did everyone just sit around and wait for the heat of their car to melt the ice? Well, it didn't look like there was much on the window. I'm sure I wouldn't be here long.

I turned on the radio and scanned through the channels. A throwback station was playing Britney, so I turned it up. I sang along loudly while I waited for the ice to soften so the wipers could push it out of the way.

Rap Rap Rap

I screamed and clutched my chest, turning to see what had made the knocking sound. Clear brown eyes peered back at me through the window.

Giles.

As I rolled the window down, I couldn't help but notice how the ends of his hair curled up just underneath his striped black beanie. He gave me a confused look, and I prepared my best charming smile in return.

"Hey Giles, I was just head—"

"What are you doing?"

I inhaled sharply through my nose but did not drop my smile. I hated being interrupted, and if these initial interactions were a good indicator, Giles was about to test my patience.

"I was about to drive to the store nearby. I need to pick up a few thi—"

"No. Why are you just sitting here parked in the driveway? I pulled up five minutes ago and you haven't moved."

My smile finally dropped at his harsh tone. Politeness could only get me so far. It was clear I'd have to work extra hard to get on this guy's good side.

"You've been watching me for five minutes?"

He shrugged. "I was waiting to pull into the driveway. When you never backed out, I figured I might as well come see what the hell was taking you so long."

"So nice of you to check on me," I said in a sickeningly sweet tone. "I'm just waiting for my windshield to melt. You see, there's some ice on it, and I can't see—"

"You're waiting for your windshield to melt," he repeated and looked at me as if I was the biggest idiot on the planet.

"That's what I said. I can't see anything right no—"

"You're just sitting here. Waiting?"

"Yes," I huffed.

Giles opened the door of my backseat and felt around on the floor.

"What are you doing?" I asked as he produced a plastic stick-looking thing from my backseat. "What is that? And can you please stop interrupting—"

"Here," he said as he opened my door and shoved the foreign object into my hands.

"What am I supposed to do with this."

"It's a scraper."

I stared at him blankly.

"You use it to scrape."

I took the device and slowly got out of the car, fearing him outright calling me stupid. I examined the piece of plastic. It had bristles on one side and a plastic fan on the other. What had he called this?

"Umm I—"

"Jesus." He let out an exasperated sigh and snatched the stick back.

He proceeded to move to the front of my car and use the stick to chip away at the ice on the windshield.

Oh. That made a lot of sense.

I crossed my arms.

"Thanks," I called out over the scraping noises. "I appreciate the help. They never have to clear ice off the window in movies."

He paused to stare at me.

"The movies? Seriously?" He cocked his head and examined me.

I just laughed nervously and shifted my gaze to the mountains.

"Don't get out much, huh?"

"It's not that," I protested, although there was truth in his words. "I just grew up in Florida. We usually stayed pretty local for vacations. My parents weren't into the whole 'ski trips in Aspen' thing."

"Aspen is overrated."

"Right, sure. I was just using it as an example since it's famous and all."

I rocked back and forth on my boots, unsure what to say next. Giles wasn't exactly a chatterbox, and anytime I spoke to him, I felt like I was a giant pain in his ass.

"So maybe I should give this whole scraping thing a try." I held out my hand, but he didn't give it over.

"I'm almost done," he said and continued with what he

was doing. After a few seconds, he tossed the stick back where he found it.

"Do you know how to use your defrosters?" he asked.

"Ummm…" I trailed off, too scared to give him an honest answer.

"Move it." He pushed past me and leaned over the driver's seat to the central control unit. "Look at this."

I leaned in next to him to see. There wasn't a lot of room with us both leaning through the same doorframe, so I was forced to press my side against his. He smelled good. And his body felt warm against my freezing one. I shook my head and focused on what he was showing me. He pointed out a knob that was next to the heat settings.

"Push this one for rear defrost and this one for front defrost. It'll help melt the ice faster next time this happens."

"Ah, of course, there would be a button for that. Duh. Thanks." I stood up and put a few steps of space between us before crossing my arms and rubbing my hands up and down them. How did anyone live in these frigid conditions?

Giles exited the driver's side and leaned against the doorframe, eyeing me disdainfully.

"You should wear a warmer coat than that. You'll freeze to death."

Thanks, Sherlock.

"I know. That's kind of what I was trying to do right now. Buy some warmer clothes."

He stared at me blankly.

"Okay, well…"

Still nothing.

"It was great running into you again." I walked past him and re-entered the car. "I'm sure I'll see you around at the lodge."

I reached for the door to slam it closed, but Giles was faster than me. He gripped the top of the window so that when I pulled, the door didn't move an inch.

This guy was wearing on my last nerve.

Taking an exaggerated breath in, I glared at the towering man in my way. My polite smile and sweet voice had dissolved entirely at this point.

"What's your problem," I barked.

He chuckled. "I can't let you drive anywhere right now."

"Why not?"

"Because it's people like you that have never driven in the snow and don't know what they're doing that cause accidents. You would be a danger to yourself and everyone on the road."

"Have you seen this monstrosity that I'm driving? There's no way this thing slides anywhere."

"I appreciate your heavy machinery, but the answer is still no."

"But I need food. And clothes. Like you said, I'll freeze to death."

"Should have come better prepared."

"But—"

"What's all that commotion down there?"

Our face-off was thankfully interrupted by Bev walking down her front entrance and toward us.

"I'm trying to watch my show, and all I hear is you two yammering on about something."

"Hey, Aunt Bev." His evil demeanor was replaced with a warm smile as he hugged Bev. "I just stopped by to make sure you still had power. I know that tree branch has been threatening your line ever since that big storm a few weeks ago."

"I'm fine, as you can see." She patted his chest and then directed her attention to me.

"How are you settling in, Mattie? Do you need anything?"

"Actually, yes. I'm trying to head out to buy a few necessities, but your nephew has detained me." I smiled at Bev and glared at Giles, sure she would be on my side. "He said I can't drive in these conditions."

"Well, you can't," she said matter-of-factly.

"Excuse me?" My mouth hung open in shock.

"Roads are slick, and you aren't used to it. I'd kick myself if something happened to you or someone else on the road."

"Told you." Giles smirked at me.

I stuck my tongue out at him.

His mouth hung open. "Did you just—"

"Giles will drive you."

"What?" we both replied in unison.

"These conditions are nothing for a local. He'll get you to the store just fine, and you'll be able to get whatever you need."

"Bev I can't. I've got to—"

"That's enough, Giles. You were raised to be a gentleman, and a gentleman helps out when the newest town resident is in desperate need of a sweater and a snack. Isn't that right?"

"Fine," he grumbled. "We'll take my car." He stalked off to a truck parked in the street.

"Great." I smiled at Bev hoping my disdain for her nephew wasn't written all over my face.

"Have fun," she called out.

As soon as the truck pulled into the gigantic parking lot I sprung out of the door. That had been the most awkward car ride of my entire life. After making small talk about the snow, or the town, and receiving nothing but grunts in return, I gave up trying to communicate with him. At least now I could do my shopping in peace and get the rest of this interaction over with as quickly as possible.

The driver-side door slammed behind me. I whipped my head around to see Giles exiting the truck.

"You're coming in too?" I knew my tone gave away my disappointment.

He shrugged. "Too cold to wait outside."

"Of course."

We walked side by side to the automatic entry doors. I grabbed a cart and headed for the grocery section.

To my dismay, instead of wandering off someplace else, Giles fell into step beside me.

"So," I started, still determined I could win him over. Whatever preconceived notions he had about me were clearly wrong. "Giles is an interesting name."

He shrugged and examined an apple as I threw a few ready-made salads into the cart.

"Were you named after someone?" I pressed when he didn't respond.

"My grandfather."

"Oh my god," I said excitedly, stopping the cart. "I was named after my grandmother. Mattie is short for Matilda.

That's so crazy we were both named after our grandparents."

He looked bored. "Is it?"

I faltered at his dry response and continued to push the cart forward. "Well, more like crazy coincidence than actually crazy. It's just interesting is all."

"Is it?" he repeated, and it took all of my self-control not to shove his chest and push his smug face away from me.

"I guess not," I finally relented.

We continued in silence as I grabbed what I needed. Apparently, I had no self-preservation techniques because my brain continued to send messages to my mouth to make small talk.

"So, snowboarding. That's an exciting career."

His eyes grew wide in surprise before he tore them away from mine.

"You googled me?"

"My coworker had heard of you, so I might have done some research."

"If you were any good at researching, you'd know I'm retired."

"Well, it's still impressive that you were able to do it professionally. You must be really good."

"I used to be better. It's all downhill once you're in your thirties."

"That's not a very good attitude to have."

He looked at me pointedly. "It's just the truth."

"I guess if you're comparing yourself to a younger you, then sure. Our bones get creakier, and our muscles get sorer. But you were still one of the best in the world in your prime, and I'm sure you're still, like, in the ninety-ninth percentile of snowboarders now. That's something to be proud of."

I didn't know why I was yammering on about his snowboarding career, but the fact that he had responded with more than one word had sent me into a vocal frenzy. I was desperate to keep the conversation going.

That desperation was one-sided because Giles didn't say anything after that.

I sighed and trudged through the aisle toward the clothing department. I threw a few sweaters into the cart and kept moving to outerwear. There were just a few coats to choose from, and only one appeared to be in my size. It was, unfortunately, neon orange with camo pockets.

"Shoot, not a very big selection."

"Nothing here good enough for you?" Giles was resting an arm on the coat rack and staring down at me.

I balked at him. "That's not what I meant. There's just not a lot of options."

"Sorry, it isn't up to your standards."

Stuffing the coat into the cart, I glared at him. "What are you even talking about? I'm from Florida. That in no way makes me a snob, or rich." I angrily marched on. "And you're one to talk, Mr. hot-shot-professional-snowboarder. You're the one that probably thinks this place is beneath him."

As if on cue, one of the workers walked up to us. "Hey Giles, twice in one week, huh?"

"Yeah, man. Just one of those weeks."

I rolled my eyes. "Whatever, that doesn't prove anything."

A smirk started to form on his lips before he coughed to disguise it.

After I grabbed a pair of black rubber-soled boots, we hit the checkout line. The rest of the transaction happened without either of us speaking a word. Why should I bother trying if he was so determined not to be polite?

Back at the car, I stuffed my purchases into his trunk. I climbed into the passenger seat and prepared myself for another uncomfortable drive.

He slid into the driver's seat and started the engine. The cool air blasted from the vents, and I began to shiver.

"Why does it take so long for the heat to get going?" I asked through chattering teeth.

"The car engine has to heat up, Einstein."

"Thanks, so much for the science lesson," I mumbled.

He chuckled, and I spun around in my seat to face him.

"You know what, I don't know what your deal is, but you could at least try to be civil toward me. You don't even know me. I promise I'm a nice person. I just want to help with the lodge. I'm not some corporate monster that's descended upon your town despite what you might think."

"I am being civil."

"You call snippy responses or ignoring me, civil?"

"I drove you here, didn't I?" He was glaring at me now.

"Only because your aunt practically forced you to."

"Hey, look. I'm sorry if I'm not falling all over you. I'm sure that's what you're used to, right? Just because you usually get everything you want from guys doesn't mean I have to bend over backward for you."

I laughed bitterly. "Me? Get everything I want from men? That's a good one."

He pulled out of the parking lot but snuck a glance at me. His hard eyes had softened ever so slightly.

"Seems like there's a story there."

"There's not."

He whistled. "Must have been bad. Nasty breakup or something?"

"You could say that," I muttered, staring out the window.

"Did you drive the last guy away with your ditzy attitude? Or was it your affinity for sticking your nose in other peoples' business?"

I whipped my head around. "Why don't you shut the hell up."

He took his eyes off the road briefly to glance at me. At least he had the decency to look contrite.

I crossed my arms and resumed staring out the window, not caring that I had just made a scene. He had been baiting me all night. He had wanted an outburst out of me, and now he had one.

Screw him. Honey could only get you so far if the fly turned out to be a hornet.

After another minute, Giles sighed. "Look, I'm sorry. That was way out of line."

I didn't respond or turn to look at him.

"I might not like that you're here, but it doesn't give me an excuse to make personal jabs at you." He cursed under his breath. "Look, I've got a lot going on right now. It's not an excuse to be a dick, but it is what it is. I'll try to stay out of your way while you're here for the next few weeks."

My ears perked up. "Well, I might be gone then, but someone from my company will be here after that. Hopefully, you don't treat them this poorly."

"The trial period will be up in a few weeks. Then this will all be over," he insisted.

"Well, I plan to wow your aunt right into signing a contract with us."

"Sorry to break it to you, but that won't happen. I have a partial stake at this lodge, too. I only agreed to the trial period because she begged me to give it a chance. I will not be so generous when it comes to signing a long-term contract."

My mouth hung open. "But I thought Bev was the primary decision maker."

He shrugged. "Technically, she is. But I've got a lot of history with the lodge too. Plus, we're family. She's going to take that into account in the end."

"We'll see about that," I said.

He opened his mouth as if to say something else but thankfully shut it.

I'm not sure what his problem with me was, but it sure as hell wasn't going to get in the way of me doing my job. Once Bev saw how much of an asset I could be, then I'm sure she would sign the contract. She had said it herself. They were drowning. I just needed to make a good impression tomorrow and hit the ground running with whatever work needed to be done.

Giles Stone was not my problem, and I refused to spend one more iota of energy being worried about winning him over.

Chapter Eleven

"Good morning." I swept into the lobby bright and early with a drink carrier full of coffee in tow.

Bev was sitting at the front desk. Unfortunately for me, Giles was seated beside her.

"Well, aren't you Ms. Rise-and-Shine?" Bev took one of the cups I handed her and sipped it gratefully.

"I got up a couple of hours ago. I wanted to make sure I got here early enough to have time for a tour. Plus, I had to check out that cute cafe across the street from your house. It's adorable in there."

"Lucy's place," Bev said.

"I love that everyone knows everyone here."

"It's a small town. You'll get to know all of the locals soon enough."

"Good morning, Giles. Coffee?" I handed him a cup in what I hoped could be considered a peace offering.

To my genuine surprise, he nodded and took it from me without a fight.

"Thanks," he said.

"So, are you ready to give me the tour? I'm so excited to see everything. Are the rooms all the same inside? Can I see an example of every layout?"

Giles side-eyed Bev.

"You're quite the burst of energy." She chuckled before finally eyeing my new vibrant coat. "Um, that's a loud coat you've got yourself there."

Giles smirked into his coffee cup.

"Isn't it fun," I replied, shaking it off my shoulders. "The store didn't have many options, but I feel like now that I have it, I might as well embrace it."

"I might need sunglasses if you're going to show up every day wearing that," Giles said. This time there was a playfulness in his voice.

I laughed maniacally. "That's funny," I choked out.

They eyed me like they thought I should be medicated, so I cleared my throat to try to bring it down a notch. My nerves were getting the best of me. I had been up since five a.m. and had already consumed four cups of coffee. My jittery energy was not giving off the stellar first-day-on-the-job impression I wanted.

"So," I started again. "The tour?"

"Right, yes." Bev got up and came around to the other side of the desk.

She took my coat and placed it on a nearby hook.

"Off the main lobby, through this hallway, are twenty-five rooms." We walked down a short hallway, and she pointed out the different types of rooms. "Straight through this hallway, there's an exit and a stairwell. The stairs take you to a second and third floor with twenty-five additional rooms each. The only other way up to the rooms is through the elevator off the main lobby. If you head out the exit in the stairwell, it'll take you to our fenced-in spa area. We have a ten-person jacuzzi that's popular with the guests after a long day of skiing."

We poked our heads outside briefly, and I saw the spa area in question. It looked clean and had a few chairs scattered around. I made a mental note to buy some string lights to hang over the top.

"Do you have a map of the lodge anywhere?" I asked as we closed the door to the outside.

"Nope, I know this place like the back of my hand."

"It's just they can be helpful for guests. I can whip one up in photoshop and print some out. We can place a few in the hallways."

"Sure, if you think the guests will like that. I guess we do get a lot of questions about where the hot tub is. People tend to stop paying attention when you tell them where everything is located during check-in."

"About check-in. We have this great software I can hook the hotel up to. It tracks room occupancy and allows guests to check in directly from their phones."

Bev looked at me unconvinced. "I'm sure that's great and all, but a lot of guests like to check in at the front desk. It's part of the small town charm to welcome them and give them local recommendations."

"Right, of course. And they still have that option. This would just be for people checking in late that maybe want to get straight to sleep or something like that. Trust me. It's a great time saver."

"If you say so." Bev gestured toward the stairs. "Let me show you the basement. Not much to look at down there, but it's where the laundry machine is and the supply closet."

We walked down the stairs, and Bev opened the door.

"There isn't a lock or anything on it to keep guests out?"

"Haven't ever bothered with one. Usually, guests aren't wandering around down here."

"Might be a good idea to add one, just in case."

I surveyed the small basement. There was a large industrial washing machine and shelves stacked with linens and other supplies, as well as an old green couch in the middle of the room.

"We dragged that thing down here years ago. Sometimes it's nice to sit down here when you're doing a bunch of loads and folding everything."

"Of course," I said. "This setup looks pretty organized. Do you keep an inventory of everything?"

Bev laughed. "So many questions."

"Sorry. I'm just excited to jump right in."

"We don't have an inventory list but feel free to knock yourself out."

I pulled out my phone to make a to-do list.

Bev led me upstairs and through the hallway, back to the lobby area.

"You've already seen this room, but let me give you the lay of the land." She gestured to the front desk. "Obviously, this is our check-in area. We've got two employees that take most of our night shifts. In the center, we've got what I like to call our gathering area. We light a fire most evenings."

"Have you ever done a complimentary happy hour for guests?"

She shook her head.

"Might be a nice idea to do once a week. Builds a sense

of comradery and often leads to glowing reviews, and all we have to do is invest in a few bottles of wine."

I jotted down a note.

"Welp, that's pretty much the tour."

"What's that room used for?" I pointed to the space beyond the fireplace that I had noticed yesterday. It was sparsely furnished and separated from the main lobby by a half wall.

"We used to offer a complimentary breakfast that we served in there. But since most folks that come here are looking to get an early start on the slopes, we never got many takers. We transitioned to coffee and muffins by the front desk for people to grab and go. Now this room basically sits empty."

I walked over to it and examined the room. An extended bar area, likely used as the breakfast buffet, ran along the right back wall. I noticed the room had an exterior exit that led to the main street, which was just a block away from the ski resort.

There was also a double door on the left side. I walked over and poked my head through to discover a small kitchen.

"It almost seems like it used to be a restaurant."

"Once upon a time, when my parents owned this place, it was. They served homestyle meals to locals and anyone visiting. I used to love coming in here as a kid. Made the whole lodge feel alive."

"Why did it close?"

She shrugged. "Too much work, I guess. They had it open for at least two decades before calling it quits when they got older. It had been shut down for years by the time my sister and I took over the place."

I looked at her in surprise.

"Oh, I didn't realize you had a sister. Will I get to meet the other owners?"

She leaned against the wall and stared out the window.

"Unfortunately, my sister and brother-in-law passed away last year. It's one of the reasons I'm so in over my head now. It's hard to do this without them."

"Oh, I'm so sorry. I had no idea."

She waved me off.

Bev's sister. She hadn't mentioned any other siblings. And if Giles was her nephew, did that mean… Shit, had he just lost his parents?

"So Giles's parents…" I trailed off.

She just nodded. "I miss them like crazy. And I know it's killing Giles. They were so proud of him. Used to talk the guests' ears off about their professional snowboarder son. This place is a constant reminder of them." We stood there in silence. "You got a sister?"

"Yes. I can't even imagine losing her."

We both stood there for a moment before Bev pushed off against the wall and gestured for me to follow.

"Come on. I'll show you the computer and the books."

"Now see, this tab is where I've put all the upcoming reservations. I've got it color-coded by room type and occupancy."

I pointed out the features of the new spreadsheet I had whipped up to Giles. I had only been here a few hours, but I had already transitioned all of their upcoming reservations from a binder to the computer. Now I was trying to teach Giles my system.

"There wasn't anything wrong with the binder," he grumbled.

"Didn't you say you had another job at the ski resort?" I asked with a sweet smile.

Surprisingly that got a smirk out of him. "Bev wanted me to be here for your first day."

"Well, thank god for that." I took a chance and winked at him, and he bit his bottom lip to keep his smirk from growing.

"All I'm saying is Bev and my family have been doing this for decades, and the binder system never failed."

"You say that now but wait until someone spills a mug of coffee all over it, and it becomes illegible. Trust me, I've seen it happen."

Key Ridge Lodge was pretty dead at the moment, but Bev assured me it was because it was still the beginning of the season. The ski area only had one run open, and it would be at least another week before it opened up more. Then guests would be flooding in.

She also informed me there was a large commercial resort just thirty minutes up the road. It had become so popular at this point that a lot of their spillover traffic had transitioned to Key Ridge. The past two years had been the busiest winters they'd ever seen.

I flashed back to a memory of Garrett promising to teach me to ski one day. He and his friends would always take an annual ski trip. One year, when we first started dating, I begged to go with him. I just wanted to see the snow and browse the cute shops. He declined, informing me it was boys only and that we could do a trip just the two of us another time. Funny how "another time" never came.

The front door opened, and I was jerked from my thoughts as a tall, burly man in a red flannel shirt came barging in.

"Hey, man." The jovial-looking lumberjack hesitated when he saw me. "This the corporate hire you flew out here?"

Before Giles could speak, I threw on my most impressive smile. "Hi there, I'm Mattie."

"Johnny's the name." He shook my hand enthusiastically. "I'm obviously the better-looking cousin."

"Oh, so you're Bev's son? It's so nice to meet you."

"You, too. They didn't say you were a looker." He winked at me good-naturedly.

I giggled. "Aren't you the charmer?"

"I try. Maybe you could put in a good word with my wife. She hasn't found me charming in years."

"I'll be sure to do that."

"Don't let it go to your head. Johnny could flirt with a tree trunk."

"Ouch, cuz." He placed a hand on his heart as if wounded. "I'm hurt."

Giles turned to me. "Don't let him scare you off. He can be a bit much."

"On the contrary, I find his jolliness quite refreshing." I looked back at Giles teasingly.

He raised his eyebrows as if pretending he didn't know what I was trying to imply.

"So, Mattie. What do you think of our humble lodge so far?" Johnny leaned on the desk.

"It's fantastic. I can see why it's so popular."

Giles snorted and I ignored him.

"Any grand ideas for the place?" Johnny continued his polite line of questioning, something that was apparently not impossible for the men in this family.

"Well, definitely a lot of odds and ends that I've already written down. I do have one crazy idea that I'm pretty excited about."

"Do tell?" Johnny asked at the same time I swear I heard Giles mumble, "Spare me."

"Well, I was talking with Bev about the old breakfast place, and I brought up maybe trying to turn it into a casual lounge."

She had loved the idea. She didn't want to be over-whelmed with work, but when I convinced her I could handle it, she was practically glowing with the idea of restoring the place to some of its former glory.

Johnny looked interested.

Giles, on the other hand, scowled at my idea. "What do you know about running a restaurant?" he demanded.

"I said lounge, not restaurant. And not a ton, but I have a degree in hospitality, and Bev mentioned a few people in town who would love to help get the place back up and running."

"The guests don't need to eat here. They can go into town."

I refused to let Giles's snide remarks get to me. "It would be for more than just the guests. Bev said we already have a liquor license. We could open the place up to anyone skiing here for the day. We can have daily specials and get the Après-ski crowd."

"What would you know about Après-ski?" Giles glared at me.

"You'd be surprised by the information you can find on the internet nowadays."

Johnny chuckled.

"It wouldn't work. We've got enough going on as it is," Giles insisted.

"Bev seems to think it's worth a shot. I'm great with decorating on a budget. And I'm not talking about a full menu or anything. Just some small bites that are easy to whip up and a couple of bartenders."

"I think it's a great idea," Johnny said.

"That's because you're too nice. It's a terrible idea. It's hard enough to find staff here in the winter. We can barely keep the lights on as it is, and you want to add more to our plate?"

"I didn't think—"

"Of course, you didn't think," he snapped.

Tears were welling up behind my eyes. I wasn't used to this kind of verbal abuse on a daily basis.

"Look, I just thought it was a good idea. The space is completely unused. Wouldn't it be nice to see it come alive again? Bev said it would mean a lot to her. Wouldn't your parents have loved it?"

As soon as the words left my mouth, I sucked in a breath. Shit, that was crossing a line.

Giles gripped the desk. "You need to stop talking."

"I'm sorr—"

"Now."

He stalked off without another word, back through the front door.

I groaned and threw my head back. "Shit, I totally put my foot in my mouth. He hates me even more now."

Johnny shook off my words. "I'm sure he doesn't hate

you, and you didn't do anything wrong. Giles hasn't been himself since the accident." He sighed. "His parents are a sore subject, but you were right. They would have loved to see the energy being injected back into this place. It was their pride and joy."

"I shouldn't have said anything. It's none of my business." I hung my head feeling ashamed for bringing up such a sensitive topic.

Johnny reached across the desk and squeezed my arm like we were already familiar.

"Seriously, Mattie. Don't worry about it."

I forced a smile and nodded at him. I still felt like crap. For a second, it had almost felt like Giles's chilly attitude toward me was thawing. Now with the lounge idea, and my thoughtless comment, we were back to square one. Maybe even worse.

The next time I saw him, I would make amends. There was no way I could go through the whole trial with him hating me.

Chapter Twelve

"Here's your key Mr. Williams. Please let me know if we can do anything to make your stay more enjoyable." The forty-something man smiled and nodded at me before heading toward the elevators.

Since I arrived a week ago, more guests had started to trickle in. We had also gotten a decent amount of snow since then, and the ski resort was now over fifty percent open.

A few days ago, I had walked to the base of the hill to see the skiers and snowboarders zip down. It was exhilarating watching them. Johnny had said he wanted to take me one day, but I was too nervous to take him up on his offer.

The lodge was running smoothly too. I had already implemented several new processes to improve efficiency at the front desk. Bev and I had also started tackling the project of cleaning up the former restaurant. I was confident the space would be popular with tourists and locals by the time we finished with it.

"Mattie, delivery for you." Bev walked in and tossed a package in my direction.

I quickly tore open the white paper.

"Nice, it's the lock I ordered."

"Lock?"

"For the basement. I want to make sure no guests can accidentally wander down there."

"Want me to get Giles to install that for you?"

I shook off her offer. "I got this. I just need a screwdriver and the instruction manual."

"There should be a toolbox on one of the bottom shelves down there."

"Thanks. I'll be back in a bit."

Grabbing the lock, I headed for the stairwell. The basement smelled mustier than I remembered. I made a mental note to buy an air freshener for the space.

I spotted a red toolbox on a lower shelf and sifted through its contents until I produced a screwdriver.

Getting to work, I started to unscrew the existing doorknob. Since the thing had probably been there for decades, the screws had layers of paint stuck on them, and they proved difficult to loosen. Leveraging my other hand to hold the door in place, I used all my strength to get the screws undone. When the knob finally hit the floor, I gave myself a mental pat on the back for my handiness.

And Bev thought I might need help. *Ha!*

I opened the instructions and placed the new doorknob-electric-lock combo in its new home. This part of the process was much easier as there were no ancient screws involved. I was screwing the last piece into place when I felt a presence looming in the stairwell.

Giles was leaning against the wall just outside the doorframe.

"Oh, um, hi." I fumbled over my words.

I had only seen Giles in passing since he stormed out of here last week. I felt terrible I hadn't had the chance to apologize. But I had to admit that life was a lot more pleasant when he was avoiding me and not criticizing my every move.

"Bev sent me down here to see if you needed help."

"Nope, I'm just finishing up." To prove my point, I screwed in the final screw and took a step back to admire my handiwork. "There. All done. Much more secure."

He pushed off the wall and stepped through the doorframe to inspect the new lock. "Looks good."

"Thanks." I beamed at his minuscule compliment.

"Would look even better if it wasn't on backward."

"It's not on backward." I looked down in a panic.

He grabbed the knob and gestured to the electronic keypad.

"Shouldn't the lock code be on the *outside* of the door?"

I faltered. "Shit."

He chuckled. "Nice try, Florida."

"I'd prefer it if you called me Mattie."

"Okay." The twinkle in his eye told me he had no intention of honoring my request.

His amused expression made my stomach do a little flip. It was a welcome change from his typical scowl. Even though it *was* at the expense of my dumb mistake.

"Guess I better fix it," I muttered.

He grabbed the screwdriver from my hand and tossed it into the box behind me. "Later," he said. "Bev needs you back at the front desk."

"Fine. Fine. We'll just leave the basement as unsecure as ever."

Before we ascended, I chewed my lip and glanced back at Giles. "I'm sorry, by the way, about last week. I shouldn't have said anything about your—" I hesitated. "Anyway, I'm just sorry."

He cocked his head. I was surprised to see warmth in his brown eyes. A small smile played on his lips.

"It's forgotten."

My shoulders sagged in relief. "Thanks."

I turned to head back up the stairs, but my foot caught the ledge of the step, and I felt myself starting to fall forward. Before my face could connect with the ground, large hands were on my waist, pulling me back.

"Woah there." Giles was now directly behind me, holding me by my sides. The proximity of his warm body sent shockwaves through my veins, and my cheeks immediately flushed. I snuck a glance at him, surprised to see he wasn't pulling away in disgust. It was impossible to ignore his attractiveness when our faces were only inches apart.

My lips parted, but no words came out as we stood there for another half a second. Before I could say anything, Giles cleared his throat and snatched his hands away from me.

"Th-thanks," I stuttered, trying to get my bearings. "That could have been bad."

"Couldn't have you adding another gash to your face." He pointed to my still-recovering forehead. "Most people get broken noses out on the mountain, not climbing up a short flight of stairs."

"Ha. Ha." I rolled my eyes at him. "Wow, did you just make a joke?"

He shrugged. "It's been known to happen on occasion."

"Only if it's at my expense, right?" I teased.

"Not my fault you're an easy target."

He wasn't even trying to hide his smile anymore. It softened his whole face and made him seem a hell of a lot more approachable than his typical grimace.

"You should smile more often. You have a nice one," I said.

And just like that, his face fell. He cleared his throat again, dropping his eyes so they wouldn't meet mine.

Oh well. It was nice while it lasted.

I shook my head and walked back upstairs to the front desk. That was the most pleasant interaction Giles and I had ever had. I didn't care how brief it was. I was calling it a win.

"Excuse me." I looked up from the computer to see a brunette with long hair tucked under a beanie peering over the desk.

"Hi, there. Are you looking for a room?"

She laughed. "I'm looking for my husband. Johnny. Have you seen him?'

My eyes brightened upon realization.

"Oh my gosh, hi. You're Johnny's wife. It's so nice to meet you."

She smiled and extended her hand. "Erin. It's nice to meet you. You're Mattie, right? The new property manager?"

I nodded. "Yep, that's me. And you just missed Johnny.

He dropped by to take Bev to an appointment about an hour ago."

"Ah shoot, oh well. I thought we were supposed to have lunch." She held up a white sack. "I brought sandwiches. Any interest?"

My stomach growled just at the mention of food.

"Yes, please."

Erin swung around the desk and took the seat next to me as we dove into the food.

"I'm glad I'm finally meeting you. Johnny has been singing your praises. Says Bev seems more relaxed this week than she's been all year."

"That's the goal," I said, pleased with the news that Johnny thought I was doing a good job. One point for me in the battle of getting this long-term contract signed. "Do you work in town?" I asked her in between bites.

"I'm a substitute teacher at the elementary school."

"That must be fun."

"Fun. A living nightmare. Depends on the day."

We both laughed and continued to get to know each other.

"So, what brings you to our quaint town of Key Ridge? Rumor has it that you've never even seen snow before."

I put my hand on my forehead. "Great. It looks like my reputation proceeds me."

"That and the neon orange coat you've been walking around town in." She laughed. "Only someone that didn't have any options would buy a coat like that."

I groaned. "I swear it was all they had."

"Don't worry about it," she replied, waving off my misery. "I've got so many coats I've been meaning to donate. I'll give you one."

"That would be amazing, Erin. Thank you."

"Of course." She paused. "So, not to pry, but you didn't answer my question earlier. What brings you to town? It seems like a lot to move halfway across the country just for a job at our lil' ol' lodge."

"The company I work for manages properties. When this job came up, I thought it sounded like a fun adventure." I was purposefully being evasive, but I also didn't want to bring up the sore subject that was my ex-boyfriend and former life.

Erin nodded, seeming to sense that I was holding back. I felt guilty. This was the first person genuinely trying to get to know me, and I was being surface-level with her.

"Actually, that's not quite the whole truth." I hesitated before continuing. "I decided to move here after I found out my boyfriend was cheating on me. We lived together, and I thought we were going to get married. Anyway, I won't bore you with the gory details but long story short, I desperately needed a fresh start."

"Shit. I'm sorry. That royally sucks." She pursed her lips and looked down at her sandwich. "You know, before Johnny, my high school boyfriend cheated on me. With my friend, too. Can you imagine that? I can't believe I was so dense that I didn't realize they were sneaking around behind my back for weeks."

I choked on the bite I had just taken and started violently coughing.

"That's terrible." I managed to spew out.

"Well, I'm glad you're here. It's fun to have someone new in town." She threw her finger up as if thinking of a brilliant idea. "Johnny and I are having a bonfire this weekend. You have to come."

"That would be great." I was buzzing with energy at the thought of having plans unrelated to work. "Are you sure?"

"Positive. It'll be so much fun. Just a few friends. It's a potluck but no need to bring anything fancy."

I refrained from admitting that I was a terrible cook. Hopefully, chips and salsa would suffice as a dish.

"Sounds like fun," I replied, smiling.

We carried on for a while longer until we both finished our food. It was nice to talk to a friendly face for a change. It made me realize how much I missed Frankie. I needed to text her.

As if sensing my good mood, Giles appeared out of thin air and stood expectantly at the front desk.

"Giles." Erin threw her arms around him in an embrace.

To my surprise, he didn't recoil. I guess it was just my cheery demeanor he couldn't stand.

"Hey," I greeted him weakly.

He nodded in my direction, barely acknowledging my existence.

"Erin, Jonny wanted me to tell you that he's sorry, but he completely forgot about lunch. He had to take Bev to her appointment. It's my fault. I was supposed to go, but something came up at work."

"What came up?" I asked.

He had mentioned working at the ski resort but had otherwise been evasive about what he did. Honestly, I assumed he had money from his days professionally snowboarding, and he just worked at the resort for fun.

His brown eyes flicked over to mine. He looked almost

pained that I once again had the nerve to engage him in small talk.

"It was nothing."

I rolled my eyes at his obnoxiously vague response. Little did he know my ability to prattle on knew no bounds. "Well, what do you do there?"

He sighed as if my polite chitchat was some sort of interrogation. Erin must have caught on to his coldness because she elbowed him in the ribs.

"Giles does lessons a few days a week. He also manages the lifties."

"Lifties?"

"That's just short for the people that operate the chair lifts," she said.

I tilted my head. "Is that a hard job?"

Giles's lips turned up in a smug grin. "It's pretty much rocket science, Florida. Takes almost two hours of training to learn the ropes."

I glared at him while Erin elbowed him in the ribs again.

"Don't be rude to my new friend," she hissed.

"Thanks for trying, Erin, but I think my presence alone must offend him."

He balked. "That's not true."

Rolling my eyes, I stood up. Not even bothering to respond.

"I don't know what this weird energy is between the two of you, but maybe you can resolve it at the bonfire."

"She's coming?" Giles asked as if I wasn't standing right there. "I thought it was just going to be the usual crowd."

I shot him a look. "Sorry, I didn't realize Erin had to

run the guest list by you first. Is it okay if I come, Mr. Stone? Pretty please?"

His attitude was getting on my last nerve. Was it that hard to just be nice to me? When I had envisioned starting my life over in a small mountain town, I had pictured the locals being a lot more welcoming.

"Mattie, I'm sorry for my cousin-in-law's rudeness. I'm excited you'll be there."

Giles held up his hands as we both stared daggers at him.

"I didn't mean it like that. Of course, Mattie can come if she wants."

"Thanks for making me feel so welcome." I tried to keep the hurt feelings out of my voice, but I knew they had slipped through. Crap. I hated not being liked.

"Excuse me, I need to check on something," I lied.

His eyebrows rose, and his mouth hung open. I pushed past him before he could say anything.

Erin rushed behind me to catch up and grabbed my arm.

"Hey, seriously. Please come. It'll be fun."

"I'll think about it." I forced a smile. "Things are picking up at the lodge, so I'm not sure if I can take the night off."

"Answer me one question."

I looked at her warily.

"Have you done anything besides work since arriving?"

"Well, no, but—"

"No buts. You have to come. Besides, fitting in with the locals is super important here. I'm sure it will factor into whether or not they want to sign a contract with your company."

She winked at me, knowing my weak spot.

"Well, alright. I guess I can make an appearance."

"Great." She beamed. "And don't let the asshat in there get to you. He may seem tough, but it's all a front."

"I'm trying my best."

But the reality was that Giles *was* getting to me. Despite my best efforts, he was under my skin. Maybe seeing him outside this lodge, in his real world, would force him to warm up to me.

Chapter Thirteen

I wrapped my new black coat tightly around my neck. Erin had dropped it off after we talked, and I was eternally grateful that I didn't have to show up to this party rocking a neon orange and camouflage pattern.

The dish felt heavy in my hands. I had attempted to make cookies, but they came out slightly overdone. They were still edible, though, which was a win in my book. Garrett used to give me shit for being a lousy cook. I always reminded him that I had never seen him set foot in the kitchen in our entire eight years of dating, but he was quick to brush that fact off.

I was about to knock when footsteps approached behind me.

"You decided to come, huh?"

Giles stood behind me, dressed in his usual brown utility jacket and beanie. I hated how attractive he looked with his blonde curls poking out against his stubble.

"I was invited." I smiled at him, determined to make tonight a turning point in our relationship.

He looked down at his boots and back up at me. "You're pretty persistent."

My eyebrows shot up at his comment. "Persistent because I took a job that was offered to me, or persistent because I came to a party that I was invited to?"

He smirked. "Fair."

"Funny *you* calling *me* persistent." I turned around.

Giles took a step up so that we were standing next to each other at the doorway. "What do you mean?"

"You're the persistent one. You're so stubborn. You know I've been doing a good job, and you know I'm not out here as some corporate villain. I'm a nice person, Giles. I promise." I held up three fingers inside my mittens as if I was still in Girl Scouts. "If you'd just give me a chance, you'd see that."

He broke eye contact and scratched the back of his head. "I know you're not evil, Mattie."

"Then pleas—"

We were interrupted by Johnny swinging open the door.

"Hey, there. I thought I heard someone talking out here. Did you two come together?" He wiggled his eyebrows suggestively.

Giles ignored the comment and pushed past him. "Nope, just a coincidence."

"Hi, Johnny," I said. "Where can I set this?"

"In the kitchen." He gestured for me to follow him.

We walked through an open-concept living room that felt very homey, with matching plaid couches and a shag rug. A few people were milling about talking, and I could see more people bundled up outside in front of a large teepee of wood.

"We were just about to get the fire going. Make sure you

get some hot chocolate." Johnny grabbed Giles by the shoulder. "Come outside and help me with this thing."

The two of them disappeared through the back door, and I made my way into the kitchen. I was happy to see Erin was in there already. She was by the stove stirring multiple pots.

"Mattie, I'm so glad you came." She raised the non-stirring arm, and I rushed over to give her a side hug.

"Thanks for the invite. Your house is adorable."

"Thanks. It was my grandparents' house."

"Wow, really? That's so cool you've kept it in the family all these years." I set down my cookies on the large laminate peninsula that separated the kitchen from the living room.

She shrugged. "It's not that uncommon here."

"Can I do anything to help?"

"Can you grab the peppermint schnapps out of the liquor cabinet? It's the one next to the fridge with the glass doors."

Turning around, I walked over to the cabinet and stared at it for a moment before producing a clear bottle with a red label.

"Here you go."

"Thanks. Do you want some hot cocoa?"

I nodded eagerly. "If that's where the schnapps is going, then yes. I'm going to need the double layer of warmth if I'm going to be standing outside all evening."

She chuckled. "You'll be surprised how warm it feels once they've got the fire going."

"Sure," I said, not convinced at all.

It was like twenty degrees outside. Back in Florida, you wouldn't even catch me outside if it was below fifty.

"While you're in here, would you mind taking that dish of mac and cheese out of the oven?"

"Of course." I grabbed the oven mitt and removed the foil-covered glass pan.

"Try it for me, will you?"

I took a fork and scooped up a small amount of the bubbling mixture. I blew on it before carefully taking a bite. Flavors exploded in my mouth.

"Oh my god, that's like the best thing I've ever tasted," I exclaimed.

"Thanks, I love to cook."

An idea sprang into my mind. "Did you hear we're trying to open a lounge in the lodge? Where the old restaurant used to be."

She nodded. "Johnny mentioned something about that."

"We need someone to help out in the kitchen, any chance you'd be interested?"

"Um, hell yeah. That sounds like fun." She ladled some hot chocolate into a mug and handed it to me.

I took a sip of the warm beverage and felt my insides start to thaw. The sharp taste of the peppermint liquor added a lingering heat to my throat.

From my vantage point in the kitchen, I could see out to the yard and the soon-to-be bonfire. Johnny and Giles both lit a piece of rope, or something, on fire and placed each one in the center of the pit. A small fire started to bloom at the bottom. Once the rest of the sticks caught it would be pretty impressive.

It didn't mean I was dreading going outside any less.

Giles wiped his hands on his jeans and stood up to admire his handiwork. I bit my lip as I stared at him.

Having grown up hardly seeing anyone wearing winter clothes, I was surprised to find that I liked how men looked in them. Rugged. Burly, even. Giles especially pulled it off quite well.

Ugh, why did I have to find him so attractive?

Before I could scold myself for my intrusive thoughts, a pretty woman with dark hair wearing a red coat tapped Giles on the shoulder. She did not look happy as she pulled him away from the fire. Her arms were crossed, and she appeared to be scolding him. Giles's body language was very closed off.

"Who's that?" I asked Erin, not able to disguise my curiosity.

She glanced up before responding. "That's Julia. Giles's ex-girlfriend. They dated all through high school and on-off after he went pro and was always traveling." Shaking her head, she continued. "They should have called it quits ages ago, but since Giles moved back, she's been on him to commit to her. It's his fault for always leading her on. I always told him that if she's not the girl for you, you need to let her go once and for all."

My interest was officially sparked as I watched the two of them continue to argue in the backyard.

"Funny, Giles seems so stoic. It's hard to picture him in a relationship."

She snorted. "That stoic attitude translates to 'bad communicator' in relationship terms."

"So, are they back on right now?"

"Who knows with those two. Giles has probably led her into thinking that but now wants to free himself up for when the tourist crowd hits. I'm sure he would prefer to flirt with some blonde girl from California here on a ski trip than argue with Julia one more time." She dished out the last mug of hot cocoa and clapped her hands. "Alright, let's get everyone in here to make a plate."

After calling outside, everyone bustled into the kitchen. It was a frenzy of plates and spoons and food being passed around. I made a few polite introductions but, so far, was feeling out of place in a town where everyone had grown up together.

I couldn't help but notice Giles and Julia did not come inside with everyone else. I would pay to be able to eavesdrop on whatever it was they were discussing. For some reason, the idea of Giles as a boyfriend fascinated me. He seemed hardly capable of a warm human interaction.

Once everyone had finished their plates, we made our way outside to the roaring fire. I clutched my hot chocolate as if it could somehow raise the outside temperature by twenty-five degrees.

My teeth chattered.

I got the closest spot to the fire that I could find. Johnny and Erin were standing next to me. He was holding her in his arms. My heart ached a little seeing their happy marriage. To think I had once thought I would be engaged right now instead of starting all over.

I stood there for what felt like hours—but was probably minutes—until I couldn't take it anymore. How was I supposed to engage in polite small talk with strangers when my brain was iced over? I smiled at Erin and excused myself, eager to hide inside for a little while.

The door slammed shut behind me, and I blew my hot breath onto my frozen fingertips.

"Too cold out there for you?" Giles was leaning against

the kitchen counter. His jacket was off, revealing a black sweater that hugged his body a little too well.

"You people are out of your mind," I said. "Everyone is going to catch hypothermia out there, and we're going to make the national headlines."

He chuckled and nudged a fresh mug of cocoa in my direction. "You're so dramatic, Florida. Maybe it's too cold for you but the rest of us can handle it."

"Right, because enduring sub-zero temperatures is totally my idea of a great party." I snatched the mug he offered and gulped the warm liquid before wincing. "This tastes more like peppermint than chocolate."

He shrugged. "I might have added a little extra punch."

"Need a drink, eh?" I casually leaned on the counter next to him.

"You could say that."

We stood there in silence for a few beats as I took another sip from my cup that was basically half schnapps.

"So," I finally said.

"So," he repeated.

"I'm sorry again," I blurted out. "About that comment I made about your parents. I still feel terrible for bringing it up."

His brown eyes bore into mine. "I can't believe you're still apologizing about that."

"I told you, I'm actually a really nice person if you just get to know me."

"It isn't that." Shaking his head, he took a sip from his mug. "What you said about my parents…it wasn't even bad. It was true. They would have loved to see the lodge have a gathering spot like that again. I remember Bev and my mom used to talk about it all the time." He hesitated, and his jaw tightened. "I've been nothing but rude to you since we met. If anyone should be apologizing, it's probably me."

My heart pounded. I wasn't expecting him to say that. "Not going to argue with you, there."

He smirked down at me, and once again, I was struck by just how adorable his face was when he wasn't scowling.

"I've got an idea," I announced. "Let's start fresh with each other."

He nodded. "Works for me."

"And what better way to start fresh than with a drinking game."

Now he looked nervous.

"Truth or drink."

"Truth or drink," he repeated.

"Right. We take turns asking each other questions. You either have to answer truthfully or take a drink."

"I don't kno—"

"C'mon. It'll be fun," I insisted.

"Okay, fine. But me first." He glanced at me and then crossed his arms. "Alright, be honest. How much shit did you and your boss talk about me after I stormed out of your office that first day I met you?"

I rolled my eyes. "I thought we were starting fresh?"

"Hey, you made the rules, not me. Tell me the truth or drink up, and I'd advise being strategic when you decide to drink. That cocoa could strip paint with how strong I made it."

"Fine, if you must know, we were pretty tactful, all things considered."

He ducked his chin and gave me another smirk. "Really?"

"I might have called you an ass."

Chuckling, he gestured for me to ask the next question.

"When did you start snowboarding?" I figured that one was easy enough.

"Honestly, it's hard for me to remember not snowboarding. My dad picked it up when he was older and was excited to teach his kid. He probably had me out there by the time I was two or three."

"That's a nice memory."

His eyes darkened, and he cleared his throat. "Okay, Florida. Next question. What are you doing here? I didn't exactly get the impression you'd be the one on the ground level doing the dirty work back at your office."

"You got me there. We couldn't find someone so last minute. We almost had to cancel the trial."

"And you just thought you would come on down and give it a whirl?"

"You could say that."

"Evasiveness won't get you very far in this game."

I smiled into my cup, letting the steam from the cocoa warm my face.

"My turn." I hesitated before asking. "What was your dad like?"

He took a slow, deliberate sip.

Message received—no questions about his parents.

He continued as if nothing had happened. "Okay, I've got to know. Have you *really* never seen snow? Or were you just trying to mess with me and play up the damsel in distress card?"

I sighed exasperatedly. "I've really never seen snow. I don't know why everyone here finds that so hard to believe. And I was never a damsel in distress," I added.

He chuckled and then gestured for me to go.

"How many countries have you been to?"

"Forty-something."

He said it so casually that my mouth hung open.

"*Forty-something?* That's incredible."

He shrugged. "There were a lot of opportunities to travel when I was boarding professionally. Why, how many countries have you been to?"

"Um. Two, if you count the one that we're currently in. The other one was the Bahamas when our cruise ship docked there."

"You've *never* left the country? How is that even possible? Do you have a passport?"

"Um, excuse you. Yes, I have a passport. I just told you, I went to the Bahamas. That counts as leaving the country."

"You didn't even have to get on a plane, and you probably spent five hours there."

My mouth snapped shut. It was only three. "Well, whatever. Sorry I haven't had endless opportunities like you, Mr. hotshot."

"You don't want to see other parts of the world?"

I considered this. Growing up, I had always dreamed of going to different countries in Europe or Asia. I wasn't sure when that dream died. After I graduated from college, Garrett and I never discussed going farther than the Keys. His parents had a place down there, and it was his favorite vacation spot.

"I'm not sure," I admitted. "I used to want to travel. The opportunity never really presented itself. Then suddenly, I blinked, and I'm almost thirty, and I haven't been anywhere."

"Well, it's not too late."

"What's your favorite country that you've been to?"

He thought about it for a moment before responding.

"Probably Japan. I've had a few great boarding trips out there, and the country is all-around spectacular."

"Wow, I'd love to go someday."

"You should," he said, nudging my shoulder.

Butterflies exploded in my stomach on contact. I took a sip of cocoa to hide my flushed cheeks and ease my nerves. This easy banter between us was something I could get used to.

"Hey, what about the game," he protested after my sip. "I didn't even ask you an uncomfortable question yet, and you already took a drink."

"Oh shit, I forgot." The conversation was flowing so naturally 'truth or drink' was the last thing on my mind. "Do I get a pass on your next question?"

"No way."

He stroked his chin as if he was wracking his brain to try and think of a really good question. "What was your last relationship like?"

I winced as reality smacked me in the face.

He caught my change in demeanor. "Or your current relationship. I guess I shouldn't assume anything."

"No, definitely former." I wavered. "It's just a bit of a sore subject."

Giles raised his eyebrows, encouraging me to continue.

"We were together for a long time. We lived together. I thought he was the one, but he-he cheated on me instead."

He sucked in a breath. "Ouch."

"He was doing it for months."

"Double ouch."

"With my best friend."

"Holy shit, Florida." He rubbed his hand over his mouth. "That's tragic. How did you find out?"

"I walked in on them."

He clutched his chest. "That's it. I need a drink after that saga." He took a sip of his cocoa.

I shook my head, still in disbelief at the story, even though it had happened to me. "All my so-called friends knew about it too, and they didn't tell me."

"Some friends."

"All the more reason to start over, right?"

"Ahh. So that explains the sudden change in zip code."

I nodded. Despite his constant berating me since we met, I felt weirdly close to Giles in this moment. Like we were friends or something. This was the most I had opened up to someone outside my family in a long time.

I thought about telling him the whole truth. About the engagement. About the pregnancy… but I couldn't do it. It still hurt too much to rehash it. Plus, it made me feel utterly pathetic.

Giles shook me from my sad thoughts with a gentle nudge. Our eyes met, and I was again struck by how sincere they looked.

"It's your turn to ask me a question," he whispered.

"Same one. What was your last relationship like?"

He scrunched his eyebrows, and his face contorted into one of pain. He eyed his beverage as if he was about to take a sip before I elbowed him in the ribs.

"Do not even think about taking a drink. I just spilled all the horrific details of my breakup. It's your turn. No way it can be worse than mine."

"I wouldn't say worse. It's just not my finest moment."

He sighed. "My last relationship is also my only relationship. I met her when she moved here in high school. We were just two dumb sixteen-year-olds. After we graduated, she wanted us to go to school together. To get married young—it's common here. But I was getting sponsorship offers. I had done a few Colorado competitions, and I wanted more. So, I left. Joined a team, moved away, and broke her heart."

"That doesn't seem so bad…" I trailed off, thinking about the interaction between the two of them in the yard. Those wounds seemed fresh still.

"Well, that's probably not the worst part. Anytime I was home for a period of time, I would always hang out with her. Talk to her. I told her things I probably shouldn't have."

"Like what?" I pressed, dying to know the details.

"Like that maybe I wished we could be together."

I gasped. "You did not."

He looked guilty. "I did."

"That's awful. Why would you lead her on like that?"

He groaned. "I didn't mean to. Part of me genuinely felt that way. I dated and was with other girls, but she was the only stable relationship I had ever had. I thought that meant something."

"But it didn't?"

"It didn't," he confirmed. "And because I would always say those things she never got into another serious relationship. When I moved back for good last year, she thought we would finally be together. I had to tell her I wasn't in love with her."

"Harsh."

He nodded. "Now we see each other all the time, and I

have to see the pain all over her face. I think she still thinks I'll change my mind. But a relationship is the last thing on my mind right now."

I nodded. "I know what you mean."

"The shitty ex-boyfriend have you jaded?"

"Maybe. I mean I did spend eight years of my life with him. My best years, some would argue."

"Stop. You're in the prime of your life."

I shook my head. "Meeting people is harder now. And how am I supposed to trust that the next person won't waste my time too?"

"That's not a good way to look at it."

"And what is?"

"Think about all the possibilities. Every guy you meet could be a potential love interest. Doesn't that excite you?"

"Not really."

"Why not?"

I was too embarrassed to admit anything to him.

"Oh, come on. It's my next question. Why doesn't dating excite you?"

"Because I wanted to get married, okay?" I mumbled, barely at an audible level.

Giles raised his eyebrows. "Okay…so?"

"So, I thought I was this close"—I held up my index finger and thumb—"to getting married. I know it's not cool to admit this, but I've *always* dreamed about getting married. The fairytale wedding, starting a family, the fact that you've found your person forever. The one that picked you over everyone else."

My voice cracked on the last word, and my throat was thick with emotion. Shit. I was not about to cry in front of Giles.

To my surprise, Giles just stared at me instead of making an excuse to leave.

"I wouldn't worry about it," he said.

"How can I not? I spent eight years with the wrong guy and now I have to start over."

"The right guy won't keep you on the back burner like that. Trust me. He was never the one for you. When you meet your guy, he'll be dying to claim you forever."

I blinked a few times and finally smiled.

"Can we change to a lighter topic?" he asked.

Laughing, I thought for a minute. "Have you ever broken a bone?"

"My arm. Twice." He thought for a second. "How did you get that gash on your forehead?"

I instinctively touched the cut. "I told you," I replied sheepishly.

"Something about a golf cart?"

"I crashed a golf cart," I mumbled.

"What was that?"

"I crashed a golf cart," I huffed, this time louder.

"That's what I thought you said." He was full-on laughing now, and despite my embarrassment, I couldn't help but enjoy the musical tone of his laughter. "I need to hear this story."

I sighed. "It happened at a party my parents were throwing. Everyone drives around in golf carts where they live, it's a thing, trust me. Anyway, I got too drunk. Something upset me, and I took off in one of them. I swerved and flipped the cart. End of story."

I intentionally left the part about what had upset me out of the story, but I don't think Giles noticed. He was bent over, laughing at my embarrassment.

"It's not that funny, you know. I could have hurt someone. It was stupid of me to drink and drive."

"Of course, you're right," he replied, still laughing. "I'm just picturing you tearing across town in a golf cart."

"Whatever, my turn to ask a question," I said after he finally ceased laughing. "Will you teach me to snowboard?"

"Not after that story." He smirked. "You sound like a liability."

I scowled and shoved him in the shoulder. "Hey, I'm an excellent athlete."

He shook his head and laughed again. "Doesn't seem like it."

My lip tugging upward. Despite the embarrassing story, I felt accomplished for making Giles laugh.

"I like this version of you better," I admitted.

His laughter eased and his eyebrows shot up. "What version?"

"This version." I waved up and down at him. "The one that's nice to me and can actually hold a conversation. Not the grumpy one that was always annoyed with me. I could do without seeing that version of you again."

Sighing, he shifted his gaze to his feet. I worried for a moment that I had offended him.

"I'm sorry again about that," he muttered. "I know I've been a dick. It was hard for me to accept you coming here and working at the lodge. I know that isn't an excuse..."

"Why?" I asked.

He sighed and stared at the floor. "It's just." He hesitated before continuing. "My whole life, I've had to see this area get redeveloped. Big corporations come in and take over. They drive the locals out to replace them with tourists who will make the town more profitable. Our town has always felt relatively immune to all that, but lately, things have changed. Like the ski resort, for instance. It was family-owned until they sold it a few years back."

He paused, and I urged him to continue with my eyes.

"When Bev told me she was looking to hire outside help, I might have freaked out a little. That lodge was my childhood. It's attached to so many memories I have of my parents. I couldn't stand the thought of some profit-hungry suits stepping in and ruining everything."

"I understand where you're coming from, but I can assure you I'm hardly a profit-hungry suit. And my company is just a small firm whose owner has a passion for hospitality. We do our best to automate work and improve the guest experience without sacrificing the character of the original space." I snuck a peak at Giles to find him staring at me intently. "You would know all this if you bothered to listen to the pitch I prepared."

He grimaced at the reminder of his rudeness. "Touché. Man, I was a dick, wasn't I?"

"A massive one."

"Well, I hope you can forgive me, Mattie."

The hair on the back of my neck bristled at the sound of my name on his lips. I took another sip of my drink to hide my smile.

At that moment, the door from the kitchen to the yard slammed closed, and I jerked back in surprise. For a moment, I had completely forgotten we were at a party with other guests.

The girl that just barged in looked familiar and I realized why. It was the girl I had seen Giles arguing with earlier.

Julia.

I looked from her to him and saw that he was no longer smiling. He looked down at his drink as she looked between the two of us. I could see hurt in her eyes, and my heart ached for her. I knew our situations weren't identical, but I still related to that awful feeling of seeing the guy you loved with someone else. Instinctively, I took a step away from Giles, not wanting her to get the wrong idea.

Julia opened her mouth to say something but then snapped it shut.

"Hey," I said, trying to break the ice. "I'm Mattie. I just started at the ski lodge last week."

"Julia." She didn't even bother to look at me.

Okay, this was clearly not going to be the start of a budding friendship. I glanced out the window and waited for the awkward silence to end.

"Real nice," Julia hissed before storming toward the front door.

Giles groaned and pushed off of the counter. He started to follow Julia before spinning back toward me.

"Sorry about that. She's just hurt."

I shook my head. "You don't need to apologize. I get it."

He snatched his coat off the back of a couch and slipped it on. "I better go see if she's alright and tell her we were just talking."

"Of course."

He looked like he wanted to say more but spun back toward the door.

I let my shoulders sag, a little disappointed our conversation was over. It had been nice talking to him.

At the last moment before the door closed, Giles poked his head back through.

"Thanks for giving me another chance, by the way." He gave me a sheepish smile.

"Thanks for finally speaking more than five words to me."

He winked at me. "You were right, you know? You are nice."

With that, he let the door close behind him.

Chapter Fourteen

"Next Tuesday? Are you sure you can't get anyone in here sooner than that?"

"Sorry, it's right before the holidays. A lot of people are either sick or taking time off. Or pretending to be sick so they can have time off."

The owner of the housekeeping company was sending me into yet another circle. When I first got here, Bev had told me they had been using this company for years. Unfortunately, loyalty only ran so deep. A cleaner had only bothered to show up to work a handful of the days since I'd been here.

"You realize I'm going to have to clean these rooms myself, right?"

"Do what you gotta do."

I took a deep breath in to keep from snapping at this man. Apparently, being a long-time customer gave you no type of advantage when dealing with someone like this.

After a few more minutes of back and forth, I got him to agree to at least *try* to send someone out here tomorrow.

Hanging up the phone, I tied my golden hair back. I guess it was on me to ensure today's arrivals had clean sheets.

Leaving a note at the front desk to call my cell if anything was needed, I abandoned my station to get some rooms turned over. I entered the first suite downstairs and stripped the bed.

My phone buzzed in my pocket.

Frankie: Have you frozen to death yet?

Mattie: This is the mortuary. Mattie died days ago, but no one bothered to call and claim the body.

Frankie: Ha ha. I've been busy! So tell me everything. How is it?

Mattie: It's beautiful here. My apartment is so cozy, and most of the people are nice.

Frankie: Omg, I just fell asleep reading that. That's it!? I thought you went there for a fresh start and an adventure.

Mattie: I am having an adventure!

Frankie: How's the hot snowboarder you were telling me about?

I thought about this before responding. My answer before the bonfire would have been entirely different than the answer I wanted to give now. Ever since our conversation in the kitchen, Giles had occupied my thoughts more than I cared to admit.

When I came into work the day after, I was on edge the whole time, just waiting for him to make an appearance.

But he didn't show. In fact, the bonfire was three days ago, and he hadn't shown his face at the lodge since.

> Mattie: Ugh idk. We talked for like an hour the other day, and I thought maybe we were going to be friends, but now it seems like he's avoiding me.

> Frankie: I think someone has a crush on the hot asshole.

> Mattie: He wasn't an asshole the other day! And no comment…

> Frankie: You should go for it! You need to get over you-know-who. And what better place to have a fling than in a romantic remote mountain town?

I rolled my eyes.

> Mattie: I'm here for work, remember?

"How's it going in here?"

Bev's voice caused me to jump and drop my phone on the green carpeted floor.

"Oh, hi, Bev. Sorry, I didn't hear you come in."

"Are you cleaning the rooms again?"

I nodded solemnly.

"Damn that Howie. I swear things used to be better when his father was running the company."

Shrugging, I gathered up the sheets into a bundle. "Maybe it's time we look at other options," I said carefully.

The last time I had brought this up, Bev had snapped at me. She said I wouldn't understand small-town loyalty, and you didn't just go and replace someone you had been working with for years.

She sighed and extended her arms for me to hand her the sheets.

"I hate to admit it, but maybe you're right. It feels like it's too often now that I'm cleaning my own damn rooms."

I tried not to look too excited at her change of attitude. "That's great to hear. I have the name and number of a company the next town over. They said they're taking new clients."

She snickered. "You sure waste no time, don't you?"

"I-I just wanted to be prepared. You know. In case you changed your mind."

"Of course you did." She eyed me up and down. "You know Mattie, you've been a big help since you got here. Especially with that computer work you've done. Assigning rooms and taking new reservations is pretty much all automated now."

My chest flooded with warmth at her praise. "It's what I'm here for."

"I just wanted to make sure you knew that I think you're doing a great job."

"Thanks, Bev, I appreciate that."

"And since you've been doing such a great job with automating tasks, I figured it would be okay if you wanted to dedicate more time to the lounge."

My eyebrows shot up. "Really? That would be amazing, Bev. I have so many ideas. And I already talked to Erin, and she's excited to help in the kitchen. I figured we can start with just opening on weekend afternoons to make sur—"

"Whoa there." Bev laughed. "Let's walk and talk."

We finished grabbing all the sheets on the first floor as I

chattered away about my ideas. A fresh coat of paint and some wall decor would be first on the list. I had noticed some vintage ski posters in the basement that were dying to be framed and given a new life.

At the end of the hallway, I could see that Johnny and Erin had arrived and were waiting by the front desk. They turned around when they heard our footsteps.

"Hey, Mattie," Erin called.

"Hey," I called back.

She rushed over to me. "You've got to come with us."

"Where?" I asked nervously.

"Snowboarding."

I *had* been talking about how I wanted to learn, but the hairs on the back of my neck still bristled. While I enjoyed watching the guests shoot down the hill, I felt terrified of hurling down a mountain with no control.

"Um." I teetered on my heels nervously. "I don't know."

"You have to. There's fresh snow outside, and it's going to be epic," Johnny chimed in.

Their excitement was almost contagious, but I was still hesitant.

"But—"

"We insist. Johnny and I can take you on the bunny hill and teach you the ropes."

"Well, it does sound fun, but I'm working right now." I faked a disappointed pout.

Bev waved me off. "Go. I insist."

I chewed my lip, wracking my brain for another excuse. "I don't have a snowboard."

Erin grabbed my arm and started pulling me toward the front door.

"We know everyone that works at the rental shop.

They'll loan you one for free since you live here and know us."

"I also don't have anything to wear." My panic was increasing.

"There's a great shop I can take you to. Come on. It'll be so much fun."

Erin looked at me with pleading eyes. When I snuck a glance at Johnny, he gave me a thumbs up.

I was about to insist that I couldn't when I thought about Frankie's text.

'I thought you went there for a fresh start and an adventure.'

She was right. That is what I came here for. This was not the time to chicken out.

"Alright, let's do it," I said.

Erin squealed and dragged me through the door, rambling on about how I was bound to pick it up quickly. I nodded my head and tried to disguise my anxiousness with a smile.

Chapter Fifteen

THE JUMPSUIT I DONNED MADE A SWISHING NOISE WITH every step I took as I tried to keep my newly rented snowboard balanced in my grip. Erin had insisted I pick this one as soon as I tried it on. It was a soft cream color, but the elbow and knee areas were enhanced with neon rainbow lines. It was fun and colorful. I loved it.

"If you had told me snowboarding would involve buying a cute outfit, maybe I would have come out here sooner."

"I love that you picked that one. So many beginners want to go with boring black so they don't stand out. Where's the fun in that?"

"Why don't they want to stand out?"

"Just to avoid the jeers of the people on the chairlift."

"People will be jeering?" The fantasy I had envisioned of me softly falling a few times before gracefully making it down the hill slowly altered in my head.

"Not in a mean way. People love to poke fun at beginners, and the main lift has the perfect view of the bunny hill."

"What a great setup," I retorted, the sarcasm evident in my voice.

"Hey, don't worry about it." Erin stopped in her tracks and turned to face me, placing a hand on each of my padded shoulders. "Johnny and I won't let you look stupid. Everyone remembers their first day out here, trust me."

"Sure."

We continued to the bunny hill as I tried to pep myself up, but I remembered the conversation Giles and I had back at the bonfire. How he couldn't really remember *not* snowboarding. I wondered how many locals were just like him.

Minutes ago, I loved my new outfit. Now having arrived and seeing everyone dressed in neutrals, I realized just how loud it was.

'Look at me,' it practically screamed. My snowsuit—and my hot pink snowboard rental—was sure to attract the attention of every wandering expert's eye today.

Great.

"Here we are," Erin said.

Johnny was already there waiting for us.

"Well, don't you look festive?" He admired my suit as I did a twirl.

"Thanks. I realize that maybe standing out isn't such a good thing on the bunny hill."

"Nonsense," he replied. "You look great, and pretty soon, you'll be riding great too. Now set the board down."

I did as he told me and turned to face him before he immediately shoved me backward. It was a light shove, and I easily caught myself, but my face registered my shock.

"What the hell was that for?"

"Gotta determine your dominant foot," he said like it was obvious. "Looks like you're goofy. Giles is goofy too."

"Goofy?"

"It means your left leg is dominant, so you'll be going down the hill right foot forward."

"If you say so."

"Now, strap in your right foot."

Johnny walked me through strapping my boot into my binding, and showed me how to scoot my back foot along so that I glided over the snow.

"Alright." He clapped his mitten-clad hands. "Now that you're mobile, let's hit the lift."

He gestured toward a chairlift maybe one-hundred feet long that ascended a short, almost flat, hill.

"Why even build that? I can probably walk up there faster."

Erin laughed. "It's to get you used to the lift for when you migrate to the bigger hills. You'd be surprised how hard it is to master getting on and off."

A few people were already on the bunny hill. Thankfully, it wasn't too crowded. I observed as two people stood at the bottom of the lift. They let the moving chair hit the back of their knees before sitting down and getting carried up.

How hard could it be?

"You ready, Mattie?" Johnny looked at me expectantly.

"Ready as I'll ever be," I murmured before gracelessly gliding behind him. A few times, my boot got caught underneath my board, and I almost face-planted into the fresh snow.

"You'll get the hang of it," Erin assured me.

At the lift, I sat down easily and was scooped up by the chair. Erin went with me since it was only a two-person seat.

"That wasn't so bad." I mentally patted myself on the back as we chugged to the top.

"Getting on is easy. It's getting off where people usually eat it."

My face fell as I took in her words. At that moment, as if on cue, the person getting off the lift on skis did a sharp turn to the left and fell on their side.

"Great," I said, now nervous for when it was my turn.

"So, you and Giles seemed to be talking an awful lot at our house the other day," Erin said out of the blue.

"Huh?" I tore my eyes away from the dreaded end of the lift. I wasn't prepared for a personal conversation when I was so focused on not breaking a bone.

"He's usually not very talkative, that one. I've known him just as long as I've known Johnny. We all grew up together, basically. I know he can come across as rough around the edges, but he really is a good guy."

"Oh, um yeah." I tried my best to give Erin my attention since the lift was now stopped. The attendant tried to help the skier who was still floundering to get up. "He's given me the cold shoulder since I met him. It was nice to have an actual conversation for once," I admitted.

She rolled her eyes. "Trust me, the cold shoulder is typical for him. He's always been a little prickly with new people. You'd think he would have met tons of people while traveling the world. Instead, he used it as an excuse to keep everyone at an arms-length. I don't think he made a single close friend all those years competing. Anyway, it's just great to see him letting someone in."

I snorted. "I would hardly say he's letting me in. We had one civil conversation. I'm just happy he doesn't seem to hate me anymore."

"He definitely doesn't hate you."

"I hope not. He seems to be avoiding the lodge lately, though. I haven't seen him since the party. Maybe he's just busy, but…" I trailed off, feeling ridiculous for implying I could have a strong enough effect on Giles that it would keep him from visiting his family's lodge.

"Well, I wouldn't worry about that. I'm sure you'll see him soon." She winked at me, and before I could ask her what she meant by that, the lift started moving again.

"Oh god, we're almost at the top." Panic crept into my voice.

"You've got this. Just shift your body so that your front foot hits the ground first. Keep your tip up. Then you'll stand up when we get to the top and glide out of the way."

"That sounds like a lot of steps." Shifting my body, I waited anxiously for the impact. There were only two chairs ahead of ours now.

The next thing I knew, it was our turn. My snowboard hit the ground and Erin shouted, "stand up."

I stood on shaking legs. Before I could move, the lift hit the back of my knees, pushing me. My snowboard slid forward while my body flung around for balance. Eventually, my board flew too far forward, and the rest of me landed backward on top of it.

"Ouch." I rubbed my butt and was thankful Erin had insisted I buy padded leggings.

"That was a great first effort." Johnny was there now, too, helping me up.

"You must not have been watching me."

"Hey, maybe you fell, but you got out of the way of the lift. Them not having to stop it for you on your first try is a win."

I looked back to see that I had gotten out of the way of the lift exit, and the chairs were still moving.

"Alright, the first lesson of the day is falling leaf."

AN HOUR LATER, I HAD ONLY MADE IT DOWN THE HILL three times. I had finally mastered falling leaf, which was leaning on my heels and rocking back and forth to get down the hill. It was not an impressive sight, but I had only fallen once on the last run.

"You're doing great," Erin exclaimed when I reached the bottom.

"Thanks for taking the time to show me. I know this must not be fun for you."

Johnny had left us twenty minutes ago to hit the bigger hills, and I could tell Erin was dying to join him.

"I think I'm ready to take a break," I said, even though I kind of wanted to try a couple more times now that I wasn't falling constantly. "Maybe I'll go inside and get a coffee. You should catch up with Johnny."

"Nonsense. You need to learn how to carve now. You've got to try toe side." She glanced at something behind me. "But I'm not a very good teacher. You know who is, though?"

I shook my head.

"Giles, over here!" she shouted.

Turning, I saw Giles walking toward the ski hill's lodge carrying a snowboard. When he spotted Erin, he turned his stride toward us. He was completely covered in black snow pants and a navy-blue jacket that had the ski resort's name on it. His goggles were pushed up on his helmet, and he had a bandana covering his chin. How was it possible that he could still look so good, maybe even better, in all those layers?

"Hey, Erin. What're you doing at the bunny hill?" He glanced over at me and back at Erin before doing a double take and looking me up and down.

"Mattie?" He squinted his eyes, clearly surprised.

"Hey."

"What the hell are you wearing."

He said it like I was out here in a bikini or something.

"Um, ouch. Watch your tone, or I might think you don't like my outfit."

"You look like a ski bunny."

"A what?" I asked at the same time Erin hit Giles in the arm.

"Don't be rude, Giles. Mattie is doing a great job for her first day."

"What's a ski bunny?" I asked again, still out of the loop.

"It's just someone that tries to look hot on the ski hill and only cares about picking up men. It's implied that they aren't good at skiing—or boarding." Erin smiled apologetically.

"Hey." I glared at Giles, offended now that I knew the meaning. "I'm trying out here. And why can't I do it in a cute outfit? That's ridiculous."

He held up his hands. "It's just something people say."

"Well, they shouldn't." I lifted my chin defiantly.

He chuckled. "Okay, Florida. So, you're out here learning for real, huh?"

"Yes, and she's getting pretty good," Erin chimed in. "But unfortunately, my instructing skills are pretty lackluster. Will you help her learn toe side? I want to catch up with Johnny."

I raised my eyebrows at her sudden need to ditch me.

"I don't know." Giles stuck his snowboard in the ground and leaned against it. "I just got done with a lesson. I'm pretty beat."

"It's just on the bunny hill. You'll be fine," Erin insisted, already walking away from us. "I'll see you two later."

With that, I was left alone with Giles.

"You so don't have to help me if you don't want to." The last thing I wanted to do was bother him. "I think I was getting the hang of it."

He let out a long slow breath and stared at me before looking back to the lodge as if weighing his options.

"Let's see what you got, Florida."

He strapped in and effortlessly glided to the lift entrance while I hobbled behind him.

Turning around, he laughed when he saw me.

"Still haven't gotten the hang of that, huh?"

"It's kind of hard to walk when I've got a twenty-pound board attached to me."

"It's not so much walking as sliding the board along. Here let me show you." He unstrapped his board and walked in front of me. "Can I grab your waist?"

"Sure," I mumbled before he placed two gloved hands on my snowsuit. Despite the layers between us, my heart still dropped into my stomach. I could feel his warm breath on my face.

"Okay, so take your back foot and keep it parallel with the board. Pretend like you're skateboarding or something."

I did as he instructed, and he started walking, slowly bringing me along with him.

"There you go, much smoother. You don't want to turn that back foot. That's when it becomes more like walking, and it's a lot less efficient."

"Got it, thanks." I sounded breathless. Hopefully, he thought it was due to my tiredness and not our proximity.

We were at the lift now, and it scooped us up. My board hit the top of his board as I got situated.

"Shit. I'm sorry. I'm still getting the hang of the lift."

He waved me off. "Don't worry about it. I teach lessons all day. You have no idea the abuse my board has seen."

"Do you like teaching?"

He shrugged. "It's alright. I like it some days more than others. It's fun being out here all the time in the winter."

"It's a beautiful place to spend time."

He just nodded.

"Um. Do you miss competing?"

He sucked in a breath. "You know, it's weird to admit it out loud, but not really. I'm grateful for that part of my life and all the doors it opened. But it was a lot of pressure. It's nice to wake up every day and not feel like I'm on a downward spiral toward obsoletion."

"I never would have thought about it like that. Sounds pretty tough, mentally."

The lift halted as two skiers fell at the top. Their limbs became tangled in one another's.

I waited for Giles to ask me questions or continue the conversation. We sat there in silence for a few beats when he didn't.

"So," I started again. "I haven't seen you around the lodge the past few days."

"I've been busy. Had a few private lessons the other day."

"Got it."

"Why, did you miss me?"

My cheeks flushed, and I looked up to see Giles grinning at me. Was he flirting with me? What kind of strange alternate reality were we in right now?

"Don't flatter yourself. You usually stop by, is all."

The lift was moving again. I snapped my mouth closed, focusing all my attention on not embarrassing myself.

"How are you with getting off the lift?" he asked.

"I'm okay."

"Meaning?"

"I've fallen two out of the three times.'

He chuckled. "Just don't bring me down with you, Florida."

I scowled but couldn't answer as we were almost to the top.

My board hit the snow, and I quickly stood up. The lift nudged me, but this time, I was prepared. I let the board move forward and put my back foot on the spot between my bindings like Erin had shown me. I was about to declare victory when my board picked up speed, and I panicked. My back foot jutted out, and I was about to do a faceplant when I felt strong arms around me, tugging me back.

Looking up, I saw Giles smirking down at me. "This doesn't count as a success."

"What if I say two-and-a-half out of four times?"

He raised his eyebrows as if considering my question. "I'll allow it."

He released my waist, and I hated to admit how much I wanted his hands to stay right where they were.

"So, what did Erin teach you so far?"

"I've just been riding down on my heels."

"That's good you've got that down, at least. We should work on your toe side and carving."

He ran through a few instructions. He told me where to lean my weight and how to shift my body. As if to demonstrate, he would move slightly anytime he gave directions. I nodded along, but in reality, I was slightly distracted. He looked so in control and comfortable on a board. I mean, obviously, he did. What had I expected? But something about seeing him out here in person was different. He looked really good…

"Did you get all that?"

I realized he was talking to me. I pulled myself out of my thoughts and nodded my head. "Totally."

He leaned down and strapped in his other binding while still standing. I had to plop on my butt, or I'd lose my balance.

"Alright, let's take it slow. Start on your heel, and don't pick up any speed. When you feel ready, switch to your toe and then back to your heel. You can exaggerate the movements to start with."

He gave a quick demonstration until he was twenty feet down the hill.

"Your turn," he called up to me.

"Okay, don't look stupid," I muttered under my breath. Me eating shit was not the visual I wanted Giles to have of me.

Placing my hands behind me, I pushed up from the ground. Once upright, I scooted myself down the hill on my heels. I did as he instructed and slowly let off my heels to transition to my toes. My board shifted beneath me. Once the nose was going straight forward, I picked up a little speed.

"Ahhh!" I panicked and leaned into my heels so hard that I fell on my butt.

"That was close." Giles gave me a thumbs up. He was still below me on the hill because I had only moved forward about two feet.

"Don't placate me!" I shouted back.

He chuckled and gestured for me to keep going.

I continued to try, and Giles continued to give me feedback. It took me five attempts of falling and getting back up, but at the end of the run, I finally managed to dig into my toes. Sure, I fell on my knees as soon as the board shifted, but I was getting more comfortable with the movements.

On the next run, I only fell twice and was able to transition from my heels to my toes a few times. At the bottom, I stopped on my heels and pumped my arms in victory. Unfortunately, that movement caused me to lose balance. I started to topple over before Giles rode up and grabbed me.

"Whoa there." He laughed. "Good run, but you know I can't follow you around and catch you all the time, right?"

"Why not?" I pretended to pout.

His grin widened as he stared down at me.

Time stopped for the next few seconds. His hands lingered around my waist, and his face was so close that I could smell his minty breath. Instinctively I licked my lips, and I swear he moved an inch closer to me.

Giles cleared his throat and stepped away. Looking

down, I tried to mask my disappointment. For a moment there, it almost felt like he was going to kiss me…

That would be ridiculous, though. He had just gone from my moody nemesis to a casual acquaintance. I was imagining things because I was lonely. Plus, me and Giles? The part owner of the lodge? Talk about unprofessional. No way Bev would be pleased with that development.

"Um, so are you going to buy me a hot chocolate for being a good student or what?" I finally broke the silence.

"You think you deserve that, huh?"

I unstrapped my bindings and picked up my board. "Come on," I whined. "It's been hours, and I'm exhausted. I need a break."

"Fine, let's go." He picked up his board and led the way to the wood cabin building that housed the rental equipment, food, and plenty of comfortable chairs to relax and warm up on.

"So, how did I do today?" I was unabashedly fishing for a compliment. There were a few other beginner snowboarders on the hill today, and I had shown way more improvement than any of them had.

Giles just shrugged and gave a noncommittal, "you did okay."

"Okay? Did you see the other chumps out there? I was practically boarding in circles around them."

He threw his head back and laughed. "You're dreaming, Florida. You all looked like a bunch of newborn gazelles trying to walk for the first time."

"Hey." I shoved his shoulder but laughed along with him. "Admit you're impressed with me."

"You're relentless." He held open the door to the main

entrance of the cabin for me. "Fine. You did alright. Now stop badgering me and buy me a hot chocolate."

I looked at him, appalled. "Excuse you. I thought that was my reward for a job well done?"

"I gave you a free lesson." He pointed out as we walked over to the food service counter.

Rolling my eyes, I turned to the cashier. "Two hot chocolates, please."

I fished around in my giant snowsuit for my credit card, but the teenager behind the counter handed over two cups without payment.

"Here you go, Giles."

"Thanks, man," he replied before turning away and handing me one.

"Don't we have to pay?"

He smirked. "I work here, remember? Consider it a perk."

I gratefully took the piping hot cup and sipped it cautiously.

"Fireplace?" Giles gestured toward the large one in the center of the room, surrounded by chairs.

"I think fireplaces in every building and a constant supply of hot chocolate might be my two favorite things about living in a mountain town."

"It really is the only appeal."

We sat down at a small two-person table. I shed my mittens so I could stick my frozen hands as close to the hot flames as possible.

"I don't know how you spend all day every day out here. It's freezing."

"I'm acclimated. I've lived in cold temperatures my whole life. Your blood is just too thin."

"That's a myth…I think."

"Your purple hands say otherwise."

"Hey, they're just a dark red." I flexed my hands as my fingertips started to thaw.

We sat there in silence for a few beats, sipping our cocoa. It should feel awkward to sit with him like this, but it didn't—not really.

"Thanks again for teaching me. I know being on the bunny hill can't be that exciting for you."

He smiled and took a sip. "I can think of worse ways to spend an afternoon."

My face grew hot at his comment. "You probably didn't even learn on the bunny hill," I joked. "Probably just went straight to jumping off cliffs."

He chuckled. "Not quite. My dad was definitely out there on that exact hill towing me around with a leash."

I smiled at the thought of a miniature Giles riding a tiny board.

"That sounds like the cutest thing I ever heard."

His eyes looked bright and happy with the memory of his dad. I decided to take another chance on asking him about his life.

"So." I approached the subject cautiously. "What were your parents like?"

His face hardened at the mention of them, and I immediately regretted bringing it up again. Why did I insist on being so nosy? Especially when things were going so well between the two of us.

"They were the best. The warmest people you could ever hope to meet."

I waited for him to elaborate, but when he didn't, I

stared back at the fire. Not wanting to push him further, I desperately searched my mind for something to say.

"My parents are warm too, not just because they live in Florida." I wanted to hit myself for how stupid that sounded and for bringing up my parents, who were very much alive. "Sorry, that was a dumb thing to say," I muttered.

The corner of his lip tugged up slightly. "No, tell me about them."

"Well," I started carefully, not wanting to gush too much. "They're great. They've always been so supportive of my sister and me. Even with the whole Garrett thing…" my voice trailed off. The last thing I wanted to discuss with Giles was my cheating scumbag of an ex-boyfriend.

"What's your sister like?"

"Beautiful. Amazing. Adventurous. Pretty much me, but better."

He gave me a puzzled look. "I could argue that all of those words describe you too."

My cheeks flushed. I hoped my sunburnt face disguised it. I should have worn more sunscreen, but who knew you needed to lather that on when you were surrounded by five feet of snow?

"If you met her, you'd get it."

"I don't think I would."

I glanced up, and our eyes locked for a few heartbeats.

"Hey, you two." Erin popped up out of nowhere and had one hand on the back of each of our chairs.

Giles cleared his throat and started to fidget as if we had just been caught doing something inappropriate.

"Sorry, did I interrupt something?" She winked at me.

"Stop that," I mouthed silently at her.

Had she gotten Giles and me alone together on purpose? From the huge grin that was plastered across her face, it sure seemed that way.

"No, good timing," Giles said, standing up. "I've got to check on something. I'll see you two later."

He walked away, but before he was out of earshot, he turned back. "Good job today, Florida."

"Thanks," I called after him, his back already turned again.

Erin looked at me expectantly. "So? How did it go?"

I shrugged. "It was fine. I've almost got turning down."

"Not that." She waved off my comment and rolled her eyes at me like I was missing something obvious. "How did it go with Giles?"

I tilted my head. "Fine? He was a good teacher. I'm not sure what you want me to say."

"Ugh," she huffed. "Don't play clueless with me. I can see the little flirtatious eyes you've been throwing at each other."

My eyebrows shot up in surprise. "Erin, nothing is going on with us."

"And at my party? You two were alone all night."

"It's not like that, I swear." As I was trying to convince Erin nothing was going on between Giles and me, my heart sank to my stomach because I realized that maybe I *wanted* something to be there.

"Whatever you say. Go get yourself cleaned up. We're grabbing food and drinks in town tonight." Erin instructed me. "And I'll drop this whole you-and-Giles thing for now, but just know that I think there is a spark there. I'm calling it now."

"You're way off base," I insisted while secretly hoping she was right.

Did I have a crush on Giles Stone? I couldn't even remember the last time I had a crush on a man. I had been with Garrett for so long that I wasn't sure I even remembered how to flirt. I sighed and knocked back the remainder of my room-temperature drink. It didn't matter what I was feeling. There was no way it was mutual.

Chapter Sixteen

Setting my curling iron down, I scrutinized my appearance. My lashes were coated in dark mascara, and I had applied enough bronzer to tone down my cheeks' redness. Did it look like I was trying too hard?

I tugged at the cropped sweater I was wearing before pulling it up over my head. Rushing to the closet, I picked through my slim wardrobe before settling on an oversized maroon crewneck sweatshirt. This would make me look more casual.

A knock sounded at the door.

"It's open," I called.

Erin poked her head through the doorframe before walking inside.

"You almost ready?" she asked. "Damn. You clean up nice."

Heat went straight to my cheeks. "Really? I just threw this on."

"Uh-huh." Erin crossed her arms and gave me a

knowing look. "Just so you know, I'm not sure if Giles is coming tonight."

"Oh. Why would that matter?" I asked, feeling like I had been caught.

Maybe I just wanted to look nice for my first time out on the town. It definitely wasn't for anyone in particular.

"You just put those effortless beach waves in your hair for fun?" Erin leaned against the kitchen sink, smirking at me.

"This is basically how I always look," I insisted, even though I had spent thirty minutes longer getting ready than I typically did.

"Whatever you say. Let's head out. Johnny is already there."

Grabbing my coat, I followed her out of my apartment and down the stairs.

"We can just walk. It's only halfway down Main Street."

"Great." I shivered, crossing my arms over my chest.

"Are you limping?" Erin eyed me.

"No. Maybe? I'm so sore," I whined. "Can we just drive?"

Erin laughed and grabbed my shoulders, pushing me forward. "We're not driving. It's two blocks, *Florida*."

"You better not start with that nickname too." I glared at her.

"Wouldn't dream of it."

Erin was right. We were at the front door of the Ridge Tavern and Tap in under ten minutes. I'd be lying if I said my quads weren't burning, though.

"Here we are," she announced before pushing open the worn wooden door.

The Ridge reminded me of an old western saloon that

had been turned into a college dive bar. There was wood everywhere. Old pictures and paintings adorned the walls. The bar and tables took up the right half of the establishment, while the left half housed two pool tables and a few other games.

"This is charming." I followed her inside.

"I don't know if charming is the word I would use, but whatever floats your boat," she replied as we approached the bar.

"Wife," Johnny called from a barstool and kissed Erin on the cheek.

"What are you having, Erin?" the gray-haired bartender asked.

"I'll have a gin and tonic. Mattie?"

"Same." I smiled and then whispered to Erin. "See? Everyone knows everyone. That's charming."

Johnny snorted and pointed a finger at the bartender. "Dave is *not* charming. Last year he got so drunk he puked on the pool table before passing out in the snow. It took three of us to drag him home."

I scrunched my nose and eyed the other side of the room. "*Those* pool tables?"

"Maybe," Johnny said, winking at me.

Erin and I took the seats next to Johnny while Dave slid us our drinks.

"You hungry?" he asked us.

We put a food order in for every appetizer on the menu. After a day of falling in the snow, I was completely ravenous.

"I think my stomach is going to cave in on itself," I complained after five minutes.

Erin giggled. "You're so dramatic. It'll be up soon."

She must have been a mind reader because, at that moment, Dave set down plates of nachos, mozzarella sticks, and chicken wings in front of us. Silence ensued as we all devoured the food.

I was mid-bite on a particularly messy chicken wing when the bell by the door chimed, signaling someone had entered. I barely registered it, but I did clock Dave raise his hand, and wave at the new arrival.

"Giles," he greeted.

I whipped my head around to see Giles wearing a thick fleece pullover and black jeans at the doorway.

"Hey, cuz." Johnny gestured for him to join us.

He sauntered over to us, greeting me with a small side smile that caused my stomach to flip.

"Hey." He rested his hands and leaned on the back of Erin's barstool.

"Hi." I smiled at him.

He gave me a funny look in return. "Florida, you got a little something on your face."

My face paled, and I dropped the chicken wing I had been shoving down my gullet. I looked around frantically for a napkin. Erin slid me one across the table with a huge smirk on her face. Snatching it, I quickly dabbed my face.

"It's still there." Giles's grin was bigger now.

I wiped my face with more urgency.

"Not quite." Giles chuckled as Dave handed him a beer.

"Well, excuse me for trying to enjoy a messy food." I relented, dropping the napkin, and picking the wing back up.

As soon as I was done, I excused myself to the restroom. Once there, I saw that I did have a few dots of sauce all the way up my cheeks.

"Shit," I whispered as I took a damp paper towel to them. So much for looking nice tonight.

I reentered the bar to find Johnny and Erin moving toward the other side.

"Johnny owes me a rematch in pool. Why don't you and Giles play on the other table."

Giles raised his eyebrows to see if I would protest.

"Eh. Sure," I replied, following them over there.

I glanced at the pool table and remembered Johnny's story about Dave and the puke.

"Um, what about darts instead?" I proposed.

Giles shrugged. "Whatever you want, Florida."

Uncontrollable butterflies were flapping around in my stomach as he brushed past me. *Why* did he always have to smell so good?

Be cool. I coached myself.

I took a huge sip of my drink before setting it down on the high-top table next to the board. I held out my hand for Giles to hand me a dart. Our palms touched briefly, and I felt a jolt of electricity in my veins.

"Did you just want to play for fun?" he asked.

"Um, probably. I don't even know the rules."

"We can play for points," he suggested. "Bull's eye is fifty." He continued to rattle off the scoring while I nodded and tried not to stare at his mouth.

"Got it?" he asked.

"Uh, yep."

He shook his head, a smile playing on his lips. He held his hand up and moved it back and forth slightly before releasing the dart he was holding. It landed directly on the bull's eye. My mouth hung open.

"You're hustling me," I accused.

He chuckled. "How could I be hustling you? We're just playing for fun."

"It's not fun if you're going to be shooting bull's eyes all night while I struggle."

He shrugged. "What do you want me to say? I've played a lot."

Raising his hand again, he threw another dart that landed just next to the center.

"You're up." He gestured for me to take his place.

I shuffled to the spot and closed one eye as I held the dart up to my eye line. In all honesty, I don't think I had ever played this before.

I took a deep breath in and released the dart. It hit the wood a few inches next to where the board was hanging before clattering to the ground.

Giles snorted next to me before slapping his hand across his mouth to stifle his laughter.

"Shut it," I said, already readying the next dart. This one hit the wall on the opposite side of the board but stuck in place this time.

"Do I get points for that?" I asked sheepishly.

Giles removed his hand to reveal a huge smile. "I think that's a negative five."

"This is going to be a long game," I said, groaning.

"Can I give you a pointer?" He took a step closer to me so that he was directly at my side.

"Su-sure." I mentally cursed my voice for cracking.

He placed a dart in my hand. "Okay, raise your hand." I followed his instruction. "Now, loosen your grip. Just keep your thumb and index finger on the back of it… yeah, there you go. Now, point your body at your target. Don't let your eyes leave the spot. When you release the dart, you've got to follow through." He was leaning in closer to me now, and I gulped nervously. "Okay, try it."

His breath on my neck caused me to blink a few times inadvertently, and I shot the dart haphazardly. It ended up hitting the wall just above the board.

He let out a sigh and dragged his hand over his jaw.

"Um. I think that was technically closer," I said, biting my lip.

"Maybe we should start with taking a few steps closer to the target."

After thirty minutes and another drink, I was now managing to hit the board every time I threw.

"Nice one," Giles exclaimed when I hit just a few inches away from the center. He held up his hand for a high five, and I beamed at his praise.

"You've been my teacher all day," I joked.

"I guess I have." He took a sip of his beer. "How's the tailbone holding up, by the way?"

I groaned. "It's so sore. I'm going to sleep so hard tonight."

"It's going to be worse in the morning," he warned.

"Ugh. Can't wait."

"Hey, you two," Erin said in a singsong voice. She was approaching us with shot glasses.

I started shaking my head on instinct. "No way. Absolutely not."

"Suit yourself, but you might change your mind when I tell you it's karaoke night, and Dave just finished setting up the machine." She gestured to the only empty corner of the bar where an older woman was stepping up with a microphone. Abba started to blare through the speaker system.

"Oh my god, yay!" I squealed before downing the shot she handed to me. "I love karaoke."

Giles looked pained. "Of course, you do."

"Will you sing with me?" Erin asked excitedly.

"Obviously. What song should we do?"

We debated before selecting a well-known boyband throwback and raced to the stage when the older woman finished.

Erin and I smiled as we sang the lyrics and even did a little impromptu dance number. I caught Giles staring at me. Feeling brave, I winked at him because I was already making an ass of myself. He bit his lip to stifle the smile I could see trying to form.

Erin and I sang our hearts out until the song ended, and we breathlessly stepped down from the stage and handed the mics to two college-aged girls.

"Nice one, babe." Johnny planted a kiss on her head.

"Very impressive," Giles said, trying to keep his tone serious.

"You guys got next, right?" I asked, still grinning.

Johnny snorted. "In your dreams. Giles would never be caught dead up there."

"Is that right?" I stared at him, and his brown eyes didn't leave mine.

"That's right."

"What if I persuaded you?" I challenged.

"Impossible."

"Please?"

"Nope."

"What if I went up there with you?"

"Not going to happen."

"Come on. Let me teach you something today."

He couldn't keep the smile from his face as he shook his head at me. "There you go again with your persistency."

"It's part of my charm," I replied sweetly. "C'mon. What do you have to lose?" I held out my hand as the previous song ended.

Erin and Johnny watched our back and forth silently, waiting to see who would win the battle.

"If anyone records this, you're dead," Giles announced before grabbing my hand and marching up to the stage with me.

"What song do you want to do?" I asked, gleeful that I had won.

"Something easy," he muttered. "You better choose fast, or I'm out of here."

I picked a well-known Motown duet that every English-speaking person in the world knew the lyrics to.

"We've got this," I said before giving him a thumbs-up.

The music started up, and I belted the lyrics at him. To his credit, as uncomfortable as he was, his voice wasn't half bad.

I danced around him as he stood stiffly with one hand on the mic and the other in his pocket. When the first chorus came around, I started jumping around, and the whole bar sang along too.

Trying to loosen Giles up, I grabbed his hand from his pocket and forced him to twirl me. That finally got him to crack a smile. By the time the chorus rolled around again, he was jumping around with the rest of the bar. He looked like he was actually having fun with it and I couldn't keep the smile off of my face.

The song ended, and we stepped off the stage, laughing.

I beamed up at him. "See, that was fun, right?" I asked through heavy breathing.

He smiled down at me. "If you say so, Florida."

I smacked his arm. "Shut up. You were having fun and you know it."

"Wow, hell must be frozen over because I never would have thought I'd see my cousin on a karaoke stage." Johnny was at our side now, clapping Giles on the shoulder.

Giles shrugged him off, but his smile remained.

A hand grabbed my arm and I glanced to my right to see Erin smirking at me.

"What?" I hissed. "We were just having fun."

"Sure," she whispered before raising her voice to address the group. "Johnny we should probably head home. I'm completely wiped. Giles can you walk Mattie back?"

"You don't have to," I insisted, turning to him and cursing Erin in my mind.

"It's no problem," he said as we all grabbed our coats and exited the lively bar.

We said our goodnights to Erin and Johnny before turning to walk the short way to my apartment. Our footsteps crunching in the snow was the only sound for the first minute. Giles finally cleared his throat.

"So, is Key Ridge everything you thought it would be?"

"It's different than I expected. More real."

He glanced over at me. "You thought it would be fake?"

"Not exactly. I guess before I came, I was just picturing a fantasy. But Key Ridge is just as real as anywhere else. Real people, with real lives, and real problems. It isn't just this vacation paradise."

"Some people would love for the world to think that."

"Like money hungry corporations?" I guessed.

He nodded.

We walked a few more steps in silence. The side of his arm kept brushing mine, effectively causing my stomach to do somersaults. I kept sneaking glances at his profile.

"I'm glad you came here," he said.

"Why?" I asked. I couldn't keep the surprise from creeping into my voice at his admittance.

"It's been nice having someone around that hasn't known me my entire life. It's easy to talk to you."

"It's easy to talk to you too," I murmured. "And I know the feeling. Before I moved here, I had the same friends since college. It felt like they knew me so well that we had run out of things to talk about if that makes sense."

"Or maybe they just stopped trying."

I bit my lip. "That's probably more likely."

"Are you doing okay with all that? Not missing your old life too much?"

"What's there to miss." Bitterness crept into my voice as I once again shoved all thoughts of Garrett and my ex-friends out of my mind.

"What about you?" I asked, changing the subject.

"What about me?"

"You said competing was too much pressure, but what about the rest of it? Do you miss your old life?"

He hesitated before responding. "I'm not sure that life-style was ever for me. It was lonely traveling all the time. I'm not much of a talker so it was hard to get close to anyone. The people that actually cared about me were always right here..." his voice faded.

Without thinking I grabbed his hand and gave it a quick squeeze.

He looked at me, eyebrows raised in surprise, before the corner of his lip tugged up.

We were in front of Bev's house now. I stopped and turned to face him.

"Thanks for walking me home."

He nodded. "Of course."

I took a step toward the stairs at the same time he moved to step past me. Suddenly we were only inches apart. Giles stared down at me and my eyes flicked to his lips. Before I could think, I took a small step forward. He lingered close to me for a moment. His eyes searched mine before his gaze shifted to the ground.

Shaking his head, he cleared his throat. He took a step back, effectively killing whatever moment was happening between the two of us.

"Goodnight, Mattie," he said before walking back in the direction we came.

"Night," I called after him, my voice only slightly shaky.

Climbing the stairs, I thought of nothing except for how good it felt to be that close to Giles Stone.

<h1 style="text-align:center">Chapter Seventeen</h1>

Hi Mike,

Everything is going well at The Key Ridge Ski Lodge. Please see below for some of the changes I've implemented to date:

- Updated guest booking system
- Implemented automated check in and check out
- Hired a new housekeeping team
- Created a guest survey to gather feedback after checkout
- Incentivized reviews with a 5% rental discount code

In addition to these changes, we are actively working on getting the lounge area up and running. The plan is to have it open Thursday-Sunday. There will be a full bar and a basic menu that will be easy to keep up with. There will be a happy hour coinciding with the ski hill closing to hopefully gain

new nonguest generated business. I'll keep you updated.
Thanks for all your trust!
Mattie

Mattie,
Glad to hear everything is going smoothly over there. I had no doubt you would be successful. FYI we have some promising leads for your replacement once we've secured the contract. Please see the resumes I've attached.
Mike

Staring at the last line of Mike's email, I sighed and closed the laptop. I couldn't bring myself to look at the resumes right now. Knowing I would have to leave eventually, and actually facing that reality, were two completely different things. I was finally getting comfortable here. It felt strange to think about leaving. I wasn't sure how I felt about returning to Florida and all the memories I wanted desperately to leave behind.

After the golf cart incident, I finally deleted all social media from my phone so that there was no way I could see any of Garrett's or Nadine's posts. I couldn't mentally handle it. But right now, my hand was itching to hit that redownload button and see exactly what they were doing. Frankie's voice was in the back of my mind, scolding me for even thinking about doing that. Shaking her hypothetical words out of my guilty conscience, I reached for my phone.

"How are you feeling today, Florida?"

Jumping, I jerked my hand away from my phone as if I had just touched a hot burner.

Giles raised his eyebrows. "Did I scare you?"

"Sorry, I was just a little zoned out." I forced a smile. "You were right. My tailbone is even more sore than yesterday."

Should I bring up last night?

"So about last night." Giles interrupted my thoughts. "It was fun…" His eyes shifted to the floor.

"Definitely," I agreed. My brain seemed incapable of coming up with something else to say.

"Right," he replied, drumming his fingers against the desk, and rocking back and forth. "So, I heard the plans to fix up the lounge are in full swing."

I eyed him nervously and nodded. "That's the plan."

"Bev mentioned it to me. I thought maybe you might need some help or something. A ride, maybe? There's a hardware store in the town over and a secondhand furniture shop."

"You-you want to help?" I stumbled over my words, surprised he was being so cooperative.

He scratched the back of his head, and his eyes darted around the room, looking anywhere but at me.

"Yeah, I know I was jerk about the idea when you first brought it up. I was still salty you were here. It's a great plan, and I want to help."

"Well, if you're sure, I'd love some help." I smiled at him.

"I am," he said, finally meeting my gaze. "When did you want to go?"

I glanced around the empty lobby. It was noon, so any guests checking out had already done so, and check-in wasn't until three.

"Bev did say she could take over the front desk today."

"Great. Text her."

Slamming the door to Giles's truck, I was instantly transported back to my first day here when he took me shopping.

He was so closed off and I was so desperate to be liked. Now he was giving me snowboarding lessons and letting me talk him into Karaoke. I bit back a smile at the memory.

"What are you thinking about?" he asked, staring at me.

"Just your amazing singing voice."

"Oh god." He rolled his eyes and turned away from me. "Please never bring that up again."

I laughed. "Why not? You were actually pretty good."

"Just like you were actually pretty good at snowboarding?" He raised his eyebrows.

My mouth hung open. I tried to look offended, but I couldn't keep the laughter out of my voice. "Hey, give me a break. It was my first time."

He chuckled. "I'm just messing with you. I was impressed."

"You better be."

Leaning forward, I fiddled with the radio. After scrolling through a few stations playing commercials, I came across one of my favorite Christmas songs and turned it up to sing along.

Giles hit the power button and glared at me.

"It's not even Thanksgiving yet. No Christmas music in my car."

"But it's snowy," I whined. "I've never listened to Christmas music with an actual snowy backdrop."

"I don't care. It's too early."

"Please?" I pleaded and gave him my best puppy dog eyes.

He glanced at me and rolled his eyes.

"Fine. But just one song."

"Yay," I cheered and pushed the power button.

My one song turned into five.

Giles pretended to look pained, but the corner of his lip tugged up as he snuck glances at me, singing along. He still refused to join in despite my best efforts.

The mountains whizzed by on the scenic highway between towns. Giles exited and pulled into the parking lot for the hardware store.

"This is so charming," I said, climbing out of his truck and slamming the door.

The store was petite, with a wooden sign and a front porch—a far cry from the large commercial stores I was used to seeing.

"You've got to stop saying everything is charming just because we're in the mountains," he said, side-eyeing me as he held the door open.

"What? Just because it's a place you buy tools it can't be charming?"

Giles led me down an aisle that held the paint selections. I eyed them and stroked my chin. "What do you think about doing something dark?"

"You're asking me? I don't have a creative bone in my body."

"C'mon Giles, help me." I nudged him playfully, and the half-smile he gave me in return made my heart flutter.

"A dark blue would look good against all the wood."

"That's exactly what I was thinking," I exclaimed, grabbing a swatch with several different navy variations.

We were pondering over a few choices when a man in an orange vest rounded the corner and joined us in the aisle.

"You two need a paint order?" he drawled.

"Yes actually. I think we're going to go with this one." I pointed to a deep blue that reminded me of the ocean on a stormy day.

His eyes moved over me slowly as he took the sample from my hand. His thin lips widened into a smile. I fought the urge to roll my eyes at his blatant attempt to check me out.

"I haven't seen you around before, and I know everyone. What's your name, sugar?"

Before I could answer, Giles placed himself in front of me. His stance felt protective, and his eyes were dark. "Back off Earl."

"Oh shit, I didn't see you there, Giles. This your new girl?"

Giles curled his fingers into fists as he glanced back at me.

"She works at the lodge."

"I'm Mattie," I interjected, feeling ridiculous that they were talking about me as if I wasn't standing right there.

"Mattie, huh?" My name on his cracked lips made me cringe. "Is Giles here showing you a good time? Because if he's not, I know all the best bars in the area. I could take you out som—"

"Just the paint, Earl," Giles snapped.

"Geez, so sensitive. I was just tryna be nice." Earl backed off, taking our sample with him behind the paint counter. He plugged a few things into a computer. "I've got a few other things I need to take care of first. I should be able to have this ready for you in an hour if you want to stop back."

"That's perfect." I put on my best polite smile. "We've got other errands to run. We'll come back when we're done."

Giles was still glaring at Earl, so I nudged him. "Let's go," I hissed under my breath.

Finally breaking his stare, he met my eyes and nodded.

"See you folks in a few. Nice to meet you, Mattie."

"You too," I lied.

As soon as we were out the door, I breathed a sigh of relief. "Well, the workers aren't nearly as charming as the facade."

"Earl is a creep," Giles mumbled. "Don't come back here without me, okay?" He looked genuinely concerned.

"What would I come back here for? Fishing gear?" I joked.

"I'm serious." His sternness startled me.

"I-I won't come back," I promised.

We sat in a heavy silence as Giles drove us to our next destination.

He finally sighed and glanced over at me. "I'm sorry, it's just that I've never considered some of these people from an outsider's perspective. Earl is harmless when you can handle yourself, but…I wouldn't want him taking advantage of you."

My eyebrows shot up. "Excuse you. You don't think I can handle myself?"

"You're too polite."

"So?"

"So. He would push you. Take advantage of that. You've got to be harsh with guys like him."

"Giles, I'm nice, not stupid. I know how to handle guys like that."

He glanced at me and then back to the road, clearly not believing me.

"I'm serious. You don't think we have creepy men in Florida? I can handle myself."

He still looked unconvinced as we pulled into our next stop. It was an old house that had been converted into a thrift store.

"If you say so," he said, slamming his door.

Inside, old shelves were lined with every knickknack imaginable. Ceramics, glassware, art pieces. In the back, I spied rows and rows of furniture.

I was already planning on painting the existing, worn-out chairs black, but I still needed to pick up a couple of tables to create more seating. Some wall art would also be nice. Bev had given me a very modest budget, but I was confident I could make it work.

"What about this one?" I ran my fingers over a long wooden table. It must have been fifteen feet long. "We could do open seating and fit a ton of people here."

Checking the price tag, I winced.

"Scratch that. This alone would take up the entire budget."

Giles waved off my concern. "Don't worry about the budget."

"Bev told me specifically—"

"I said don't worry about it. I got it."

"Giles, you don't have to do that."

He shrugged. "I want to. It's my place, too."

Gazing at the table, he absent-mindedly started tracing the grain in the wood. There was sadness in his eyes, but I didn't dare bring up his parents again.

"Well, I think we should get it, then."

He nodded. "It's perfect."

We continued to browse the store as I selected paintings and decor of various sizes.

"Look at all the stuff we've found." I admired my pile of collections.

Giles snorted next to me. "You mean the stuff you found."

"Add something to the stack then."

He shook his head. "I don't have an eye for stuff like this."

I grabbed his arm and tugged him around the store, pointing to various pieces.

"We're going for eclectic. Random even. The whole point is to not think too hard about it."

"A neon sign would be cool," he finally said. "We had an ancient one hanging in there for years before it crapped out."

"I love that," I squealed with excitement, tugging on his sleeve.

He raised his eyebrows and stared down at me. "Did you hit the caffeine a little too hard today?"

I waved off his comment. "Do you know where we could get a neon sign?"

"Johnny can make us one. He did one for their basement a while back."

"That's perfect. A neon sign always draws the social media crowd."

"Excuse me?"

"You know. People see a picture of a cute neon sign and want to go to that place so they can take the same picture. It's a thing, trust me."

"I changed my mind. I don't want one anymore," he deadpanned.

I ignored him. "What should it say? Maybe a cute phrase or a pun or something." I put my hand over my face, trying to think of the perfect words.

"Don't worry, I got it," he insisted.

After we paid, we gathered everything—aside from the massive table they would deliver later on—and piled it into Giles's truck.

"This is so exciting. You have to help me get everything together."

Giles started driving back to the hardware store to collect the paint. "Have you always been such a peppy person?" he asked dryly.

"Have you always been such a prickly person?" I teased.

A grin tugged at his lips, and his clear brown eyes glanced from the road to me. "Answer my question, or you owe me a drink."

"I didn't realize that game would be forever ongoing." I laughed. "But to answer your question—I think so? I've just always felt like everything is going to work out. And even if it doesn't work out the way I want it to, everything will still fall into place like it's meant to..." My voice trailed off at my last words. The pain I had been suppressing from my recent betrayal was bubbling to the surface, and I fought to push it down.

Giles seemed to sense my change in demeanor because his next words were soft. "It's okay to be upset sometimes, y'know? It doesn't mean you're not still a positive person."

"I know that." I fiddled with my hands, not caring that my words didn't sound convincing even to my own ears.

We pulled into the hardware store. He sighed, turning toward me. "For the record, anyone that hurts you is an asshole. You don't have to put on a front and pretend it's okay when it's not."

He knew exactly where my mind had wandered to.

"They're not worth it," I said.

"But you are." He leaned toward me. "If you don't let yourself feel the pain, you'll never get over it."

His intensity had me speechless. I couldn't help but feel like he was talking to himself when he spoke those words.

"I'm going to run in by myself and grab the paint. I really don't think I can handle Earl talking to you again."

With that, he slammed the door and was gone, leaving me swimming in my thoughts.

Chapter Eighteen

"Phew, that was a rush." Bev wiped her brow and held her hand up for a high five.

I slapped it gleefully, feeling electrified from such a busy morning. It was the first night of the season the lodge was at full occupancy. It was thrilling to see the lobby abuzz with so many people.

The past few days had been a blur of nonstop activities. Giles and Johnny had already painted the lounge and the existing chairs. Bev had helped me place the art I bought. The table had arrived yesterday. Erin was already tinkering around in the kitchen, coming up with a simple menu.

"Did you hear how many guests asked about the new lounge?" I asked excitedly.

"I have ears. How could I not hear? That fresh paint really draws your eye right to the lounge when you walk in."

"It looks so good," I agreed.

My phone buzzed in my pocket, and I ignored it,

scrolling through the computer's list of reservations to see how many guests we had left to check in.

My phone continued to buzz relentlessly so I finally reached for it to see what the big emergency was.

Frankie: OMG!!!

Frankie: PICK UP YOUR PHONE NOW!

Frankie: Did you know?

Frankie: Mattie!!

My stomach sank.

Mattie: What are you talking about?

The next message was just a picture of Garrett and Nadine in a field. He was sitting behind her with two hands on her stomach. She was looking lovingly back at him and holding a picture of a sonogram up to the camera.

The blood drained from my face as I stared at it.

Frankie: Did you know she was pregnant!?!
I can't believe this! WTF. Is that why they
got engaged two seconds after you
broke up?

I was still staring at the photo. At Garrett's smile. At how genuinely happy they both looked. I had been trying to pretend like this wasn't real. Like what Garrett had revealed to me wasn't true. Now that was impossible. It was plastered all over the internet for the world to see and revel in their bliss. I couldn't hide from this anymore.

A lump formed in my throat and my eyes started to burn.

Shit, I could not cry here.

I squeezed my eyes shut and took a deep breath through my nose and out my mouth, trying desperately to remain composed.

"You, okay?" I peeked through one eye to see Giles staring at me. Concern flooded his eyes.

"Of course." I plastered on the best fake smile I could muster.

He searched my face, clearly not convinced of my show. My eyes were glassy from trying to hold back tears. I blinked a few times and pretended to look something up on the computer.

"So, what brings you in?" I asked in a cheery voice.

"Um, Johnny finished the sign. The neon one for behind the bar? I figured we could show you and put it up."

"That's fantastic." Bev clapped her hands excitedly.

"How exciting," I said, still not making eye contact.

Usually, distracting myself with conversation was enough to compose myself, but these tears roared at the back of my eyes and threatened to explode.

"It's in the lounge already." He grabbed my arm across the desk. The gentle touch of his hand just made me want to lose it more. "Come see it. You too, Bev."

I nodded.

Staring at the ground, I watched my feet shuffle into the next room. I could feel Giles's stare boring into me, but I refused to meet his eyes. One sympathetic look from him, and I was sure to start bawling. I kept taking deep breaths through my nose, fighting back the tears with everything I had.

Johnny and Erin were already in the lounge. The neon sign was leaning against the bar, covered by a tarp.

"You ready for the reveal?" Johnny asked.

There were excited cheers from the group as Johnny and Giles both grabbed a side of the tarp.

They both ripped the tarp away to reveal a neon pink and blue sign. I glanced up but could barely see the words through my wet eyes. I blinked a few times to clear my vision.

SKI BUNNY

"Ski bunny?" Erin asked, crossing her arms. "Is that supposed to be funny?"

Giles shrugged. "It's cute."

Bev chuckled. "I think it's clever. It'll look great above the bar."

Silence followed, and I knew eyes were on me. I realized I hadn't said anything yet. I needed to show my approval.

Damn it, say it looks great, Mattie.

My face was bright red, but I finally looked up and opened my mouth to address the room.

"It looks gr—" My voice was interrupted by a choked sob. To my horror, tears started flowing freely down my face.

"Mattie, what's wrong?" Giles stepped in my direction before I bolted out of the lounge.

"She probably thought you were making fun of her." I heard Erin whisper behind me.

Too hysterical to stop and explain, I raced out of there as fast as I could. The bathroom off the lobby had a line already. I brushed right past it toward the stairwell. I took the stairs down two at a time and closed the basement door behind me. Once in the solace of the dark room, I sank onto the sofa and cried my eyes out.

It had been ages since I had cried this hard. Letting it all out, my chest heaved up and down. I ripped open a new pack of tissues and dried my endless stream of tears.

Why couldn't I be as over this as they were?

What was wrong with me?

They treated me like shit. I shouldn't be wasting time being upset over them.

These thoughts that entered my mind just made me sob harder until I was on the verge of dry heaving.

I hated myself for this outburst. But my disgust with myself just made me cry harder.

Finally, after a violent hiccup, my sobbing decreased to sniffles, and I blew my nose. My face felt swollen. I was terrified to look in a mirror.

A soft knock sounded at the door, causing me to jump up. I decided to pretend I didn't hear it.

"Florida, open up. It's me." Giles soft, muffled voice made its way through the closed door.

No one could see me like this, especially not him.

"No," I responded weakly.

I heard a sigh through the door.

"Please, Mattie."

His voice sounded slightly pained. My hand hovered over the doorknob.

"Have you been standing out there this whole time?" I asked, suddenly horrified that he had overheard my embarrassing crying sounds.

"Yes, and it's been killing me. Please, let me in," he pleaded.

After a few more seconds of deliberation, I slowly

opened the door. Giles had been sitting on the ground, leaning against the wall. He jumped to his feet as soon as I had the door cracked. As if worried I might change my mind, he snuck his hand between the door frame and wedged his body through.

He looked me up and down. I covered my blotchy face, horrified he was seeing me like this.

"Please, don't look at me," I muttered pathetically.

"Mattie, what's wrong?" he asked, grabbing my wrists and pulling my hands away from my face. "You scared the shit out of me. You sounded hysterical in here."

"I can't believe you were eavesdropping." I attempted to glare at him, but my face fell into a puddle of sadness.

He placed a hand on each of my shoulders and pushed me back toward the couch, forcing me to take a seat.

"I wasn't eavesdropping. I was worried about you." He bit his lip and continued to stare at me despite my instructions. "This-this wasn't about the sign, right?"

His expression was so earnest it almost made me laugh.

"The sign is cute," I said.

He leaned back, sighing. He ripped his beanie off and ran a hand through his hair. "Then what's wrong?"

I stared at the floor, not giving anything away. "It's so stupid. I don't want to talk about it."

"Mattie—"

"No, really. I'm so embarrassed. I just want everyone to forget this ever happened."

"Not likely."

I groaned and cradled my forehead in my hands. "I can't believe I lost it like that."

Giles didn't say anything. I snuck a glance at him

through my fingers only to find that he was staring at me intently.

"Let's get back out there. I should get cleaned up."

I sprang to my feet, but his hand grabbed mine, holding me in place.

"Please talk to me," he whispered.

"It's nothing, I promise." I forced a pathetic smile and tugged my hand away from him.

I turned the door handle, only to find that it was locked. The keypad was still on the inside of the basement door since I hadn't found the time to reinstall it. Giles was standing behind me now, looking over my shoulder as I tried to enter the four-digit factory code.

I let out a frustrated sigh as I tugged the door to no avail.

"What is it?"

"It's locked." I continued to shake the handle violently.

"Why did you lock it?"

"I didn't. The stupid thing must be malfunctioning. The code isn't working either."

"This is why you're supposed to install these things with the keypad on the *outside* of the room."

"I know, I know." I took a step back and assessed the lock. "Can you open it with your tools or something?"

He shook his head. "Toolbox is upstairs."

"Oh," I said flatly.

I started to bang loudly on the door, but Giles grabbed my hands.

"Whoa there. Let's not freak out the guests." He steered me back toward the couch, and I reluctantly followed. "Everyone knows we're down here. Someone will be by to check on us any minute."

"Okay," I mumbled.

He leaned back and resumed staring at me. "Now that we're stuck here, are you sure you don't want to talk to me?"

"You did this on purpose." I pouted, eyeing him warily.

He smirked. "I don't think I could have anticipated you still not fixing that damn lock."

We sat there in silence for a few more minutes. I opened and closed my mouth a few times, scared to finally say the words out loud.

"Remember how I told you my ex cheated on me?" I finally whispered.

Instead of responding, he inched closer to me on the couch and nudged my knee with his to encourage me to continue. I wasn't sure if his knee pressing into mine was comforting or making me nervous. Maybe it was both.

"I didn't exactly tell you the whole story." I took a deep breath, ready to blurt it all out and get it over with. "Right after it happened, I found out he had proposed to her. That hurt. Like a lot. I had been with him for *eight years*. That was supposed to be me…" I trailed off as tears began to form in my eyes again.

"Mattie," Giles whispered. He was lightly stroking my upper arm now in a circular motion.

"She's pregnant." I forced the words out of my mouth, and tears fell as I did so. "I know I should be over it. They're clearly happy and ready to start their family." My voice cracked, and Giles reached out to tuck a piece of my hair behind my ear. "But it still hurts. I thought I was supposed to be with him forever. I thought she was *my friend*. I feel like they got to live happily ever after, and I got everything taken away from me. It isn't fair."

"It's not fair," Giles agreed.

"I don't even have friends anymore." I looked up at him. "I feel stupid for getting so upset over people that don't care about me at all."

"You shouldn't feel stupid. That's an insane way to have a relationship end. Anyone would be hurt by that. And most people would let it stop them from living for a while. You've been trying to pretend everything is fine for weeks. I know you're strong, but you don't have to be okay, Mattie."

"I'm not that strong." I sighed before continuing. "Remember that golf cart accident I told you about? After I found out she was pregnant, I was way too drunk and got upset. That's why I crashed it. I'm pathetic."

"You are *not* pathetic." He raised his hand cautiously before wiping away one of my tears with his thumb. "You came out here to start over. That takes guts. And look at you now." He nudged my shoulder. "You're turning this place around. You can stand outside even when it's below thirty degrees. You're *basically* a professional snowboarder."

I laughed at his last two comments and wiped my eyes.

"And you're wrong about not having any friends." He hesitated. "I'm your friend."

I smiled but dropped my gaze as I thought about our tumultuous relationship. "Really? Sometimes it feels like I annoy you."

"If this is about when we first met, I told you I'm sorry."

"It's not that." I shook my head. "I just mean—I know it's none of my business, but whenever I ask you personal questions, it seems like you're closed off. And I know I'm one to talk because I haven't exactly been forthcoming either…"

His eyes looked pained, and I regretted bringing this up.

"Sorry, I shouldn't have said anything. I guess I just wanted you to know that if you do want to be friends, then I'm here if you ever want someone to talk to."

He covered his mouth with his hand and slowly dragged it down his face.

"I do want to talk to you. It's just hard for me to talk about my parents."

I reached over and took his hand, squeezing it in mine.

"You don't have to."

"No, I want to." I waited for him to continue, not wanting to push him. "They died last year in a car accident."

Tears pricked my eyes again, this time not for my pain but for his.

"It was a bad snowstorm, the roads were icy, and visibility was shit. A semi crossed into their lane and hit them head-on." He was staring at his feet, his voice thick with pain. "I wasn't even here. I was in Canada doing some bullshit competition I had no business being in. I'd been having some problems with my knee. I should have retired a couple of years ago, but I was too stubborn. My mom kept asking me when I was going to slow down. When I would have time to visit more. I always just brushed her off, knowing I'd move back here one day. But one day was too damn late." His hands were balled into fists as anger crept into his voice. I cautiously grabbed his hands with mine and sat there with him in silence for a few moments, tears running freely down my face.

"I-I can't even imagine what that must feel like," I finally said.

"It doesn't feel great," he mumbled.

"But you can't blame yourself for not being here. You could have never known that was going to happen."

He shook his head. "I should have prioritized spending time with them."

"Were they proud of you?" I whispered.

He raised his eyebrows and looked at me, surprised. "I guess so."

"Bev told me they would always tell guests that you were their son. They must have been so proud of everything you were doing."

Giles squeezed his eyes shut. When he finally opened them again, a tear rolled down his cheek.

"I don't want to say the wrong thing because I have no idea what you're feeling. But you can't control what happened," I said as his eyes bore into mine. "You can hold on to the memories you have, though. And the knowledge that they loved you and were so proud of yo—"

His lips were on mine before I realized what was happening. His mouth devoured mine hungrily. He licked my lips, and I parted them, inviting him inside. He kissed me even deeper, and I kissed him back, too stunned to even register what this meant.

Moving his hands to my cheeks, he held onto my face, ensuring I kept my mouth glued to his. I leaned back slightly, and Giles followed me. He gently nudged me back further until I was lying down on the couch with him on top of me. He wedged his knee between my legs, and I moaned against his mouth. I snuck my hands underneath his shirt and was about to start exploring his chest when a loud knock sounded at the door.

Giles ripped his mouth off mine and jumped back. He

was standing and moving away from the couch before I could even register what had just happened.

"Is everything okay in there?" Bev asked through the door.

"We're locked in." His voice was deeper than usual, and he cleared his throat. "The keypad isn't working."

I heard the sound of the knob being unlocked. I jumped up and smoothed down my hair.

Bev flung open the door. She eyed us both up and down. I'm sure I looked a mess from the hysterical crying. Also, the whole being kissed by a different man after *almost a decade* thing. Yeah, I'm sure that wasn't doing much for my composure. Giles, on the other hand, looked completely calm and collected, like nothing had happened.

"We've got to get this lock turned around," Bev finally said.

"I'm getting the tools and doing it right now." Giles glanced in my direction and nodded before racing back up the stairs.

I took a few shaky steps toward the door and tried to smile at Bev on my way out. She grabbed my arm and squeezed it.

"I hope everything is okay." Her voice was comforting.

"I'm sorry about my outburst. I feel silly."

"Don't even give that a second thought." She wrapped me in a side hug and led me upstairs. "I've lost count of the number of times I've broken down in this very lodge. At least you didn't lose it in front of guests."

"I guess that's true."

"Why don't you go home and take a nice hot bath? You've done so much work this week. You deserve a break."

"Thanks, Bev."

I gave her a reassuring smile and we parted ways once we got to the lobby. Giles brushed past me with the toolset. Despite my pleading eyes begging to talk about what had just happened, he didn't even glance down at me.

Walking back to my studio, I felt numb. Talking to Giles had felt amazing at the time, but now I felt foolish. He was dealing with so much grief that he probably thought I was being melodramatic.

"Ugh," I groaned, grateful for the cold air hitting my face.

And what was that kiss about? Had he done it to shut me up? Did it mean something?

I licked my lips from the memory. Kissing Garrett hadn't felt *anything* like that. I tried to remember back to when we had first gotten together. I had thought he was cute, and I remembered getting butterflies the first time he kissed me at a party. But this intense desire I was feeling now…Garrett had never made me feel like this. Giles's body on top of mine was running through my mind repeatedly.

Shaking my head, I tried to rid myself of the thought. Unfortunately for me, I couldn't get my mind to stop fantasizing about doing it again.

Chapter Nineteen

BEEP BEEP BEEP

Groaning, I leaned over the side of my bed and felt around for my phone to snooze the alarm once again.

Last night I had stayed up until four a.m. tossing and turning. I cried again over Garrett. Then I got myself so worked up about the Giles situation that I managed to shed a few tears over that too. There's no way he was *actually* into me. It was just him feeling vulnerable and confused.

Then I cursed myself for being so self-deprecating. Of course, he could like me. Why not? But then I broke down again, convinced no one would ever truly love me and that I'd be alone forever.

Overall, it was not an enjoyable night.

I finally checked the time on my phone.

Shit.

I should have been at the lodge a few hours ago. Before I could race to put pants on, I saw I had two texts from Bev.

Bev: Don't worry about coming in today. We're expecting a big storm, so It's going to be slow, and you deserve a day off.

Bev: Hope you're feeling better.

I cursed in frustration, thinking again about yesterday.

The fact that I had cried in front of everyone was already bad enough. Now I had to stress about facing Giles again after that kiss.

That *really* good kiss.

It was impossible to keep my thoughts from drifting back to yesterday. He was a great kisser, and judging by how confidently he had moved his hands, he was probably great at everything else too.

I had always thought Garrett and I had an okay sex life, but it had gone downhill recently. Now, with the truth finally revealed, I could see why. It was probably difficult for him to keep a sex drive up for two women.

I tried to remember the last time Garrett and I had even had sex, and it dawned on me that it was months ago. No wonder just a few minutes with Giles on top of me had me all hot and bothered. I was desperate for some action, and I hadn't even realized it.

Sighing, I walked over to my tiny kitchen and started to brew a pot of coffee. I stared out the window. The sky looked dark, and the trees were blowing violently in the wind. This must be the precursor to the storm Bev had mentioned.

I poured myself a very strong cup of coffee and put the pot back for the rest to brew. Garrett had always hated when I did this. "You're ruining the rest of the pot," he would say. Since I was always the one up early enough to make the coffee, I ignored him and continued to pour myself a cup as soon as there was enough in the pot. He never even noticed unless he caught me doing it. Then he would complain bitterly about the taste.

I collapsed on the couch and pulled out my phone to get some much-needed advice.

> Mattie: I need your help.

> Frankie: Are you okay? I'm soooo sorry I sent that picture. I was just in shock.

> Mattie: It's fine. I knew, and it was about time I accepted it.

> Mattie: I actually need help with something else….

> Frankie: ??

> Mattie: Giles kissed me yesterday.

> Frankie: WHAAT!? How was it??

> Mattie: Kind of amazing…

> Frankie: AHHH I'm literally screaming!! He's so attractive. I've got a google image search pulled up now to get the visual of him making out with your face.

> Mattie: 1. Gross. 2. Stop stalking him. I need your advice. What the hell do I do now?? I'm dreading running into him again. It's going to be so awkward.

> Frankie: Why? Did it seem like he wasn't into it?

> Mattie: I mean, I think he was? It seemed like he was trying to take it further before we got interrupted...

> Frankie: Then take it further!!!

> Mattie: Like a rebound?

> Frankie: LOL you can try, but you are so not a rebound girl.

> Mattie: I could be!

> Frankie: You dated your high school bf for 3 years. Then you met Garrett and immediately got together. Now here you are 8 years later, a single serial monogamist.

I groaned, reading her words. She was right. I was a relationship kind of girl. I loved them. And getting married was still very much high on my priority list. It was tough for me not to start fantasizing about a future with a guy as soon as he showed any interest.

> Mattie: It would be different with Giles. I can't live here forever. It would have to end when I moved back home.

> Frankie: Oh, I fully expect you to move there if you start something with Giles. Have a nice life!

> Mattie: Ha. Ha.

Chewing my lip, I scrolled through my messages until I saw Giles's name. Bev must have given him my number back when I first started. The only text exchange we ever had was him telling me Bev had to do something in town and was running late one day. My fingers hovered over my phone as I debated what to type.

Mattie: Hey, can we talk about what happened yesterday?

I hit send and immediately threw my phone across the room onto the bed.

Ugh, why couldn't I play it cool?

Now I had to anxiously wait for his response.

I started to tidy the kitchen while periodically checking my phone for a message from Giles. After the tenth or so time, I had finally given up. If he wanted to pretend like nothing happened, I could do that too.

Unfortunately, after I stopped obsessing about Giles, my fingers were itching to redownload social media to see what my former friends were commenting on Garrett's big announcement. Instead, I decided to shut off my phone and stick it inside a cabinet to avoid temptation.

The wind was howling outside. It felt like the perfect time to cozy up under a blanket, watch a movie, and hide from reality.

———

A LOUD BANGING SOUND AGAINST THE WINDOW STARTLED ME out of my nap. I jolted up from the couch. Racing over to the window, I saw that it was just a tree branch getting thrown around in the wind.

The time on the microwave told me that it was already almost eight p.m. After binging three movies and eating all the junk food I could find in my studio, I must have dozed off on the couch.

I was about to open the fridge and rummage through the bare contents when a massive gust of wind threw another branch into my window. At that exact moment all of the lights in my apartment turned off.

I screamed instinctively.

The power must have gone out. The white snow outside reflected some light through the windows, but I could still barely see a thing. I took two steps toward the living room before colliding with the edge of the table.

"Shit, ouch." I rubbed my thigh. That was definitely going to bruise.

I remembered seeing a box of what looked like camping supplies in the closet by the bathroom. Carefully, I made my way there and started rummaging through the disorganized mess.

I pulled out a lantern and fiddled with the power button a few times only to realize the batteries must be dead. Groaning, I continued to rummage. My eyes adjusted slightly to the dark, and I came across a few candles and a lighter. This would have to do for now.

I set two candles on the kitchen table and two on the coffee table and lit them. They gave off a very dim glow. It was better than nothing.

I remembered Bev had left some books on the bookshelf. I snagged one that looked like a mystery thriller. I wrapped a blanket around myself and curled up on the floor to put the book right next to the candles.

I had only gotten through a few chapters when a banging at the front door made me jump.

Instinctively, I ducked under the coffee table like I was worried someone was trying to break in and kidnap me. When the banging continued, I realized it was probably just

Bev checking on me. I walked over to the door, still wrapped in my blanket. It had only been twenty minutes or so since the power had gone out, but it was already chilly in here.

I opened the door to find Giles standing there in a large coat with the hood up. His brow was creased, and his jaw was locked. His arms were full of wood and a large square box. He looked very irritated.

"Hey, what ar—"

"You don't answer your phone?" he asked, moving past me into the entryway. I closed the door behind him.

"Sorry, it was off." I had forgotten about my phone.

"I called you like a hundred times." He set down the stuff he was carrying and glared at me. "You can't have your phone off in a storm like this. How was anyone supposed to know you were okay?"

"Shit, I didn't even think about it."

"You're damn right you didn't think." He tore off his mittens and ran his hands through his hair. "It's freezing in here."

"Well, duh, there's no power."

"You have a wood-burning stove." He gestured toward the cute black piece of furniture with the pipe going up to the ceiling.

"Oh." *So that wasn't just for decoration.*

He groaned as he stooped down to the stove, opened it, and placed pieces of wood inside. "So, you were planning to just freeze to death in here?"

I shrugged pathetically. "It hasn't been that long. I figured the power would come back on eventually."

"Not tonight it won't. The main power line to the whole town is down, and the storm is too bad for them to fix it.

They'll have to wait until it blows over, which likely won't be until morning."

He held a lighter to the bottom of the woodpile. When a small flame flickered to life, he shut the door and stood up.

"Thank you." I smiled weakly.

Giles paced around the apartment. He opened a few cabinets before pulling out my phone.

"No food at all in here, but I found your missing phone." He handed it to me and gave me a look like he expected me to explain, but I just grabbed it from him and set it on the table.

"I've been meaning to get to the grocery store, but I've been busy."

"Well, I didn't have much at my house, but I brought some granola bars and a few other things to get you through the night."

Giles mentioning his house captured my interest.

"Where do you live?" I asked.

His eyebrows shot up, and the tension in his brow lifted.

"On the other side of town."

"What's your house like?"

"Why?" He was looking at me as if I had lost my mind.

I shrugged. "Just curious is all. I've never heard you mention it before."

"It's just a cottage two blocks off of Main Street. I like to be close to everything."

"Sounds cute," I replied, trying to picture his house.

"It's not *cute*."

"Oh, I'm sorry. Does that word offend you too?"

He groaned in frustration. "The only thing that offends me is people not answering their phones in the middle of a huge storm and forcing me to race down here to make sure that they're still alive and not buried under a pile of snow in a ditch somewhere."

I smirked and tilted my head at him. "You thought that I, Ms. Florida herself, was outside in this weather?"

"If you had just answered your phone to confirm that, then I would have known for sure," he countered.

"Alright, I give. I'm sorry. I'll keep my phone permanently glued to me from now on."

"Good."

He placed a bag on my table and then walked over to the closet that was still open. Grabbing the lantern, he moved back toward the table and removed the backing.

"You brought batteries?" I asked, hopeful.

He grunted in response as he continued to fiddle with the lantern. Seconds later, lamplight illuminated the room.

I frowned. "That's barely stronger than my candles."

"It is pretty old," he said. "But it'll have to do."

"Did you bring anything else?"

"Like what?"

I sat down at the table. "Like a game or something."

He cocked his head, and his frown deepened. "I was a little preoccupied with making sure you were okay."

"Well, physically I'm fine, but I *am* a little bored."

He rolled his eyes. "It's been less than an hour. You're that reliant on technology?"

I jutted out my bottom lip in a pout and nodded. The light flickered softly over his features. He looked adorably disheveled right now. Although he was scowling at me, I couldn't take my eyes off his mouth. The one that was on mine just yesterday.

"So yesterday…" My voice trailed off, and I hoped Giles would help me out here.

Instead, he crossed his arms and raised his eyebrows, waiting for me to continue.

"It was-it was nice?" My words came out like a question I was desperate for him to confirm.

Unfortunately for me, his posture changed. He sighed deeply, running his hand over his face before looking at the floor.

"I shouldn't have done that."

My face fell. I relied on the dim light to hide my evident display of disappointment.

"Why not?" I asked.

"It's just-I'm just-Look. I'm a mess right now. I'm trying to figure a lot of shit out, and I'm not very good company. You and me—that would just complicate things. Especially since you work at the lodge."

I blew out the breath I had been holding. "I see."

"And I don't want to lead you on or anything. Believe me. I've learned my lesson with that."

"So, you didn't like it?" I practically whispered. I hated myself for needing his approval, but this was my first inter-action with a man other than Garrett in years, and he was hurting my ego.

"Fuck—no. That's not what I meant. Look, I'd be lying if I said I hadn't thought about doing that for a while now. But that isn't the point. The point is that we shouldn't be doing that. It's not any good for either of us."

My heart started to beat faster at his words. He'd been thinking about doing that for a while? It wasn't just me?

He knocked on the table a few times with his fist before announcing, "I should get going. Stay inside, okay?"

He started to move toward the door before I jumped up to stop him. "Wait," I pleaded, grabbing his arm.

Raising his eyebrows, he stared down at me.

"What if it's not such a bad idea?" I licked my lips and stared hungrily at his mouth.

"Mattie."

"Giles, we're both adults. And we both want this, right?" I took a step closer to him. He didn't back away. "Maybe we're both trying to figure things out right now, but this doesn't have to be one of those things."

"What are you saying?" his voice was thick, and the tension between us was palpable.

"I want you. Let's forget about everything else for now."

He bit his lip, still looking unsure but also not backing away from me. "I can't Mattie. Trust me. I wish I could."

I frowned and backed away from him. "I get it. You're right."

He stood there staring at me for another moment before shaking his head. "I better get going."

"Right, of course. Get home safe."

"Just…just text me if you need anything."

He turned away and exited through the door.

I groaned and cradled my head in my hands. I had practically begged him to make a move and he had rejected me. I cursed myself for being so resistible. Before I had a chance to wallow in my self-pity more, another knock sounded trough the apartment.

My heart slammed against my chest as I cautiously approached the door. I swung it open to reveal Giles standing there, his eyes dark.

"Fuck it," he said before bringing his hands to the back of my neck and pulling me in, covering my mouth with his.

My hands went straight to his hair. I raked my fingers through his messy waves.

He kissed me slowly at first then with growing need as he slammed the door behind him and backed me into the table. I gasped as he took his hands off my face and placed them at the backs of my thighs before hoisting me on top of the table. Grabbing at his thick jacket, I pushed it off his shoulders before he took his hands away from me for a moment to shrug it off.

I wrapped my legs around his torso, eager to pull myself even closer and feel his body against mine. When he grabbed my waist and yanked me toward him, I felt his arousal pressing into me, and I moaned against his mouth. It had been too long since I had been touched like this.

Warm hands moved from my lower back to the front of my sweater as Giles lifted it up and tugged it over my stomach. I lifted my arms, and he tore it off me, leaving me completely bare since I hadn't been wearing a bra.

"Fuck," he said as his eyes slowly roamed over my body. "I've wanted to do this for so long."

I gasped as his mouth moved to my neck, and his hands drew slow circles on my stomach just below my breast. He gently caressed the bottom of one, and I threw my head back, almost undone by the smallest brush of his fingertips.

His fingers moved slowly to my nipples as he gently started to play with them while his mouth moved south to my other breast. I gasped as he took me in his mouth, his tongue gently rolling over my nipple.

"Giles," I moaned as my hands tangled in his hair, desperate for more.

His mouth went to my other breast as I grinded against him, desperate to shed the rest of our layers.

His mouth covered mine, suppressing another moan as he cupped my ass between his hands and lifted me off the table. I straddled him and kissed him deeply as he walked us over to the bed, where he turned around and fell back onto it, letting me fall on top of him before he rolled us over, pinning me against the sheets.

"Are you sure?" he asked against my mouth.

"Yes," I breathed as I fumbled with the button on his jeans. He took over and had them off in seconds before pulling down my own sweatpants in one fluid motion.

His hand brushed the inside of my thigh, and my legs fell open for him, needing to feel his touch. He slowly rubbed his fingers against me before slipping one inside. I gasped and raised my hips, desperate for more. He slid another one inside me before moving them slowly, in and out while rubbing his thumb in circles over the exact spot my body was begging to be touched.

"Giles," I panted, my voice thick with desire. "Please."

He moaned against my neck and released me. The area his hand left was pulsing for more. He fiddled with the pocket of his jeans for a moment before disposing of a foil wrapper on the ground.

"You sure?" he asked, again.

"Giles, please. I need you inside me now," I whimpered, desperate for release.

His mouth covered mine again as he slowly slid inside me.

I gasped at the overwhelming feeling and dug my fingers into his back.

He moved expertly inside me and with one hand, resumed playing with my nipples as he rocked back and forth on top of me. I wrapped my legs around his hips, willing him to go deeper. The pressure was building inside me as I kissed him hungrily.

"Fuck Mattie, you feel amazing."

I thrust my hips up to increase the intensity. I was right on the edge. Finally, with one deep thrust, I moaned his name as I finally came undone.

Chapter Twenty

WAKING UP, I YAWNED DEEPLY AND STRETCHED MY ARMS above my head. Squinting my eyes, I saw that daylight was already creeping in through the blinds.

My body was sore and satisfied, a feeling I hadn't felt in years. Maybe ever. A smile played on my lips as I opened my eyes and turned over. I expected to find a still shirtless Giles. Instead, the bed was empty, and I jolted up, scanning my surroundings.

Getting up, I threw on an oversized hoodie and checked the bathroom—the only room I couldn't see from the bed —but he was nowhere to be found. The only sign he was here, and that I hadn't fantasized the entire thing, was the bag of food he had brought over that now lay on the floor after our escapades on the table last night.

"Shit," I groaned. Here I was sleeping soundly, dreaming about waking up for part two. Meanwhile, he was probably already regretting what we did.

My phone caught my eye in the kitchen. I walked over

to retrieve it, desperate to text Frankie about this turn of events. There was a yellow Post-it note stuck to my screen.

Keep this turned on, please.

I smiled. Maybe he didn't regret it.

While I waited for my phone to power on, I made a pot of coffee. Dings started sounding, and I eagerly snatched up my phone to read my missed messages.

> Giles: Are you okay? Pretty much the whole town has lost power.

> Giles: Mattie? Hello?

> Giles: Answer your phone!!

While I felt bad that I hadn't seen these, a part of me felt pleased he was concerned. My face fell at the last unread text.

> Bev: Hey Mattie, the lodge lost power, but we've got a generator backup. No worries over here. I'm going to send Giles to check on you since I don't think I left any emergency supplies at that apartment.

That's why he stopped over? Because Bev had asked? I groaned and cradled my face in my hands. He wasn't worried about me. He was just fulfilling a duty. And I just threw myself at him like some desperate woman that hadn't been touched in forever. No wonder he left this morning so quickly.

I texted Frankie.

Mattie: I slept with Giles.

I didn't even have a chance to set the phone down before it rang.

"Hello," I answered.

"Tell me everything," my sister demanded.

I gave her a recap of last night and this morning. Including how I had awoken to Giles already gone and finding out that his aunt was the one that had asked him to check on me.

"I'm so pathetic," I said when I was done recounting the tale.

"Um, no, you're not. He goes over to check on a hot girl in the middle of a power outage, and he ends up getting lucky? That's like every guy's fantasy. No way he regrets that. I'm sure he was just as desperate as you were."

"I don't know about that."

"Well, I, for one, am proud of you for sleeping with someone else. Now we can forget that ex of yours, what's-his-name, ever existed."

"It was pretty amazing," I murmured.

"Dude, I believe it. That man is gorgeous."

"Do you have the Google image search of him pulled up again?"

"I'm just making sure I have the proper visual. Goddamn, I'm a little jealous."

I groaned. "Well, don't be too jealous. I doubt it'll happen again."

"Not with that attitude. When are you seeing him again?"

"I mean, probably at the lodge today, unless he tries to avoid me."

"Well, you better look extra good, just in case."

I took Frankie's advice to heart and made sure to spend a little extra time on myself that morning. My normally messy bronze hair was curled to perfection in large bouncy waves, and I had on my favorite black V-neck sweater. It wasn't low enough to be unprofessional, but it did show enough of my chest that I hoped it would play with Giles's imagination. I threw on my favorite pair of jeans and black boots before grabbing my coat.

You've got this, I told myself. When in fact, I had no idea if I had this. Something told me this situation with Giles was not going to be simple.

Once outside, I walked carefully over to the lodge. Someone had shoveled the driveway and path, so it was a lot easier of a walk than I was anticipating.

I took a moment to look up and around me in awe. The mountains were drenched in feet of snow. The early morning sun danced off them, and the white peaks were glistening like diamonds. Even the cold air was starting to grow on me. I took in a deep breath and savored the crisp, fresh feeling.

At the lodge, I threw open the back door to see a line of a few guests waiting at the front desk where Bev was standing. I rushed over to help.

"Busy morning?" I asked her.

"A lot of guests that were supposed to come in last night are here this morning because of the storm."

"Got it." I waved to the next couple in line. "I can help you get checked in right over here."

The first hour of the day flew by as Bev and I worked the front desk. My brain had no time for excess thoughts. The minute the rush slowed down, however, I found myself scanning the lodge looking for a certain someone.

"Did Giles come over last night?"

'Er-what? Why would he come over?" I sputtered, my face turning red.

Bev raised her eyebrows and looked at me through her thin glasses. "Because I asked him to check on you when the power went out. He didn't come?"

"Oh, right." I laughed nervously. "He did. He brought over some batteries and food."

She patted me on the back. "I'm glad you were taken care of."

I nearly choked on the sip of water I had just taken.

At that moment, Giles and Johnny walked into the lobby together, and my heart started pounding out of my chest. He either looked even better than usual, or my attraction to him was now feral after experiencing his hands all over my bare skin.

"Morning," I called out in a voice that sounded robotically cheery even to my own ears.

Giles lifted his hand in a small wave. He looked like he wanted to head straight to the lounge, but Johnny sauntered over to the front desk, a huge grin on his face.

"Morning. How did you like your first big snowstorm, Mattie?"

Giles raised his eyebrows next to his cousin and started to shift from foot to foot. He looked like a guilty kid that had just been caught doing something he wasn't supposed to.

"It was exciting," I exclaimed, and I swear I saw Giles

smirk at the floor. "And the town looks so beautiful this morning. I think the snow is really starting to grow on me."

"I was hoping you'd say that. You've got to come snowboarding with us later. Erin is going to meet me down here in a couple of hours."

Biting my lip, I glanced out the window again. "I don't know about that. I'm still not very good."

Since the day of my first lesson, I had gone once more with Erin. We had made it onto one of the bigger lifts, and I managed to get down without falling. But a three-year-old could still ski in circles around me.

"You've got to experience a powder day. It's the absolute best thing. Tell her, Giles."

Giles shrugged. "It is pretty great."

"Plus, you're less scared to fall because if you do, you'll land in a pillow of powder, and you won't get hurt," Johnny said.

"Well, maybe. Bev might need me here."

"Don't use me as an excuse." Bev looked up from the computer. "I'll be fine here for a few hours."

"Then, sure. I guess." I finally caved. In truth, I did enjoy snowboarding, and taking the afternoon off sounded like fun. I just wished I was more confident on a board.

"Great, when Erin gets here, we'll come get you." Johnny tapped the desk and then headed over to the lounge.

Giles was about to follow him when I asked, "Are you coming too?" I tried to keep the hopefulness out of my voice.

He stopped and finally looked at me. "I'll be out there, but I've got to work."

"Ah. Duh." My lips were starting to hurt from smiling so big. Why was I such a dork?

He lingered for a moment and opened his mouth like he might say something but then glanced at Bev and back at me.

"I'll see you later, Florida."

"Bye," I called after him, too loudly, before slumping down on the stool behind me.

I suppressed the urge to drop my head onto the desk in front of me. Apparently, I sucked at playing it cool.

"Have a nice stay," I said to the last guest checking in today.

Glancing over to the lounge, I saw Giles and Johnny still working. They had hung up everything to my specifications and were now unpacking boxes of old glassware from the original restaurant behind the bar. Normally I would have joined them, but Bev and I had a steady stream of guests coming to the front desk all morning.

"Phew. Finally, a lull. I need a solitaire break," Bev announced as she pulled up the game on the computer and started clicking away.

I forced a small chuckle and snuck another glance at Giles. He just took off his sweatshirt and was wearing a black T-shirt that hugged his lean muscular arms. Those same arms that had me pinned to my bed yesterday...

Nope. Stop that right now.

But memories of last night kept flooding my mind, and I hated how little self-control I had. If Giles had asked me to meet him in the basement, I would have let him take me right there on the worn sofa.

My face was getting hot, so I fanned myself with one of our brochures.

"You, okay?" Bev asked.

"I'm fine. Totally fine," I mumbled.

Just then, Johnny walked out of the lounge and down the hallway, probably to get something from the basement. Seeing Giles alone had me springing from my seated position.

"I'm going to see if Giles needs any help," I said.

Bev didn't look up from her game as I walked over to him. I didn't want to give him a chance to escape.

"Hey, can I help?" Before he responded, I grabbed two glasses from the box he was holding and unwrapped them.

"I think I've got it under control," he teased.

"So…" My voice trailed off.

"So?" He raised his eyebrows, not helping me out with this awkward encounter at all.

"Are we going to talk about last night?" I whispered.

He looked from side to side to make sure no one was in earshot before lowering his gaze back down to me.

"What's there to talk about?"

"Um, just…" His nonchalance caught me off guard. "What now?" I asked.

He sighed and grabbed my elbow, steering me away from the bar and to a more secluded corner.

"Look, Mattie." Usually, I loved when he said my name, but this tone had me nervous. "I had a great time last night. Really great. But I told you yesterday I just don't think the two of us starting anything is a good idea."

"You said we couldn't go anywhere. Why can't we just

have fun right now?" His words stung and I felt pathetic for wanting him as much as I did. "I like you."

Dragging his hand over his face, he glanced from the floor back to me. "I like you too. Which is even more of a reason not to go there again."

"But—"

"I had a moment of weakness yesterday. And can you blame me? I mean, look at you. And you're so fucking nice and a good listener. It's been hard to pretend like there's nothing here."

"Then why do we have to pretend?" I whispered.

"It's easier this way. If we start something it'll just get messy. Let's just focus on the lodge and working together, okay?"

My face fell, and I didn't bother to hide my disappointment.

"I'm sorry, okay? This isn't because I don't like you or because last night wasn't amazing…" he trailed off as Bev and Johnny walked into the lounge.

Bev looked back and forth between the two of us. "Why are you two huddled in a corner?"

I glanced behind me and gestured to the posters hanging on the wall. "Just admiring how good these look here."

Bev raised her eyebrows. She didn't look convinced.

"Giles, can you come take a look at something our accountant sent over?"

"Sure." He gave me a small apologetic smile before following Bev out of the lounge.

Johnny eyed my sullen face. "You okay there, champ?"

"Of course." I straightened my posture and forced my lips to turn up.

He glanced from me to Giles and gave me a knowing look. "That sad face you had a minute ago wouldn't have anything to do with that cousin of mine, would it?"

The hairs on the back of my neck bristled. I tried to play it cool. "What? I don't know what you're talking about?"

He shrugged. "If you say so."

"Hey, you ready to shred?" Erin picked the perfect moment to walk in and interject.

"Definitely," I replied, desperate to get far away from Giles and nurse my bruised ego.

"Isn't this perfect?" Erin shouted as I took a small tumble, laughing as I fell.

"You were right," I called back.

We had been out in the snow for hours now. If I thought boarding was fun before, I didn't know what I was missing. Cruising in the fresh powder felt like floating. And Johnny was right. I was never nervous about falling like I was when the terrain was a bit icier. This was helping my confidence. I could feel myself improving, even though I still needed to stick to easier terrain. The only downside was now that the resort was mostly open, the crowds had started to flow in. Dodging people while learning to snowboard was challenging.

If only my ex-friends could see me now. Back home, I had never even tried surfing. Now I was full-on cruising down the side of a mountain. Part of me wished I still had social media so I could rub my new adventurous, thriving self in their faces.

"You're crushing it." Johnny stopped next to me and threw up his hand for a high-five. "I can't believe you just started learning."

I laughed. "I'm just glad I haven't broken anything."

He continued down the hill while Erin plopped down in the snow next to me.

"So, I heard a rumor."

I eyed her warily. "What?"

"That Giles went to check on you last night and didn't come home."

"Oh, uh, what? That's weird. Who told you that?" I stumbled over my words.

"Johnny." Her smile was smug. She knew I was lying. "He was there when Giles left to check on you. Then, when he was shoveling the driveway at the lodge this morning, he saw Giles walking out of your apartment."

"Um. He just—he forgot something." My excuse was pitiful and Erin knew it.

She laughed. "You can deny all you want, but I see the way you two look at each other. It was only a matter of time before you ripped each other's clothes off."

"Erin!" I hit her on the side of her puffy coat.

"So, you admit it."

"Please don't tell anyone. He doesn't want anyone to know."

She rolled her eyes. "He can be so stupid."

"He just doesn't think it's a good idea for us to start anything since I work at the lodge."

"Like I said, stupid. You two started something the moment you got here. I sensed it at our bonfire."

The shaking of my head was barely perceptible underneath my helmet. "It wasn't like that. He didn't even like me when I first got here.

"He's stubborn and stupid, but he definitely likes you now."

"Even if he does, he already told me nothing is going to happen again."

"Again?" Erin smirked at my admittance. "We'll see about that. Fifty bucks says that resolution lasts less than a day."

"Why don't we just get down the hill?"

"Fine, fine."

Erin stood up and took off. I placed my palms on the snow behind my back and pushed myself up much less gracefully. Leaning back on my heels, I slowly turned myself so that the front of my board pointed straight. The powder was so deep I had to lean far back on my board so that the front didn't sink into the fresh snow.

The part of the hill we were on today was crowded. I was hyper-focused on not getting too close to anyone else as I made my way down the hill. The green hill, which was the easy flat one I was on, intersected at times with more difficult terrain. The skiers and boarders shooting down those sections intimidated me.

I was just arriving at a point where my flat hill intersected with a steeper one. After looking both ways a few times, I continued.

Moving my board was becoming second nature, and my thoughts shifted to Giles. Was Erin right? Would he really change his mind? I hoped she was right. All I wanted was a repeat of last night.

"On your right!" A loud shout sounded out directly behind me.

I looked over my shoulder in a panic. All I saw was a sloppy skier coming directly at me at full speed. I dug my toes in to try to turn and get out of the way, but the sudden movement had me off balance.

Right before I was about to fall, the skier hit me full force. The collision knocked the wind out of me and pushed me right off the edge of the flat green terrain and into a steep sea of trees.

Chapter Twenty-One

I screamed as my adrenaline kicked in.

I was no longer on the main run but surrounded by trees and barreling down the ungroomed terrain. I flung my body out of the way of a few trees and was shocked to find my board was still underneath my feet as I continued to fly down the steep hill. The trees were getting denser and denser as I tried desperately to avoid hitting them.

I sunk into my heels quickly to avoid a large trunk, but there was another tree just next to it. Before I could react, my body slammed into it. My limp form ping-ponged off it, but my board was buried deep in the snow and wasn't moving freely. As my body flew forward, but my board stayed stuck, I felt a snap somewhere near my ankle. Pain shot up my leg before I face-planted into the deep snow.

The snow engulfed me, and I panicked. I couldn't breathe.

I clawed desperately to free my face, my heart pounding a mile a minute. Gasping for breath, my face finally came up for air, and I looked bewilderedly at my surroundings.

All I could see were trees in every direction. I pushed myself out of the powder and winced. My whole body was in pain, and my head was throbbing. I reached up to touch my helmet, only to find that it had shifted back on my head. I touched my forehead. Warm, wet, and sticky. Blood. Shit, I must have reopened my stitched gash— or gotten a new one. I couldn't tell.

I tried to pull my board so that it was in front of me, but just that tiny movement caused me to yelp in pain. My ankle hurt badly. It felt broken. I dug around in the snow and struggled with the binding for a few minutes before I was finally able to release my boots. I brought my legs out in front of me while my board stayed stuck in the snow. Moving around in this much powder was a ton of work. I was sweating and breathing heavily by the time I had gotten resituated.

Now that I was out of immediate danger, I took in my surroundings. Just trees everywhere, and to my alarm, there were no fresh tracks. I knew experts liked to do tree runs from talking to Johnny and Erin, but it appeared no one had been over here today. This wasn't good. I typically didn't have service out here, but I pulled out my phone anyway, only to see that I had shattered my screen with the fall. It wouldn't even turn on now.

Shit.

I couldn't walk, my head hurt so badly I saw spots every time I turned it, and I couldn't call for help. I was stuck.

"Help!" I finally shouted. "Help!"

I continued to scream my lungs out for what felt like an hour, but at no point did anyone shout something back. My alarm was slowly turning into fear.

They would have to find me, right? Johnny and Erin

would know roughly the place they last saw me. It would probably just take them a minute to realize I was missing, and then it would take a while to locate me. Someone would be combing through these trees soon enough.

My snowsuit might be brightly colored, but it was thick and warm. At least despite the piles of snow around me, I wasn't cold in the slightest. I leaned against the tree that was next to me and took deep breaths in through my nose and out through my mouth, trying to remain calm. There was nothing I could do but sit here and hope someone found me soon.

My eyes drifted closed. I took some snow and smacked myself in the face with it to try to stay awake. I didn't know too much about concussions, but I knew that if I had one, I probably shouldn't fall asleep. Still, despite my best efforts, I felt myself fading.

The next time I remembered looking up, it was starting to get dark outside. I scrambled upright in a panic that I had dozed off. Shit, the sun was setting. That meant it was like, what? Four-thirty? I had been stuck out here for over an hour now.

"Help!" I screamed. "Help!" I continued to yell until my throat felt raw. Being stuck out here in the dark felt a lot more hopeless. I refused to go out like this.

I swear I heard someone yelling back in the distance. Maybe up the hill a bit. It was hard to tell surrounded by these trees.

"Help!" I shrieked again. "I'm over here!"

"Mattie?" I heard someone calling my name now. There was no mistaking it.

"Over here."

Tears of relief pricked at my eyes as two men I'd never seen before in red ski patrol jackets appeared.

"She's down here," one of them called up the hill, and two more men in red jackets appeared.

"Are you hurt?"

"Just my ankle. And my head." I winced as I touched the large bump that had formed on my forehead.

"Let's get you out of here."

They started to pack me into a gurney-looking thing.

"We're bringing her down now, have the ambulance there waiting." I heard one of them say into a radio.

Once I was packed into the bag, the men expertly maneuvered me through the trees. It felt like I was in the middle of nowhere, but after just five minutes, we were back on the main hill that I had strayed from.

I breathed a sigh of relief as we made it to the bottom. There were flashing lights everywhere and quite a crowd. The two men that brought me down helped hoist me into the ambulance.

"We would have found you a lot sooner if that skier that ran into you had come forward earlier. Good thing you wore this outfit. As soon as we put the call out that you were missing, he remembered colliding with you."

I guess my obnoxious outfit came in handy after all.

The ski patrol backed away from the ambulance, and the E.M.T. closed the door.

"Wait, I was with my friends—"

"They're probably still out looking for you. There was quite the search party."

I groaned in embarrassment.

"Don't worry, we'll alert everyone that you've been found, and your friends will be notified you've been sent to the hospital. We can't waste any more time getting you checked out, though. That's a nasty-looking head injury you've got yourself there."

THE DOCTOR TOOK MULTIPLE SCANS OF MY HEAD BEFORE determining it was just a slight concussion. Unfortunately for me, it looked like my snowboarding days were over since I had fractured my ankle pretty badly.

"You're lucky. It could have been a lot worse," she said, showing me my X-Ray. "Those trees can be really dangerous."

"You don't have to tell me twice."

"We'll get this set in a cast and have you on your way in a few hours. We won't have to keep you overnight as long as you have someone that can monitor you at home to ensure there's no turn for the worse."

"I live alone. Can I just call someone if I notice a change?"

She raised her eyebrows. "You can't monitor yourself. What about your husband?"

I squinted at her in confusion.

"Someone claiming to be your husband showed up here about thirty minutes after you arrived. He's been demanding to see you, rather rudely, I might add. But we explained to him you were already in the middle of getting your scans."

"What? I don't have a—"

At that moment, Giles burst into the exam room. He looked angry.

"This guy." The doctor pointed at him. "Sir, I told you we would come to get you as soon as—"

He held up his hand, dismissing her. "No one should have to wait an hour to see their significant other. That's ridiculous."

I looked at Giles like he had grown two heads. Was my concussion messing with me?

"Well, I'll leave you and your *husband* alone for a moment." The way she said husband implied she didn't buy what Giles was trying to sell. "Someone will be in shortly to set your ankle."

As soon as she left, I crossed my arms and gawked at Giles. "My husband?"

He shook his head and walked over to me. "These assholes weren't giving me any information because I wasn't family."

"So, you lied?"

He shrugged. "They weren't going to let me come back here and see you."

I rolled my eyes. "I'm getting released soon."

He sat down in the chair next to my hospital bed and rested his head in his hands.

"You look exhausted," I said.

He ran his hands down his face. "Searching through trees and rough terrain for hours is pretty tiring."

"Ugh," I groaned, slumping back in my bed. "You were searching too? I'm so sorry. This is so embarrassing."

"That's not the word I would use."

"I fell off the side of the hill, and everyone on the whole mountain was searching for me. What would you call that?"

"Scary? Terrifying?"

"I guess it was pretty scary."

"I know, but I meant for me—for all of us. You scared the shit out of me, Florida. I was worried about you." His gaze was fixated on me.

My cheeks grew hot under his stare. "You were?"

"Obviously. When I got to the hill earlier, Erin was already in a panic, reporting you missing to ski patrol. I guess they had already done two laps and couldn't find you anywhere. It felt like a punch in the gut knowing you were lost. I know firsthand how dangerous boarding can be, especially for a beginner. We searched for hours. I've been over every surface of that fucking hill. When it started to get dark, I was—we were all panicking. When I got to the bottom of the last run and found out you had already been taken away in an ambulance, I got here as fast as I could."

"I-I appreciate you searching for me," I stumbled over my words. "I'm sure it's all part of the job, right?" I joked, trying to lighten his intense demeanor.

"That's not it at all." He lowered his head into his hand and kneaded his forehead. "Mattie, I'm sorry about earlier, but after today...I-I can't pretend I don't feel anything."

"You can't?" Hope fluttered inside my chest.

"Today has been the worst day I've had in a long time. Probably since..." He trailed off, but I could imagine what he was thinking. *Since my parents' accident.* "And all I could think about was that bullshit conversation we had this morning. How I brushed you off after the most amazing night. I'm such a prick."

The corner of my lip tugged up. "It wasn't exactly how I was envisioning the conversation going."

He scooted his chair closer to my bedside and gently grabbed my hand, tracing light circles into my palm. "I'm sorry about that. I know I shut you out. I've been so used to shutting people out my whole life that it just felt easier than facing whatever this thing is between us." His eyes were locked on mine.

"You don't owe me an explanation."

"I do, though."

My throat was dry. I gulped anxiously. I reached for the water on the stand next to the bed, but Giles was faster than me. He grabbed it and held the straw to my mouth before I could object.

"You don't have to baby me," I said before taking a long sip.

Giles chuckled, and the corners of his eyes crinkled. "You just had a serious accident. Sorry for treating you like you're a little fragile."

"I'm not fragile at all. In fact, I can't wait to get back out there."

His face broke out into a full smile, showing off his white teeth. "You don't think your ankle is going to slow you down?"

"Psh, this? This is nothing."

"Okay, Florida. Whatever you say."

The door swung open, and two different doctors entered the room.

"All right, it's time to get you in a cast so you can be on your way," The older one said in a comforting tone. "Sir, if you'll just wait outside."

"Nope, I'm good right here." Giles leaned back and crossed his arms.

The doctor rolled his eyes at his stubbornness but didn't object.

"You are all set," the doctor said, admiring his handiwork. "Now, whatever you do, make sure this doesn't get wet. If it does, you might have to come back in and get it set all over again."

"Got it, thank you."

"I'll have someone bring in your discharge paperwork, and you should be good to go home. Also, you've got another visitor in the lobby. Should I send her in?"

I nodded. "Sure."

Seconds later, Bev burst through the doors and was at my bedside, giving me a gentle hug.

"Mattie, thank god you're alright. We were all so worried." She glanced at Giles and then back to me with a knowing twinkle in her eye.

"I'm sorry I caused such a panic today."

"It's not your fault," he interjected. "If that stupid skier hadn't run you off the hill and then proceeded not to tell anyone..." He clenched his fist, and his eyes darkened.

"Well, it's over now." Bev patted my shoulder. "I'm just happy you're safe and sound."

"Speaking of that, the doctor said that since I have a concussion, someone needs to monitor me tonight. I wa—"

"You've got a concussion?" Giles rose from his chair and was at my side, examining me. "I thought it was just the ankle."

"They said it's minor, nothing to worry about. I can go home as long as someone is monitoring me. So, Bev would you min—"

"No," Giles interrupted me, shaking his head. "You'll stay with me. I've dealt with concussions before."

It felt like there was a ball in my throat that I couldn't swallow.

Stay with him?

I couldn't stay at his house. My cheeks flushed at the thought of it.

"That's okay, really," I insisted hurriedly. The last thing I wanted was for Giles to see me in my ratty pajamas, completely couch bound.

"It's better this way. You might need help getting around on that ankle too. Bev, can you stop at the apartment and get an overnight bag together for Mattie? I'll drive her straight to my place when she's discharged."

"I don't think—"

"If you think you're leaving my sight after today, you're out of your mind," Giles snapped, glaring down at me."

I gulped at his intensity.

"I'll just go get that bag then." Bev started to leave.

Relenting finally, I told her where she could find my toiletry bag and asked her to pack me some sweats. She almost ran into the doctor on her way out as the one from earlier came back in to discharge me.

"You're good to go, Mattie. We've got your insurance on file. Here are some crutches to use for that ankle. We'll bring in a wheelchair to get you out of the hospital. Now, who am I discharging you with, and who will be monitoring your concussion?"

"That'd be me." Giles held up his hand.

"Ah, the *husband*. Let me just go over a few things with you." She gave him some instructions.

I tried to listen too, but my stomach was doing somersaults. After last night I hoped I'd be seeing Giles's house, especially his bed. But I wasn't hoping to be in such a vulnerable position while doing so. Also, despite his change of heart, his words earlier about not wanting anything to happen between us kept echoing in my mind.

"Okay, Florida," Giles said, springing me from my thoughts. He had a wheelchair now and was gently grabbing my arm to help me into it. "Time to go home."

Chapter Twenty-Two

The tires crunched through the snow, and silence filled the car on the short drive. My thoughts spiraled. He kept sneaking glances at me, and I pretended not to notice. Finally, I felt compelled to say something to ease the tension between us.

"Did they tell you the reason they found me was because that skier recognized my description? I guess my bright outfit wasn't so bad after all, huh?"

"Glad that thing was good for something." Giles frowned and gripped the steering wheel tighter. "And don't worry about that guy. I got his ski pass taken away."

"You didn't have to do that."

"Yes, I did."

I bit my lip, unsure of what to say next. The broken phone in my pocket poked me, reminding me that I should call my family and let them know what had happened.

"Shit," I mumbled.

"Are you okay?" He glanced at me, alarm flashing across his face.

"I'm fine. I just broke my phone when I fell." I reached into my pocket and pulled out the shattered device. "I need to call my family."

"We're almost to my house. You can use my phone to call them when we get there. Johnny has an old phone or two lying around you can have until you get a new one."

"Thanks, that would be great, actually."

He nodded and turned the wheel, navigating us off the main road. His street was more residential, lined with cabins, bungalows, and small ranch homes.

"Here we are," Giles said as he pulled into the short driveway of an adorable house with blue siding and a wooden front porch.

"It's so charming," I said before opening my door.

"Of course, it is," he muttered. "Wait, stop. Let me come around and help you."

He rushed over to my side and placed my arm around his shoulders. When he lifted me out of the car, pretty much all the weight above my bad ankle was supported. He walked me over to the front door, where a black bag sat on the porch. Bev must have dropped off my stuff already.

Opening the door with his free hand, he ushered me inside. If the outside was adorable, the inside was positively cozy. The entryway led straight into a staircase. Turning left led you into a quaint living room with a brick fireplace and an oversized tan sofa.

Giles helped me take off my shoe and walked me over to the couch, where I plopped down.

"I love your house," I said, craning my head so I could catch a glimpse of the dining room and kitchen that were also off the living room.

"Ah, thanks." Giles ran his hand along the back of his

neck. "I don't really get too many visitors. Sorry, it's not cleaner."

"What are you talking about? If you don't think this is clean, then I'm glad the power was out when you came to my place yesterday," I joked.

"The cleanliness of your apartment wasn't exactly top of mind." He smirked. "Let me grab the rest of your stuff."

His words caused a stir in the pit of my stomach, and suddenly my whole body was hot at the memory of last night. How had that been just one night ago? It felt like a week ago at this point.

Wait, would we share his bed tonight? Or would he want me to sleep on the couch?

Ugh.

Dating was hard.

Giles brought in the rest of my stuff and closed the door with his foot. I watched him from my perched position on the couch, waiting to see what he would do with my black duffle. To my disappointment, he just set it down in the entryway without a second thought.

Couch it is.

Giles hovered nearby. He ran his hand across his jaw, glancing around the room.

"Are you hungry?" he asked.

"Starving."

"Do you like Chinese food? That's the fastest delivery in town."

"I'm literally already drooling at the thought of an egg roll."

He walked into the kitchen. "What do you want?"

I called out my answer as he relayed the order to the restaurant over the phone.

"Fifteen minutes." He re-entered the living room and tossed me his phone, which I clumsily managed to catch. "Why don't you call your family, and I'll head upstairs for a few and give you some privacy."

"Thanks." I smiled at him. "For everything."

He bit his lip like he might have wanted to say something else, but he just turned on his heel and went upstairs.

I dialed my mom's number as soon as he was out of sight.

"Hello?" My mom's confused voice came through the line.

"Mom? It's Mattie."

"Mattie? What number are you calling from?"

I ignored her question. "Look, I don't want you to freak out, but—"

"Ron, get in here. Something's wrong," my mom yelled.

"No, no. I'm fine. I just got into a small accident today."

"Oh my god."

"What happened?" my dad yelled in the background.

"It's nothing. I was snowboarding an—"

"I told you to be careful out there," she scolded.

"I was, I swear. Someone ran into me, and I fell. I fractured my ankle, and I have a small concussion." I decided to omit the part about me being stuck on the mountain alone for hours.

"Oh no, sweetie. That sounds serious," my mom cooed. "Do I need to get on a flight out there?"

"No," I insisted hurriedly. "I'm fine."

"Is anyone helping you? You probably shouldn't be alone right now."

"I'm staying with a friend."

"What friend?" They both asked my dad in a harsh tone and my mom in an inquisitive one.

"No one you know," I hissed.

"Is it a boy friend?" she asked as if I was still in high school or something.

"It's none of your business, but if you must know, yes, it is a *boy*. But we're just friends. His family owns the lodge I've been working at."

"Do you think that's a smart idea?" My dad asked at the same time my mom told me to send her a picture.

"Look, I've got to go. I just wanted to call and let you know what happened, but I need to give Giles his phone back."

"Okay, but call us if you need absolutely anything."

"I will. Love you both. Bye."

I hung up the phone before they could think of another question to keep the conversation going. Glancing up at the staircase, I saw no sign of Giles emerging. I strained my ears but heard nothing. Quickly, I plugged in the only other number I knew by heart.

"Hello," answered Frankie on the second ring.

"It's me. I can't talk long," I whispered.

"Mattie? Whose number is this?"

I rattled off the details of today's events, except this time, I disclosed the entire story. My sister gasped in all the parts I expected her to, but like I predicted, she was only half as interested in my brush with death as she was with where I was currently staying.

"He insisted on taking care of you? Mattie, that's huge."

"Do you think? It's not like I had a ton of other options. He could just be being nice."

"No way. If he didn't want you there, he would have let you stay with Bev. And I'm sorry, did you say he told the hospital he was your *husband*?"

"Just so that they would let him come back to the room."

"And he spent hours searching for you."

"A lot of people were searching."

"Mattie, get over yourself. He obviously likes you and—"

The staircase creaked, causing me to jump and hang up the phone in a panic, as if Giles could somehow hear what my sister was saying on the other end of the call. He emerged onto the landing, his hair was damp, and he had changed into a hoodie and gray sweatpants.

"Sorry, didn't mean to interrupt your phone call. The food should be here any minute."

"No, you're fine," I said in a voice that sounded too high-pitched. Clearing my throat, I continued. "I was done anyway."

He sauntered over to the couch, and I handed him back his phone. His warm hand brushed my fingertips, causing me to shudder. He smelled good, even better than usual. It must be the scent of his shampoo that I was so obsessed with. I fought the urge to ask him what brand he used. Disappearing into the kitchen for a moment, he returned holding an ice pack.

"Here. You should ice that bump on your forehead. It's really starting to swell."

"Um, thanks." I took the pack from him and placed it gingerly across the bump. I winced as the cold pack made contact with my wound.

The sound of a doorbell chimed. Giles walked over to

answer it, making the brief exchange with the delivery driver. As soon as the door closed, the smell of delicious fried food wafted through the entire house. My stomach growled audibly. Apparently, spending hours stranded on the side of a mountain worked up quite the appetite.

"That smells amazing." Drool pooled in my mouth. I reached for my crutches, but Giles shook his head.

"Stay there. I'll make you a plate and bring it to you. We can eat on the couch."

"Are you sure? I would hate to make a mess."

"Don't worry about it. I do it all the time when I'm by myself."

I tried to picture it. Him living here by himself. Eating on this couch, watching a movie, cooking.

"Do you cook?" I blurted out.

"Sometimes. I'm not very good at it. Do you?" he asked, handing me a plate of rice, chicken, and two egg rolls.

"Not really. Garrett and I usually ate out…" My words fell off when I realized I was bringing up my ex-boyfriend. "Never mind," I mumbled.

Giles sank into the couch next to me but didn't say anything. He turned on the tv and tossed me the remote. "Your pick since you had a pretty eventful day and all."

"Did something happen today?" I feigned ignorance, expecting him to laugh.

"Too soon." he winced. "And I take concussions very seriously. I will drive you back to the hospital if you start claiming memory loss."

"The time did actually go by pretty fast out there," I said in between shoveling in bites. "I think I was fading in and out for a bit because it got dark so quickly."

Giles looked like he was in pain. "Please spare me the details. It's making me sick thinking about you stuck out there all alone."

The concern in his voice made my heart flutter. I avoided responding by scrolling through the movie selection. I decided on a romantic comedy I had already seen twenty times. The exact distraction I needed right now.

"This, okay?" I asked.

He shrugged. "Whatever you want."

"It's a rom-com," I warned. Garrett had always given me a hard time if I deigned to select anything that wasn't action-packed.

"I'm good," he insisted, continuing to shovel in food.

My legs were propped up on the couch. If I stuck my foot out just an inch more, I could brush the side of his knee.

Stop that, I warned myself as I pressed play on my selection.

We sat there in comfortable silence, eating our food and watching the opening scenes of the film.

There was a beach scene playing out in the movie, and the leading man was surfing.

"Have you ever surfed?" I asked Giles.

He glanced over at me and looked back at the tv. "A few times, yeah. I prefer winter sports, but it's fun."

"Are you naturally good at it because of snowboarding?"

"It definitely helps."

"I'm jealous of your athleticism."

He smirked. "I'm not that athletic anymore."

"Oh, please." I nudged his leg with my blanket-clad food and gave him an exaggerated eye roll. "You know what's not athletic? Sliding down the side of a mountain and your limp body ricocheting between tree trunks. You probably could've done that run in your sleep."

"It *is* a pretty easy Black."

My mouth hung open. "Hey, I was kidding!" I threw the pillow behind me at his head.

He chuckled. "In your defense, it was ungroomed and there was about three feet of fresh snow."

"In my defense, I've gone snowboarding *three times* in my entire life. You're literally a professional."

"Retired professional," he clarified, setting his empty plate down on the coffee table.

I polished off my last egg roll and leaned forward to set my plate on top of his. "Still, that's so impressive to be that good at something. You went to the Olympics."

"It was a great life," he admitted.

"Did you always know you wanted to move back to Key Ridge?"

He glanced over at me, considering my question. The movie kept playing, forgotten in the background. "I think so, yeah. I mean, there was a time in my life when all I wanted to do was get as far away from this town as physically possible. But I think something I realized when I was traveling and moving around so much is that nowhere ever felt like home the way this place does." He fiddled with his hands in his lap. "I just wished I realized that a little earlier."

The sadness in his voice crushed my heart. It must be so hard for him to be back in this town without his parents. He must be reminded of them everywhere he looked.

"What about you?" he asked me. "You've lived in the same place your whole life. How come you never left?"

I bit my lip. "I'm not sure. I guess I've never really been anywhere else. I feel like we have the opposite problem. You were dying to get out, and I was always too scared to. It was comforting being close to things I'd known my whole life. I never even really thought about leaving until my life imploded."

"And now that you have?" he looked at me expectantly.

"Now that I have left, I'm really happy I did. I think I've had more fun, met more people, and tried more things these past few weeks than I have in the past few years."

A smile played on his lips as he pretended to watch the movie. "I'm glad to hear that."

"You are?" I challenged him to say more, but he simply nodded and said, "Yeah."

"You know what I'm glad about?" I asked, deciding to be bold.

He glanced at me, his brown eyes darkening slightly. "What?"

"That you gave me a chance."

He turned his body so that he was facing me and put his arm across the back of the couch, propping his head up against that hand. "I'm glad you didn't write me off as an asshole."

I laughed. "Well, I did at first, but I decided you deserved another chance."

He smirked and his gaze remained locked on mine.

"Would you mind if…" His voice trailed off.

"What?"

"Can I hold you?"

Butterflies exploded in my stomach. "Okay."

I carefully shifted on the couch until my back was next to him. He gently grabbed my waist and pulled me back toward him so that I was resting against his firm chest. He brought his mouth to the top of my head and kissed me.

"You really scared the shit out of me today, Florida."

"I didn't realize you cared that much," I whispered as he drew slow, deliberate circles on my arm.

"Honestly, me either," he said.

"Does this mean," I gulped, nervous about getting the words out. "Does this mean you don't think it's such a bad idea if we start something?"

I felt his warm torso go up and down as he sighed deeply. "At this point, I don't really care if it's a bad idea or not." He tilted his head and grabbed my chin, tipping it to the side, so I was forced to look at him. "There's no way I can stay away from you now."

He leaned in slowly. My heart pounded as he captured my lips with his. The kiss was slow and sweet, unlike the urgency and the need of last night. His tongue slipped into my mouth and softly flicked against my own. Every coherent thought left my brain as he continued to kiss me. After a few long minutes, he released my mouth and planted a kiss on my forehead before resuming staring down at me.

"I'm happy I'm here," I whispered.

He grabbed the back of my neck and stroked my cheek with his thumb before kissing my mouth again. "Me too."

We ended up talking through the rest of the movie. We discussed my career and how I liked it, but sometimes I wasn't sure what my next move was going to be. He told me that he wasn't sure what the future held either but that he was excited about the freedom of retirement. He talked about his parents. What it was like to grow up in this town with them.

By the time the credits were rolling, I feared I had fallen head over heels for this guy. Frankie was right. I was a serial monogamist, and Giles was evidently my next victim. I only hoped he was feeling the same way.

"We should probably get you to bed," he finally said. "It's been a long day."

I laughed. "Understatement of the year. Can I use your shower first? Now that I've been fed and I'm rested, I'm realizing how disgusting I feel."

His eyebrows shot up. "Shit, I should have asked you earlier."

"No, no. It's fine. Can you hand me my crutches?"

"I could just carry you," he offered.

"No way, I'm too heavy."

He side-eyed me. "Please, Mattie. I can carry you."

"I don't kno—" Before I could get the words out, Giles had stood from the couch and placed one arm underneath my legs and the other on my lower back.

"Grab on."

I shrieked with laughter and clutched the back of his neck as he lifted me off the couch with ease.

"Giles put me down."

He smirked. "We're already almost there," he said as he walked me past the entryway and up the first few stairs.

I was about to object again when I noticed pictures lining his staircase. Squinting, I took them all in. There were many of Giles at various ages in life. One was him as a preteen standing with a man and a woman.

"Are those your parents?"

He glanced at the photo I was looking at. "Yep. That was at one of my first competitions."

"Did you win?"

"I did. My dad was so excited he took the entire family out to dinner to celebrate." He smiled at the memory, and I squeezed his neck.

At the top of the stairs, he went straight to the vintage-tiled bathroom. He set me down on my good leg and continued to help support my weight by holding me around my waist. I limped gingerly forward and grabbed the shower wall. I lowered myself to a seated position on the bathtub ledge.

"Can you help me get my cast wrapped?"

"Right, yes." Giles raced downstairs to grab the cast cover the doctor gave me at the hospital. When he returned, he also had cling wrap and the black bag that Bev had packed for me.

"I've had a few breaks myself." He grabbed my leg and started to place the plastic wrap around the cast. "This will help keep the seal completely waterproof underneath the cover."

Thanks," I murmured, distracted by his hands brushing my calf as he delicately wrapped the cast.

When he was done, he stood up and took a step back. He crossed his arms and looked from the shower, to me, to back to the shower again.

"I can shower by myself," I said, horrified at the idea of him setting me in there naked.

He scratched his head. "Probably easier if you take a bath."

He pulled a lever by the spout and turned the handle.

Water spewed out of the faucet and started to collect in the basin.

"Sure, you don't need help?" he asked, his lips forming a playful smirk.

I groaned. Looking like a geriatric patient who needed rehab assistance was not going to up my sex appeal.

"What?" He looked confused by my displeasure.

"Nothing, just please leave me to wallow in my self-pity."

He laughed. "You're so dramatic, Florida."

I shooed him out of the room. Delicately, I peeled my sweatpants away from my cast and off my legs. When I finally lowered myself into the water, I exhaled deeply. It felt amazing, to say the least.

I inspected Giles's shampoo and soap collection. I took a sniff of one of them and smiled. Yep, that was him. I finished washing up as fast as I could from a seated position before opening the drain and grabbing a towel.

"Do you need help?" Muffled words from behind the closed door.

"Have you been standing there this whole time?"

"I just wanted to make sure you didn't slip and fall."

I rolled my eyes, but a smile formed on my lips. "I'm fine, and I do not need any help."

Unzipping the black bag, I found my comfiest flannel pajama pants and slid them on along with one of my over-sized T-shirts. I hopped slowly over to the door and unlocked it to find Giles leaning against the hallway wall. He sprung off it when he saw me.

"Feel better?" he asked.

"Much." Suddenly I felt shy again. "Um, so I'm pretty tired."

"Right. Right. Let's go to bed."

"Can you help me back down to the couch?"

He rolled his eyes. "You're obviously not sleeping on the couch. You can sleep in my bed."

"I couldn't put you out like that. Please, I'll take the couch."

He grinned and looked at me like I had amused him. "I wasn't really planning to sleep on the couch."

"Right, duh. I just didn't want to assume anything," I said hurriedly.

"Is that alright with you?" He took a step toward me and grabbed my waist.

"That's fine-totally fine."

He chuckled and helped me to the door to the left of the stairs. He supported most of my weight.

His bedroom had the same wood floor as the rest of the house but was covered in a plush gray rug. The bed was surrounded by a simple black iron headboard, and there were several photographs of snow-covered mountain peaks hanging around the room.

"I love your room," I said as he sat me down on the side of the bed closest to the wall.

"Thanks." He moved to the other side and hesitated for a moment before taking off his shirt. "I run hot," he explained needlessly.

We both got situated underneath the covers. I let out an audible moan as soon as my head hit the pillow. "I just realized how insanely exhausted I am."

I already felt myself drifting off as strong arms wrapped around me. My head found a spot in the curve of his neck as I floated off to sleep.

Chapter Twenty-Three

IT FELT LIKE I HAD ONLY BLINKED, BUT LIGHT WAS ALREADY seeping into the room the next time I partially opened my eyes. Squinting, I turned over to find that Giles had once again already vacated the bed.

"I must scare him off in my sleep," I muttered.

Then the smell hit me. Bacon. It was wafting up the stairs and through the open bedroom door.

I sat up and stretched my arms over my head before dropping them quickly and wincing. It felt like I had been in a car accident. My entire body was stiff, and when I lifted my shirt, I found dozens of bruises dotting my body.

My snowboarding career was definitely over.

I hobbled over to my crutches and awkwardly made my way to the stairs. Once there, I assessed my best course of action. Never having used crutches before, I did not feel confident in my ability to wield them properly on a staircase.

Thankfully, Giles popped his head around the banister

after just a few moments of my deliberation. "I thought I heard something. What do you think you're doing?"

"Trying to figure out how to get down these stairs without falling and winding up right back in the hospital."

Snickering, he climbed the stairs and placed one hand on my waist before taking my crutches and leaning them against the wall. "Ready?"

"You don't have to carry m—oof." Mid-protest, Giles lifted me into his arms and carried me down the stairs. He dropped me off at the bench by his front door and ran back up for my crutches.

"You know, I've got to wear this stupid thing for like six weeks. I need to learn how to fend for myself without you transferring me everywhere."

"I don't mind." He flashed me a grin, and my heart flipped.

Before I could shuffle over to the couch, there was a knock at the door.

"That's probably Erin and Johnny. They wanted to stop by yesterday, but I told them you needed to rest."

"You did?" My heart sputtered at his thoughtfulness.

He opened the door and immediately had to move out of the way as Erin burst through.

"Oh my god, Mattie. I'm so so so so sorry." She flung her arms around my neck, and I patted her back. "I should have never left you alone. I thought you were right behind me. And then when we couldn't find you and your phone was going straight to voicemail? It was so scary. Can you ever forgive me?"

I waved her off. "There's nothing to apologize for. It's not your fault."

"You could have kept a better eye on her," Giles's gruff voice chimed in.

"We know," Johnny said, also stepping over to give me a quick hug. "And we're sorry." Was it just me, or was he talking to mostly Giles?

"You know you could have always gone with us," I teased Giles. "Maybe *you* should have kept a better eye on me."

Instead of smiling, he looked at me grimly. "You're right. I should have."

I rolled my eyes. "Alright, everyone. Stop feeling guilty right now. It's no one's fault, and I'm fine. Are you both staying for breakfast?"

Erin nodded and thrust a plate she was holding underneath my nose. "And I brought cookies."

I glanced down at them. They had frosted frowny faces and "I'm Sorry" written on them.

I sighed. "Let's eat."

For saying he wasn't much of a cook, Giles's pancakes and bacon were delicious. We all scarfed down our plates in record time.

Johnny had brought me an old phone to use, which I thanked him profusely for.

"Oh, and we had an idea for the lounge," Erin said as she grabbed everyone's plates and started to rinse them in the sink. "Since Thanksgiving is next week, we were thinking we could do a local's night for anyone that can make it. Everyone from town can come and see the place. Of course, any guests we have staying can come too. But it should be a fun practice run."

"That sounds great," I said absentmindedly.

Time had completely started to slip away from me here.

I hadn't even realized it was already almost Thanksgiving. This would be my first ever holiday away from home. A pang of homesickness hit my heart.

Giles eyed me and cleared his throat. "Hey, thanks for coming over, but I think Mattie should probably rest."

"Of course, man." Johnny stood up. "We'll see you soon. And Mattie, I'm sorry again."

"Nothing to be sorry for." I smiled and gave them both a hug as they headed out of the kitchen. I breathed a sigh of relief when the door to the front of the house shut.

"Social battery a little lower than usual?" Giles asked.

"Definitely. Plus I…"

"What?" He encouraged me to continue when I trailed off.

"I forgot it was Thanksgiving next week." I shrugged. "Just feeling a little homesick, I guess."

He nodded. "Is this the longest you've ever gone without seeing your family?"

"My parents, yes. My sister lives in a different city, so we've gone months without seeing each other before. But we've always been together for every big holiday."

"Do you wish you were going back?"

I thought about this for a moment before shaking my head. "Not really. I'm pretty happy being here."

He walked over and kissed my forehead. "I'm pretty happy you're here too."

I could get used to this.

"When do you have to work today?" I asked him as he continued to clean up.

"I took the day off."

"Giles, you do not have to do that for me, okay? I'm fine."

"Maybe I just wanted an excuse to spend more time with you."

I bit my lip to hide the grin that was threatening to break out on my face. Had I ever felt this giddy with Garrett? It was hard to imagine.

We spent the rest of the day playing games, eating leftover takeout, and being completely housebound. Giles wasn't just good at snowboarding or darts. It seemed he had a knack for anything competitive since he completely smoked me in everything we played.

"This isn't even fun," I said after losing five games of rummy in a row. "You're merciless."

"What? Do you want me to just let you win?" he teased.

"Kind of, yeah."

"Don't be a sore loser." He laid down the remainder of his cards revealing that he had crushed me again. "Want to play something else?"

I refused to lose at another game, so I finally convinced him to watch a movie instead. We snuggled up on the couch. Sighing, I felt a wave of happiness settle over me. I was so comfortable in his arms that my eyes quickly drifted closed.

It felt right to be here with him. It didn't feel like we had just met. To think I thought I'd be planning my wedding to Garrett right now, but instead, I was wrapped up in someone else's arms. Someone completely *better* in every way imaginable.

Maybe I shouldn't be falling this fast, but he was making it impossible to catch myself.

Chapter Twenty-Four

"THIS LOOKS AMAZING!" I EXCLAIMED IN AWE, TAKING IN
the new lounge.

After two nights at Giles's house, I decided it was finally
time to get back to the lodge and back to work. He had
tried to protest, but when I called Bev behind his back and
begged her to pick me up, he finally relented and drove me
here himself. I was still hobbling around and getting used to
the uncomfortable crutches, but at least there was a seat
behind the front desk I could use.

When Bev saw the two of us walking in together, Giles
hovering next to me to ensure I didn't slip, she immediately
greeted us with an "I knew it."

"You did not," Giles insisted.

"I did too."

"I didn't even know."

Bev howled with laughter at that. "Yeah, right."

He ducked his head before changing the subject. "So,
this lounge, huh? It looks pretty good."

"And Erin came by yesterday to do some work in the

kitchen. She's got a great, easy menu we'll be able to pull off. Tasty but nothing fancy." Bev surveyed the lounge with pride. "Also, what name are we going with? I was thinking about having Johnny make a sign for over the door."

"The Lounge?" Giles suggested.

"What about Marie's?" I nervously snuck a glance at Giles's face after suggesting we name the restaurant after his late mother.

Instead of tensing next to me, he threw his arm over my shoulders and pulled me into him, kissing me lightly on the side of my head. "That's perfect."

"It is perfect. Good idea, Mattie. Your mom would have loved this place." Bev patted Giles on the back.

"Thanksgiving is only two days away. Are we ready to host all of those people?" I asked.

"I think we'll be able to manage. We got a few local kids that agreed to work here on the weekends when we open for real."

We continued to discuss the details. I tried my best to remain on task and not distracted, but it was tough when Giles was rubbing my shoulders and forcing me to lean into him. When we were in the bubble of his house, he had been very affectionate with me, but I wasn't sure how it would translate out here. In his family's lodge—the whole reason he said starting something between the two of us wasn't a good idea. Apparently, he had changed his tune because here he was clearly showing anyone that took the time to look that there was something here.

And I couldn't have been happier about it.

Hours later, nighttime had descended on the lodge. I was seated on one of the armchairs by the roaring fire. Erin, Johnny, and Giles were surrounding the small table, and we were laughing hysterically over a game of Pictionary that had taken a turn.

"That in no way resembles 'taking a dog for a walk,'" said Erin through tears.

"What are you talking about?" I insisted. "There's the leash, and there's the dog." I pointed at each with my marker.

"*That's* supposed to be a dog?" Johnny held up the picture and turned it sideways.

"Leave her alone." Giles smirked. "Games are not Mattie's strong suit."

I threw the marker at his head and laughed when it made contact. "Hey, I resent that. Just because you're perfect at everything doesn't mean I'm bad."

"We should probably call it a night," Johnny said, stretching his arms over his head and yawning.

Involuntarily, I found myself yawning as well. "Agreed. This is the most activity I've had since the accident."

We cleaned up the area we were seated at and said goodnight to Johnny and Erin.

After they had walked out the front door, Giles scratched the back of his neck. His eyes darted around nervously.

"So, did you want to go back to your place or?"

My cheeks flushed, I hadn't really wanted to leave him, but I knew that I should after spending two nights at his place already.

"Oh yeah, that's fine," I said at the same time Giles said, "Or you could just stay with me."

I giggled nervously. "That's okay. It'll be good to get some fresh clothes."

"Yeah, there's some stuff I should probably get done tonight." He scratched his stubble. "Let me walk you back."

I carefully maneuvered my crutches over the icy walkway to Bev's and successfully made it up my stairs with minimal assistance from Giles.

"I'm getting pretty good with these." I smiled up at him.

"Goodnight, Mattie." He dipped his head so that it was level with mine and gave me a sweet, lingering, kiss. "I'll see you tomorrow, okay?"

"See you tomorrow." I waved at him and closed the door.

My apartment didn't feel quite as homey now that I knew what staying with Giles felt like. I changed into a pair of black sweatpants and collapsed on the couch. Flipping channels, I wound up finding the same rom-com we had watched the other night.

Smiling, I took a picture and sent it to Giles.

How was it possible that I was already waiting for the next time I'd get to see him? Is this what falling in love again felt like? Not being able to get enough of him? Saying goodbye and just impatiently waiting for the next hello?

I groaned. I had it so bad.

A knock sounded at the door causing me to jump. Could it be Bev this late?

Not bothering with my crutches, I hopped over and cracked open the door to peek out.

Giles was standing there.

Grinning, I opened the door wider. "What are you doing here?"

He held his phone up. "I saw you were watching my favorite movie."

"Do you want to come in?"

He nodded, and I laughed. He grabbed me around my waist and pulled me back on to the couch. I settled in to his chest and bit back my smile.

With that lame excuse to come over, maybe he had it just as bad as I did.

Chapter Twenty-Five

Mattie,
You never got back to me on those resumes I sent
over for your replacement in Colorado. I took the
liberty of moving the most qualified candidate
through. I had a few other people from the firm
meet with him, and he's perfect for the job. The trial
run is up the Monday after Thanksgiving, so we'll
want to meet with Bev as soon as possible to get her
acquainted with your replacement. He's already
local to the area and can start immediately. Please
get back to me ASAP.
Mike

Gnawing at my lip, I reread Mike's e-mail. It was
unlike me to blow off job duties like reviewing resumes, but
it was easier for me to pretend like that wasn't real. Like I
didn't have a replacement coming to take over for me. Like
I wasn't going back to Florida.

My heart physically ached at the thought. What was

waiting for me back there? I had no apartment. No boyfriend. No friends. No life, really.

Key Ridge felt like home right now. It felt like where I belonged. And Giles….Giles was someone I did not want to leave behind. But what if he thought it was way too early to be having these thoughts? Yes, I loved this town, but I would be lying if I said that staying here wasn't primarily motivated by our budding relationship.

I had spent the past week avoiding this dilemma by pretending it didn't exist. I didn't want to leave and never get the chance to know what Giles and I could become. I probably should have talked to him about this, but I was too afraid of what he might say. What if he told me to go back?

"What's that?" Bev asked, hovering behind me.

"Nothing." I closed out of the email, but I feared she might have already read the highlights. "Um, my boss hired a replacement for me and wanted me to let you know." Despite my desire to keep this quiet until I could figure out a way to talk about it with Giles, my duty to do my job was still too strong. I had to tell Bev.

She gave me a disapproving look. I gazed down at my cast, not wanting to meet her eyes.

"You sure you want to get out of here so soon?"

"Not really," I whispered.

"Then you should probably figure something out."

"But…" I hesitated. Bev raised her eyebrows and leaned against the desk, waiting for me to go on. "Giles and I…we aren't anything. Not really. This whole thing between us just started." I cringed at how unprofessional I sounded, but right now, I just needed advice from the aunt of the guy I really, really liked. "How can I stay just for him? Wouldn't that come across as desperate?"

She sighed. "It's not my place to tell you what to do. But what I can tell you is that the spark in Giles's eyes was completely dead up until you came into this town. Maybe you two did just start dating, or whatever it is you kids call it these days. But you'll never know what it could become if you don't stick around and find out. Every forever has a beginning. What if this is yours?"

My heart swelled at the thought.

I thanked her for the advice, and she patted me on the shoulder before leaving me alone at the front desk. Pondering her words, I thought about the best way to handle the situation. One thing was for sure, leaving did not feel like a viable option.

<hr>

"Alright, just a little bit further." Giles's arms were around my waist as I took another careful step forward.

He had insisted on blindfolding me as we exited his house. Apparently, there was some big surprise he wanted to show me.

"Giles, this is silly. I'm going to fall and break my neck."

"I've got you," he insisted, squeezing my waist. "Okay, you can take it off."

I kept one hand on my crutches and used the other to remove the makeshift blindfold he had fashioned out of a shirt.

"Oh my god!" I squealed with delight. In front of the house was a small ornate carriage being pulled by two white horses. "This is *just* like the movies."

"I figured you would say that." He was grinning from ear to ear at my delight.

He grabbed the crutches from me and put them into the carriage before helping me into the seat. There was already a fleece blanket awaiting us. He tucked me in carefully before cozying up next to me and slinging his arm around my shoulders.

"Okay, Dave," he said to the older man sitting in the driver's seat of the carriage. "Can you take the scenic route?"

"You got it, Giles."

"Is that the bartender from the Ridge?" I whispered.

"It's his side hustle in the winter." Giles winked at me.

Snow was falling softly onto the ground, and the night was lit brightly by the moon.

"This is beautiful. Thank you so much." I kissed Giles's cheek before he turned his face and kissed me back squarely on the mouth.

"I wanted to make sure you weren't too homesick for Thanksgiving. Plus, you should have at least a few fond memories of snow," he teased.

"I like snow."

He raised his eyebrows. "Because it's treated you so well since you've been here?"

"It hasn't been so bad. The storm causing the power outage worked out in my favor."

"Mine too." He smiled.

"I'm so excited to see Marie's open tonight. It's going to be packed."

He nodded. "I wish my parents could see it."

I snaked one arm behind him and the other arm across his stomach before giving him a big hug. "Me too," I murmured. "I hope they would have liked it."

"They would have loved it."

The past couple of days had been perfect. There was nothing better than that magical feeling at the beginning of a relationship when you couldn't get enough of each other.

I had already decided there was no way I could leave this. Leave him. But I didn't want to tell him that. I was still nervous about scaring him off. It seemed like it was going amazing right now, but what if he was fully planning on just saying our goodbyes whenever I left for Florida? He hadn't so much as mentioned the topic of my imminent departure. I tried not to overthink it, but if he cared, shouldn't he be more concerned that I was supposed to be leaving?

I shook the intrusive thoughts from my mind. I wasn't giving him the option to get rid of me. Once I told Mike about Marie's opening and the lodge being sold out for December, he agreed it made sense to keep me on for now. When he asked when I'd be ready to come back to Florida, I told him I wasn't sure I wanted to. He wasn't pleased to hear that, but I guess the PM department had been running relatively smoothly in my absence, so he didn't have too much to fight me on.

Giles rested his chin on the top of my head. Guilt washed over me again. I should have mentioned all this to him, but I was too worried that he would talk me out of it. To me, this felt like an epic love story. What if, to him, this was just some seasonal romance?

"We're here." He squeezed my shoulders as we arrived at the lodge. Giles jumped out of the carriage and came around to my side to help me out. I was less than graceful with my crutches, but he managed to make helping me look effortless.

Instead of coming through the main entrance to the lodge, we arrived through the back parking lot that was adjoined to the street that led to the ski hill. This would be the main entrance to Marie's. A sign now hung above the doors.

"It looks great." Giles ruffled my hair, and my chest swelled with pride at his approval.

As soon as we opened the door, we were met with warmth, loud conversation, and delicious smells. The place was already packed with a boisterous crowd.

"Giles. Mattie. Over here!" Johnny shouted from across the room. He was supposed to be the informal host for the evening, and it appeared he was taking the informal aspect of his job extra seriously.

Bev was already seated at our table. Erin was standing next to her in an apron.

"Mattie." She greeted me with a hug that I tried my best to return around my crutches.

"Hey, how's everything going?"

"So far, so good. I've got everything prepped and ready to go."

"Do you need help with any—"

"Shhh," Erin cooed. "You just sit and relax. You've done enough."

Giles pulled out a chair for me and helped me sit down before taking my crutches. Beaming, I looked around at the finished lounge. The artwork popped against the dark walls, and the chairs and tables looked great, especially the long one we had thrifted that took center stage. Even the neon sign behind the bar was the perfect touch. There was a small crowd of twenty-something girls taking turns posing for a picture underneath it.

"It looks perfect in here," I gushed.

"Doesn't it?" Erin said. "The whole town is buzzing

about it."

Bev nodded. "It's great to see this place alive again." Then she turned her attention to Giles and me. "So, did you two come together?"

I blushed at her forwardness, but Giles waved her off. "Don't give Mattie a hard time."

"Come on, spill," Erin said.

I smirked and looked to Giles, who was now shifting in his seat. "It's none of your business, but yes, we did come together. And you all know that, so I don't know why you're insisting on making a spectacle of it."

He placed an arm around my chair as if claiming me, and I smiled at the whole group. "Did he tell you about the surprise he planned for me today? It was so cute." I told them about the horse-drawn carriage as Giles continued to look uncomfortable. I could tell he was pleased with the praise, though. The corner of his mouth tugged up, and he kept squeezing my shoulder.

"Alright, it's almost time for food. Johnny, let's help with the plates." They both shuffled off to the kitchen, and just minutes later, plates of delicious appetizers were set on the tables. I dug in without apprehension. Looking around, I realized how at home I felt at this moment.

HOURS LATER, MARIE'S STARTED TO EMPTY OUT AFTER everyone was completely satiated and content. I gave Johnny and Erin a hug as they headed home for the evening. Giles and I were some of the only people left, aside from a few stray guests lingering at their tables.

"Tonight was perfect." I squeezed his hand, and he

returned the gesture.

"It wouldn't have happened without you."

A large yawn escaped me, and Giles looked at me with concern. "It's getting late. We should probably get you back."

I nodded my agreement.

"Let me go say goodnight to Bev. I think she went to the lobby a while back to talk to some people."

"I'll be here." I gestured toward my immobile ankle.

I pulled out my phone while I waited for him and saw texts from my family. I responded to their "Happy Thanksgivings," surprised to find that I wasn't feeling a nagging pull of homesickness. Instead, I felt grateful. Grateful to be here. Grateful to have moved on. Grateful to be sitting next to a guy that I couldn't stop thinking about. Everything felt perfect.

Staying was the right decision.

Setting my phone down, I glanced around for Giles. He had been gone for almost ten minutes at this point. I spotted him near the front desk talking to Bev.

His body language seemed off. His arms were crossed, and his brow was pinched. I wondered what they could possibly be talking about that could sour his mood that much. I continued to stare until he finally met my eyes. Smiling, I tried to wave him over, but he just frowned at me.

Weird.

Giles stalked over to me, now seemingly in a hurry. When he got to the table, he grabbed my elbow and helped me stand up without warning.

"Whoa." I tottered a little before catching my balance.

"Sorry," he muttered, handing me my crutches.

I raised my eyebrows at his strange attitude but said

nothing as we made our way outside.

"Did you want to stay at my place since we don't have your car here?" I asked once we were outside.

He didn't say anything but continued next to me for the short walk to my apartment.

Internally I debated what to say next, desperate to lift this bizarre mood he was in. I wondered what Bev had said to him.

When we got to the bottom of the stairs, I limped up first with him directly behind me to ensure I didn't fall. At the top of the stairs, I unlocked the door. Before I could go inside, Giles gently grabbed my arm and turned me so that I faced him.

"I think I'm going to walk back to my place."

"Oh, really? It might be kind of hard for me to get there on my crutches."

He paused, not meeting my eyes. "I'm just going to go by myself."

I bit my lip, not liking this turn of events. "Is everything okay?"

"Everything is fine. I-I'm just feeling a little sick. I probably ate too much."

"Oh," I said. I wasn't sure if I should call him out on his weak excuse or not.

He finally glanced up at me. I couldn't tell if he looked upset or angry. Maybe it was both. Maybe he and Bev had a disagreement, and he wasn't ready to share the details with me yet. I let out a sigh and decided to just let it go.

I faked a smile. "I'll see you tomorrow."

He nodded curtly and turned to leave. At the last moment, he spun around and brushed a quick kiss to my cheek before retreating down the steps.

Chapter Twenty-Six

MY LONG HAIR FELL OVER THE THICK GRAY SWEATER I HAD just pulled on. All I wanted to feel today was comfort, and that included my outfit. After such a magical night, I woke up this morning feeling sad. It probably had something to do with the absence of a certain someone in my bed. After days of being inseparable, I wasn't sure what had spooked him last night. I was determined to get to the bottom of it. I half expected him to already be here when I woke up. Ready to help me down the stairs with coffee and an explanation.

I guess it was good to experience first hand how Giles handled conflict. This was the first rough patch of our very short relationship. We would have to have a talk about this. I didn't like that he just left without cluing me in to his feelings at all. It made me feel like I didn't matter nearly as much to him as I thought I did.

That thought caused a small pang in my heart. I tried to brush it off. He did care. Staying was the right decision.

"Whatever," I muttered under my breath and put on my parka.

Before I could head down the stairs, my phone rang. I was surprised to see Mike's name on the screen since we usually just corresponded through e-mail.

"What's up?" I asked, picking it up.

"Hey, Mattie. Happy holidays."

The tone of his voice immediately had me on high alert. He sounded disappointed. Like he was ready to deliver bad news.

"What is it?" I cut right to the chase.

"A bit of bad news…"

I held my breath.

"You won't be able to stay in Key Ridge after all."

"What are you talking about? We worked it all out. I told you not to hire the replacement."

"It isn't that. I totally support your decision."

"Then what?"

"This feels unfair since I know what a killer job you've done out there, but I have to tell you I just got a call this morning letting me know that they will not be moving forward with us."

My mouth hung open in shock.

"Wha-what are you talking about?"

"I'm so sorry, Mattie. I know how disappointed you must be. And I know there's still a few days left in the trial, but since we aren't contracted with them, you're free to head back to Florida whenever it's convenient for you."

My mouth felt dry, and my throat started to constrict as I processed what he was saying. Then it clicked. Bev. This must be what she was discussing with Giles last night. This was why he was so upset.

"This doesn't make any sense, Mike. Let me just talk to Bev. I'm sure I can sort this out."

"The call didn't come from Bev."

"Then who?" My stomach dropped.

"It was her nephew, Giles. He called this morning. Bit of an ass that one. Not sure how you've managed to work out there with him these past few weeks."

I slumped against the wall in shock. How could this be happening? Why would he do this? He must have known he was doing this last night if he had called Mike first thing in the morning. My shock turned into sadness.

That sadness was quickly replaced by anger.

I needed to speak with Giles.

Now.

"I've got to go, Mike." I hung up before waiting to hear what else he had to say.

I made it down the stairs as fast as my bad ankle would allow me and turned toward the lodge, hoping to find him there.

Tears pricked at my eyes, and I sniffed aggressively to try to hold them back. I could not break down before I confronted him. He had to have some sort of explanation for this abrupt turn of events.

Ambling as quickly as I could on my crutches, I was almost to the back door when I hit an icy patch. I let out a squeal as my good foot slipped out from underneath me, and I fell directly on my ass.

Groaning, I didn't move for a moment.

"Mattie? What the hell?"

I sat up to see Giles pushing through the back door and racing to me. Before he could get to me, I scrambled to my feet and got my crutches back in place. I did not want him to have the upper hand by helping me up right now.

As soon as I met his eyes, tears started to spill out of mine.

"You really need to be more careful," he barked, reaching for my elbow.

I yanked it back, out of his reach, and glared at him.

"Don't act like you care about me right now."

His eyes hardened. "Mattie, don't be like this."

"You canceled the contract. How could you do this?" I shouted.

"I don't want to talk about the fucking contract right now." He looked frustrated, running his hands through his hair. "I want to talk about *us*."

"*Us*? Are you serious? Last night you were acting super weird. Then this morning, I got a call that your family—specifically you—decided not to sign the contract to hire my company. There can't be an *us* since you're obviously trying to get rid of me." I was full-on crying now.

His eyes darkened. "Jesus, *I'm* trying to get rid of *you*? That's a convenient narrative. When were you going to tell me that you hired your replacement?"

I froze. "I wasn't going to becau—"

"Because you hate conflict? Because you just thought you'd slip away without even telling me? Without giving me the decency of a conversation or a goodbye? Fuck that, Mattie."

He wasn't even giving me a chance to explain.

"I get it. This isn't your home. It'll never be your home."

I choked, trying to gulp down my sob. "You don't understand!" I yelled. "I wasn't going to leave."

"You weren't? Then how come last night Bev told me your replacement was coming on Monday?"

"I told her that he was hired, but—"

"Save it, Mattie."

"I wasn't going to go!"

"Whatever." His face was cold and reminded me of when we first met. "We just started dating. You don't owe me anything."

"You don't mean that."

"I was right about us. We should have never started anything. Life would be a whole hell of a lot less complicated than whatever this is."

He was just trying to hurt me now, and it was working.

"Screw you, Giles."

"Have a nice life." He crossed his arms and turned back toward the lodge.

"I wasn't going to leave, you idiot!" I yelled at his back before he disappeared through the door.

I choked on my sobs as I went back to the apartment, half expecting him to rush after me. To my dismay, when I got to the stairs and turned around one last time, there was no sign of him. Pulling myself together, I hurried up the steps and inside.

The hysterics had passed, and now I was focused on one thing only. Getting the hell out of this town as quickly as possible.

I grabbed my suitcase out of the closet and tore through the small apartment, collecting all my clothes and stuffing them into the bag.

I hated how stupid I felt at this moment. I had convinced myself Giles and I were at the start of something great. Something better than I had ever had before. I was going to move to this small town and play house with him and work at the lodge. Meanwhile, he was ready to drop me at the first sign of a misunderstanding.

You should have told him sooner, came the nagging voice in the back of my head.

If I was being honest with myself, I hadn't made the decision to stay until a few days ago. It was a scary thought, not coming home and starting a new life here. I should have talked with Giles about it earlier. I should have been honest with him.

Shaking my head, I continued to pack. It didn't matter now. Whosever fault this was, the damage was done. Clearly, we didn't matter to each other enough to try to talk it out. And if he was the kind of person to just send me on my way without a second thought, then who needed him?

You do, came the same small voice.

"No, I don't," I said aloud.

IN RECORD TIME, I HAD MANAGED TO PACK ALL MY THINGS. I found the next flight to Florida and drove myself to the airport. I had a while to kill before my plane left, but I couldn't sit in that apartment anymore. It felt too sad to wait there. I felt a little guilty for not saying goodbye to Bev, Erin, or Johnny. But I was too hurt and too embarrassed to track them down. I'm sure by now the screaming fight Giles and I had in the middle of the street had made the rounds. In a small town, people talked.

I couldn't face anyone now. It was better to just leave with my head hung low and my figurative tail between my legs.

Just the other day, I thought I'd be calling this place my new home. Now I'd likely never come here again.

I stood and stared out at the tarmac before leaning my head against the window. The cool glass instantly soothed the headache that pulsed between my eyes.

I took out my phone and typed out a short message.

Mattie: I'm coming home.

Mom: Oh dear.

Chapter Twenty-Seven

"Are you sure you don't want to go with us to the card party tonight?"

I looked up from my book to see my mom standing at the door to the patio that I had left open.

"I'm good."

"Mattie, sweetie. You've been home for a week already, and you've hardly left the house except to go to work. And you don't even go to that every day."

"I told you. Mike has been letting me work from home."

"Is that wise? Surely, you'd rather go into the office than lie around here in your pajamas all day."

"Just because I'm wearing a sweatshirt doesn't mean I'm in pajamas."

She chewed her lip, not wanting to push me too far as I'd already snapped at her the day before during a similar conversation.

"Alright, have a good night, then."

I nodded at her and returned to my book.

I felt bad for being such a dismissive jerk since arriving home, but I just wasn't in the mood to put on an act. If I felt miserable, why did I have to act any differently?

Work was even more challenging. I tried to put my best foot forward and make sure my mood didn't affect my performance, but everything felt different now.

Before Key Ridge, I loved my job and looked forward to solving problems and preparing presentations. Now, it just didn't hold the same appeal. I hated sitting through meetings, and I hated making pointless slide decks. It all felt so show-boaty after working on the floor of the lodge for a month.

It didn't help that I could sense that Mike wasn't as thrilled with my return as I expected him to be. My department appeared to have gotten along swimmingly while I was away. They were acting as if I had crashed their party by simply returning to my job.

My phone rang. I rolled my eyes when I saw the name that appeared on the screen.

"Did Mom tell you to call?" I asked without bothering with the formality of a 'Hello.'

"She said she's worried about you," replied Frankie.

"I promise I'm fine." The word 'fine' had started to sound strange to my ears after saying it so many times.

"Fine isn't thriving."

"Why do I have to thrive?"

"Um, because you deserve to."

I sighed deeply and shrugged my shoulder up to the phone, keeping it in place against my cheek while I removed my hand.

"What do you want from me?"

"I want you to tell me what's wrong."

"Nothing is wrong."

"Bullshit. You can't always do this when you're upset. You try to brush it under the rug to avoid talking about it, but it's written all over your actions. I know this is about Giles."

I opened my mouth to deny it, but nothing came out. Instead, tears pricked my eyes.

"I really liked him."

"I know," Frankie said. "And it's okay to feel sad about it."

I hesitated before dropping my bombshell on her. "I-I was planning to stay there."

"Like *stay there*, stay there?"

"Uh-huh."

"I called it."

"I know. My serial monogamy tried to strike again."

"I'm sorry, Mattie. I know how much you liked him."

"I miss him," I whispered.

"Maybe there's still hope for you two."

"I don't see how."

Chapter Twenty-Eight

"One medium latte with almond milk for Mattie."

I looked up from my phone and smiled my thanks at the barista who handed me my drink. Caffeine was a crutch I had been leaning on a lot since I returned. All of my natural perkiness had dissipated, and I was forced to drink copious amounts of coffee to try to mimic being positive at work.

I limped toward the exit. I had graduated from my cast to a walking boot and one crutch. I still wasn't the most mobile, but it was a lot easier to get around on my own.

I didn't even take notice when a tall figure stopped directly in front of me.

"Excuse me," I muttered as I tried to shove past the man.

"Mattie?" The voice came out nervous and cracked, but I still recognized it.

Garrett stood in front of me. His eyes were searching my face anxiously. It pained me to admit that he looked good. Clean cut in his favorite navy-blue suit that I had picked up at the dry cleaners countless times. He flashed me a sheepish smile that I didn't bother to return.

"Hi, Garrett." A month ago, running into him like this would have been a punch to the gut. Now all I felt was inconvenience and irritation that he was in my way.

"What happened to your foot?" He gestured to my boot.

"Snowboarding accident," I replied flatly.

"Snowboarding? Seriously? I cannot picture you snowboarding."

"Cleary, it didn't go well," I deadpanned.

He chuckled nervously. I blinked back at him in return, ready for this to be over. At least his bride-to-be wasn't with him.

As if she could read my thoughts, Nadine opened the door and came to a shocked halt when she spotted me standing in front of Garrett. She was dressed in a tight dress that came down to her ankles. A small bump was barely visible underneath the black fabric.

"Oh, Mattie. What a surprise. How are you?"

I wanted to roll my eyes at their horrified expressions and attempt at tact. As if there was any decorum that could be salvaged from this interaction.

"I'm fantastic." I gave her a sickeningly sweet smile that I hoped dripped sarcasm.

"Great. Great." Nadine's eyes darted around the coffee shop, desperate to rid herself of the reminder that her happy ending didn't have a fairy tale beginning. "I'm going to put our orders in. It was so good to see you." She didn't even glance back at me as she sauntered to the counter.

Garrett was still immobile.

"Mattie…I-I just want to say—"

"Save it." I held up my hand.

"But I just wanted to apologize—"

"What's done is done. I don't need your half-assed apologies. Nothing you could say now can absolve you for lying to me and wasting my time. You're a coward for not telling me sooner."

He looked down at his dress shoes. "I did love you."

I scoffed, in disbelief he could stand there and say that to my face. "What you felt toward me couldn't have been love, or you would never have treated me like that."

"I'm so sorr—"

"I said save it. Our lives are no longer intertwined. Hopefully, after this, we will never see each other again." I started to brush past him, but the dull rage inside me over his deceit compelled me to say one last thing. "Just so you know, I was happier these last two months without you than I ever was during our relationship."

It felt good to close the door on Garrett. Both literally and figuratively. Unfortunately, the joy I felt was short-lived as the hollow emptiness returned to my chest.

Chapter Twenty-Nine

"Mattie, I'm so sorry to have to be a little tough with you, but your performance has been slipping ever since you got back." Mike looked apologetic as he relayed my poor performance review to me. "Look, I don't need to know the details, but I can tell you're working through things in your personal life."

I just stared at my folded hands, willing myself not to cry in his office right now. Being the shining star at work had always been my pride and joy. This was not a conversation I thought I would ever be at the receiving end of.

"I know, Mike. I've been a little scatterbrained. I promise I'll do better."

He nodded. "Look, I know you. I know you're a good worker. I'm not trying to be harsh. I just want to say something before it becomes a problem."

"I completely understand."

His eyes softened. "The office will be closed for the holidays next week. Take that time to be with your family.

Don't even think about work. Hopefully, you're able to relax and come back as your normal self."

"Definitely." I nodded.

I wasn't sure that was possible. Ever since leaving Key Ridge, I had no idea who my normal self was anymore.

"Can I sit?" My mom approached the couch carefully.

I glanced at the clock. It was two in the morning.

"I guess." I shrugged as she joined me. "What are you doing up so late?"

"I could ask you the same thing," she said, nudging my shoulder.

"Couldn't sleep."

"I'm sure that would have nothing to do with all the coffee you've been downing."

"I've just been so tired lately."

"Are you sure you don't mean sad?"

I sighed. "Maybe I'm a little sad," I admitted.

"Frankie told me that you were going to stay in Colorado."

I looked at her and frowned. "It was a dumb idea."

"Doesn't sound dumb to me. You seemed happy there. You know how I know? Because you texted me maybe ten times while you were gone. Your dad and I were so worried you'd be homesick, but it seemed like you fit right in there."

"I don't know about that."

"And it seems there might be a certain guy there that was worth sticking around for."

I hesitated and hugged my knees to my chest. "I thought there was," I muttered.

She waited for me to say more but didn't press.

"You know," she finally continued when I stayed silent. "You went out there to heal a heartbreak, but I think you came back more heartbroken than when you left."

With that comment, my vision became blurry, and tears started to spill out of my eyes. I leaned my head against my mom's shoulder.

"I thought we had something," I murmured.

"Maybe you still do."

I shook my head. "He practically asked me to leave."

I recounted to her the whole tale of him hating me at first. To us slowly becoming friends. To him taking care of me. All the way to our downfall, which involved me almost hiring a replacement and not telling him and us screaming at each other in the street.

"Oh honey, that sounds like a bad case of miscommunication."

"It was horrible."

She squeezed my shoulders. "You two are still getting to know each other. Sometimes we don't handle confrontation with grace, but that doesn't mean you can't try to talk and work things out."

"He hasn't even tried to call me since I left."

"Have you tried to call him?"

"No." I bit my lip.

"Maybe you should start there."

THE NEXT MORNING, I STARED AT MY PHONE FOR HOURS. IT was impossible to find the words to say to him after these few weeks apart.

What if he had completely written me off already?

What if I was the only one suffering?

My thumb hovered over his name in my contact list, but I couldn't bring myself to press the dial button.

Get it together, Mattie. You can do this.

I stood up and started pacing the living room with my phone. Taking a deep, determined breath, I braced myself to call him.

The instant before my thumb brushed my phone, I jerked it back.

I had a better idea.

Swiping away my contacts, I pulled up an internet browser and searched for the next flight to Colorado.

Chapter Thirty

My hands shook as I stood outside. For the past forty-eight hours, I had been running on nonstop adrenaline. Now that I was here, in front of the lodge, I couldn't bring myself to approach the door. I wasn't even sure he'd be here, but it was my best first bet to finding him.

I sucked in a breath and limped forward before pausing again. My ankle was starting to hurt a little from so much standing.

"Okay, you can do this." I took rapid breaths in and out through my nose, trying to pump myself up. "Don't be a coward, Mattie."

"Mattie? What are you doing here?" My heart thumped out of my chest as I heard the voice that had been flooding my dreams since I left this place.

I turned around to face him.

Giles stood before me wearing his ski resort jacket that was dusted with a fresh layer of snow. His eyes were wide with surprise. Gently, he lowered the snowboard he was holding to the ground. Slowly and deliberately, he unclipped his helmet, keeping his gaze fixed on me the whole time.

My mouth hung open for a moment before I slowly closed it. All the meaningful words I spent hours going over in my head instantly drifted from my mind the moment I saw him.

"Hi," was all I managed to get out.

"Hi." He took a step toward me.

"I just…" I trailed off, rendered speechless by his eyes. "Wanted to see how the lodge was doing."

The corner of his lip twitched, and the skin by his eyes crinkled. "Really?"

I let out a breathless laugh. "Okay, you caught me. I wanted to see how you were doing."

He tilted his head. "I've been better."

"Yeah?"

He nodded. "I was a lot better a few weeks ago."

Relief flooded through my veins. "You were?"

He smiled and nodded his head. "What are you doing here, Mattie?"

"I told you."

He shook his head, his eyes asking for more.

"I-I missed you," I choked out. "I'm sorry about our fight—"

He closed the small gap between us and crushed me to his chest, lifting my feet slightly off the ground.

"I'm so sorry," he whispered into my hair.

"*I'm* so sorry. I should have talked to you sooner."

"I should have given you a chance to explain. The last thing I wanted was for you to leave, and I thought maybe— it felt like I was changing your mind or something. When Bev told me about your replacement, I just saw red and acted like an idiot."

"I wasn't going to leave," I said.

He grimaced. "I fucked this all up."

"I should have been honest with you."

He leaned down, and his lips brushed mine softly, his fingers tangled in my hair. After a minute, he released my mouth and kissed my forehead.

"The night after our fight, I realized how stupid I was being. I went to your apartment, but you were already gone." He looked pained at the memory.

"I didn't exactly want to stick around after that," I admitted.

"I figured as much."

I tightened my arms around his torso and inhaled his scent that I missed so much.

"Why didn't you call me?" I whispered.

"I thought you were done with me."

"I thought *you* were done with *me*."

He laughed. "Not even close."

Releasing me, he took one hand and pulled his phone out of his pocket. My brow knit in confusion as he scrolled for a moment before turning the screen to me.

I leaned in closer to see what he was showing me. It was a confirmation for a flight to Orlando arriving on Christmas Eve.

Tears welled up in my eyes. "You were going to come see me?"

He chuckled. "I thought maybe if I made a grand gesture at Christmas, you might be more willing to give me a second chance. You love your movies, after all."

My cheeks hurt from grinning so hard. "So, you're not done with me then?" I asked, pinching his side.

"Definitely not." He kissed my forehead again. "But we should probably work on our communication skills if this relationship is going to go anywhere. Can't have you catching a flight every time I mess up because, let's be honest, it's going to happen again."

"I think that can be arranged."

He glanced down at the carry-on suitcase that sat forgotten next to me.

"That all you brought?" he asked.

I nodded. "I wasn't exactly sure how this was going to go."

He grabbed my suitcase and slid his other arm around my waist, leading me toward the entrance of the lodge.

"That's alright. We can just get the rest of your stuff in a few days when I come home with you to meet your parents for Christmas."

My eyebrows shot up. "The rest of my stuff?"

"You are staying here, aren't you?"

"You-you definitely want that?"

He shrugged. "The lodge has been kind of a mess without you."

I shoved him in the side, causing him to laugh. "Yes, Florida. I want you to stay here. I'm kind of a grumpy asshole when you're not around."

I beamed up at him before pausing in our tracks.

"Wait, you want to meet my parents?"

He smirked. "Well, I do already have a ticket."

Epilogue

The sound of a car horn blared outside.

"Geez, I'm coming, I'm coming!" I yelled as I exited the front door of Giles's blue bungalow.

Technically I still lived in the apartment above Bev's garage, but I spent ninety percent of my time here. Eventually, I'd officially move in, but it had only been seven months since I'd relocated to Key Ridge permanently.

I skipped down the driveway, grateful my ankle injury had left no permanent damage. Giles was even trying to convince me to get back on the ski hill next season.

"I will not take my eyes off you this time," he had promised.

I raced the rest of the distance to the passenger side door of Erin's blue jeep and climbed inside.

"Took you long enough," she said before throwing it into drive and taking off down the street.

"What's the hurry? It's not like the hike is going to go anywhere," I teased.

She glanced at me and back to the road before letting

out a fake laugh. "Totally, I know. I just..I just don't want the parking lot to fill up."

I raised my eyebrows. We always went hiking together on Sunday mornings, but she was being a little jumpy today for some reason.

"Coffee?" I offered her my travel mug.

She shook her head. "I'm good. I'm already feeling jittery."

"I can see that, weirdo."

She ignored me and turned up the radio. The throwback Taylor song distracted me and had us both belting out the lyrics at the top of our lungs out the open windows.

Gravel crunched underneath the wheels as Erin pulled into an almost empty parking lot.

"Good thing you rushed us. It's packed."

Erin laughed awkwardly before jumping out of the car and walking straight to the trailhead. "Come on, let's get moving."

My forehead crinkled in confusion as I raced to catch up to her.

The hike she had picked this week was a short one. Just one mile uphill with an amazing view at the end. You could see the ski hill and the entire town.

Normally we chatted while we hiked, but today Erin was walking so fast that I was out of breath trying to keep up with her.

"You're really on something today," I huffed as we neared the top.

Taking a few more steps, we reached the short summit. I put my hands over my head to catch my breath and take in the views.

"Shit, Mattie. I dropped my water bottle a little ways down the hill. I'm just going to grab it and be right back."

"Wait, you can have some of mine," I called after her, but she was already gone. "Weird," I muttered and continued to stare at the peaceful view.

Moments later, I heard footsteps behind me.

"Find it?" I turned around to find Giles standing there instead of Erin.

My face broke out into a grin. "What are you doing here? Shouldn't you be at the lodge?"

He ran his hands through his hair, and he took a few steps toward me. He looked nervous.

My eyebrows knit in confusion. "Is everything alright?"

He didn't respond and instead grabbed my hands in his and stared down at me.

"Mattie…"

"Giles…"

"Sorry, I'm a little nervous." He smiled shyly before taking a deep breath. "These past seven months have been amazing. I know I wasn't the easiest person to get along with when you first came around, but you were so damn persistent in getting to know me. Now I-I feel like I've known you my whole life. I can't even remember how I functioned before I met you. I love you so fucking much, and I want you around, like all the time."

He smiled and slowly lowered himself onto one knee, taking one of his hands from mine and reaching into his back pocket.

"Oh my god." My mouth hung open in shock as I registered what was happening.

He smiled and squeezed my hand. "You make me a

way less insufferable person, and I hope I bring you even a fraction of the happiness that you bring me."

The muscles in his throat tightened as he gulped, opening the black velvet box he was holding.

"Mattie, will you marry me?"

Tears streamed down my face. Completely speechless, I nodded my head before launching myself into his arms.

"Is that a yes?" he laughed as we tumbled to the ground.

"Yes. Yes. Yes."

I pressed my lips to his, giddy with happiness at finally finding my forever.

Keep reading for a sneak peek of…

COMFORT ZONED

Available now on Amazon

Al

COMFORT ZONED

"Are you serious?" I asked, gawking at my roommate, Jess.

She rolled her eyes at me in response. She just announced that she would be moving in with her boyfriend at the end of our lease this month, and I'm sure she was annoyed that I wasn't over-the-moon happy for her.

"Al, seriously, stop being dramatic. Tom and I have been together for a few months now, and it makes sense to take the next step. I know we've lived together since college, but, like, we both need to move on and try something different." She sighed, running her fingers through her thin dirty-blonde hair. "Look, I'm not trying to be insensitive, but it feels like we're attached at the hip sometimes. I need space to explore this relationship."

"I didn't realize I was weighing you down." I picked at a loose thread on the plush couch we were sitting on.

"Stop. Don't even go there. I didn't mean it like that." Jess's eyes softened as she looked over at me. "Look, I still love you, and I'm sure we'll hang out a ton. I'll be so sick of

Tom after the first few weeks I'll be begging you to hang out and let me spend the night."

Now it was my turn to roll my eyes. I doubted that would be the case. In their five short months of dating, Jess and Tom had spent nearly every night together. If anything, I had been trying my best to avoid being the third wheel. That was why it felt like a slap in the face to hear her say that the two of us were inseparable.

Sure, that had been the case at one point. We met in college and did everything together. Parties, study sessions, cheap spring break trips to Florida. Growing up, I never had an easy time making friends. So when someone as lively as Jess took me under her wing on our first day of freshman orientation, it felt like I could finally breathe.

Gone were my anxieties about how I would manage to survive the next four years. She was the extrovert to my introvert. While I struggled to engage with new people, she thrived in every social setting. She was the reason I had any friends at all. Although, the only friends I had aside from her were more like acquaintances. I would see them at parties and gatherings Jess would coordinate, but I rarely saw any of them on my own.

Jess was my rock. My comfort zone. We had lived together every year in college and this past year after graduation. So even though she had been ditching me lately to hang out with her boyfriend, the idea of her moving out terrified me.

Should I move out on my own? Then I would never get out and see anyone.

Should I get a new roommate? The thought of living with anyone else made me physically itchy.

My spiraling thought process was making my head pound.

"I'm happy for you," I finally said. I plastered the most believable smile I could manage onto my face. "Tom is a great guy, and you're right, we have lived together for a long time. This was going to happen eventually."

She threw her arms around me. "Thanks, Al. I really am so happy."

My heart wasn't in it as I returned her embrace. It hurt that she'd waited to tell me this so close to our lease ending. I only had a few days to figure out what the hell I was going to do. And if I'm being absolutely, completely honest...I didn't love Tom.

It was a betrayal of Jess's trust to even think that about him, but I knew that the two of us would never be friends—or even interact—if it wasn't for Jess. We had nothing in common, so most of our conversations led to us discussing the weather. Occasionally, he would poke fun at my lack of a dating life while I waited for Jess to intervene. Tom loved video games, drinking, sports, and activities that involved a combination of drinking and sports.

The painful memory of being forced to join a beer-in-hand kickball league a few months back surfaced immediately. I did not possess any athletic ability, so it came as no surprise that during one game when it was my turn to kick, I missed the ball completely and fell on my ass, spilling beer all over me. Everyone got a good laugh out of that and joked about it the rest of the season, Tom leading the charge, of course.

So, yeah. Tom was kind of like the big, loud, jerky older brother that I never wanted. I had to admit he seemed committed to Jess though, perhaps his only redeeming quality.

"Okay," Jess exclaimed, jumping off the couch. "I'm off to Tom's. I'll probably spend the next few days there helping him sort through all of his crap so we can make room for mine. Let's hang out this weekend though. It'll be like our last goodbye hoorah." She pumped her fist. "Eric and Tiff are throwing a housewarming party. Let's go together."

"Cool."

Tiff was our RA when we were freshmen in college. She had been a senior at the time and acted as an older sister to us as Jess and I made one bad decision after another. I'll never forget the night I tried rum for the first time. Tiff held my hair back for hours. When she brought me coffee and aspirin the next morning, she never even mentioned how disgusting I must have been. After she graduated, the three of us kept in touch.

Although she was closer to Jess, Tiff had consistently gone out of her way to be kind to me. I didn't know her boyfriend, Eric, too well except for the few times Tiff had invited us to dinner at his restaurant. He was older than us, and we'd never had much of a real conversation. But he always footed the bill for our dinner, and he had my respect for that.

Jess lingered at the door, seemingly sensing my uneasiness over the life-altering bomb she had dropped on me.

"Love you, okay? This is going to be a good change."

The fake smile barely stayed glued to my face as she left the room. What the hell was I going to do?

Continue reading Comfort Zoned!

About the Author

Allison Speka is a long time reader of romance. She met her partner in Chicago before they both picked up and moved to Colorado five years ago.

Follow along on her publishing journey @SpekaAllison on TikTok or @allisonspeka on Instagram!